AUGUST

The Story of a Nation

Byron Gatt

Pinchicus

To my wonderful and beautiful wife Jayde, who I share our perfect family with; Lily and Freddie (Chihuahua's), Button (bunny) and Truffle (Green Cheek Conure).

And our baby niece Sadie, whose story we are excited to see unfold.

CONTENTS

PART ONE

CHAPTER ONE

Welcome To August.

"Mr Terri we're live in five minutes," The floor manager enjoys eye contact with the great man. The crew on set silent, showing the respect a man of his influence deserves. The studio lights focus brightly on him; he is the centre of this process. All around people move with a quiet yet busy mania, preparing for him to speak. The people who watch comfortably from their homes are his people. In anticipation they wait to be told what to think.

Rose the makeup girl walks over to him, eyes to the floor. This is normal of the employees that surround him. They avoid his gaze out of fear and respect. His gaze drills to the core of what you believe and who you are. His attention is on the job at hand, he is unaware of her until she is in front of him, brush out. He nods allowing her to proceed.

As Rose walks around he allows himself the momentary glance. Her form is pleasing to him, young and taught. Mr Terri would never use his influence to indulge in something so pedestrian, his importance too demanding. She leaves him with an awkward smile, her existence so inconsequential. She exists within his tremendous demeanour and superior status.

Mr Terri is alone once again with his thoughts. Sitting silently in his leather chair preparing for the rush that will come. He moves his glass of water to the right and looks into it reciting his mantra, "For August and her people". August and her people, this is why he does it all, the purpose of his life.

The fame, fortune and influence is of no real conse-quence to Mr Terri. What he does is all for the love of August. He lifts a mirror from beneath his desk, looking at the makeup girls work. He thinks to himself, next time she is at his desk he will ask her name. The mirror reflects back a man of distin-guished features.

Charles Terri is 53 years of age and thinks himself in good shape. He is a well fed man, a slight chubbiness in his cheeks. He is not a glutton but does enjoy some of the finer things in life. The surveys all say this chubbiness gives him an approachable quality. The makeup girl did a good job covering the slight redness of his cheeks and nose. This feature brought on by many a bottle of wine. The makeup around his eyes toned down the darkness brought on by many sleepless nights thinking about his nation. It also brings out the striking green which was such a feature. His eyes are piercing, a key feature of his. The surveys say this feature rates well with his female audience, the mothers of a nation.

Mr Terri's influence is far reaching and weighs heavily, when he speaks millions listen and act. He takes their subser-vience as proof that what he does is for the good of August, for the good of all her people.

This influence given so graciously by the people is often sought by Politicians. They speak to him and ask for his opin-ions. Truthfully seeking his support. The subservience of his audience gives him the ability to elect or depose government members; it is a responsibility he shoulders with honour.

Mr Terri worked hard for this responsibility. He worked hard to become the leading political commentator in all Au-gust. His show is watched by 131 of the 184 million registered viewers. He prides himself on being a beacon of truth, showing the masses what has been hidden from them. For all his time on the air he has done much good, so much that he is often touted as the next Augustan President. A position he would take if it held as much power as his current.

"Two minutes left", the floor manager chirps from

below the great man's desk, sitting atop the stage. 120 seconds before he is with his people and they are with him. Butterflies are often there, but tonight unusually calm. There is a commotion behind the camera, Tony comes rushing through. The floor manager catches him before he is able to reach the almighty desk, made from oak taken from trees in the North. It is not the first time the floor manager and Tony have had a disagreement.

"Mr Terri he barged through, I told him we were nearly on air." The sweat was visible on the floor managers brow.
Mr Terri lifted his hand towards the two men. "Thank you for your concern. I'll make sure he is gone before we are on air." The floor manager walks quickly back to his position; he is disillusioned every time Tony is in the studio. Mr Terri's polite smile turns to a stern stare, focusing on Tony, "What are you doing here?"
"There was a problem with the last shipment; the detonator didn't go off until some of them were safely away from the ship".
"How hard is it to blow up a ship?" Mr Terri barks, Tony avoids his gaze, hanging his head in shame. "This is for August, if we do not stop the immigrants from coming in she will crumble. There are three million in the slums, how many more would you like to let in?"
The floor manager runs over, "30 seconds".

Mr Terri leans forward in his chair, "Find a solution, I will not have them taking August as their own."

The countdown from 10 started, Mr Terri straightens himself. Tony rightly chastised, exits the studio. Mr Terri questioned his resolve at times, whether he really wanted what was best for August. Three, two and:

"Good evening my fellow citizens, family and friends." Mr Terri places his hands on the desk palms down. He keeps a firm hold of the camera. The audience has a deep respect for him. Mr Terri is aware of this and holds them to it.

"It is with great disappointment that tonight I must tell you another boat load of immigrants has illegally landed. Intending to make August their own. The government sits and waits hoping for a resolution while they pack the slums. Something must be done. We must not be afraid to say that this is OUR nation." Mr Terri's hands come off of the desk and into tight fists, he can feel the viewers gaze on him. "The latest boat load has shown what these people feel for our great land. CONTEMPT. Not only did they sneak in with the all characteristics of criminals, once here they destroyed the ship on which they came. They do this to make it impossible for our authorities to turn that ships around. If I was a less humane person I would say let them swim."

Mr Terri's hands go up to the camera halting the audience. "We mustn't act as they do, we will not terrorise them as they have us. I want you all to think, what kind of people are the government allowing in?

"The kind of people who would endanger the lives of their own countrymen for devilishly selfish wants. What attitudes do they hold towards our countrymen?

"I was once a man of great compassion, welcoming all. Then I saw the strain on the good people of our nation. I travelled from town to town and saw the jobless. Their livelihoods taken because an immigrant would do it for much less. I saw the homes being repossessed. Most sadly I saw the despair on the faces of our great people. This will continue to be the fate for generations Augustan citizens if we do nothing.

"My fellow citizens we must act to keep our country safe. I say to Madam President, the boats leave or you do". Mr Terri's gaze was for her, a threat and reminder of his power.

CHAPTER TWO

Roderick Pravo is one of the immigrants Charles Terri proclaimed a criminal. He came to August illegally on a boat sailed by smugglers. Men whose priorities lay in taking money these unfortunate people put away for their safety. He remembered the journey with a deep horror. Seeing the dead body in the container caused him to become much more isolated from those around him, his humanity scarred. He hoped the ship coming into port would change this. Bring him back to a world he was fast leaving.

Roderick was now waiting by the shore, watching the waves softly strike the pier. The movement reminded him of those many weeks, he lost count but for the last two. The waves became a part of life and when he stepped back onto dry land his body missed the movement.

During the journey from the homeland, they were locked in those containers. Unable to move the man after he died, watching and smelling the unmaking of a body. The image sat with him. His wife cried constantly on the journey, in between falling in and out of consciousness. Fearful that she wouldn't make it. Roderick was fearful that she would add to the smell, to the despair that was contained.

Upon coming into port the doors opened and the men threw the body over board with so little care. Roderick hadn't known the man but wished more dignity for him. He was just a body for so much of the trip and in so much of his memories. Still he deserved the dignity inherent in being human.

Long ago when Roderick was not an immigrant, before

the container, he was a man who studied the ocean and her waves. The next wave came and he allowed it to take the memories of being so much more. The memories which caused the most pain.

Roderick and his wife came to August, running from a tyrannical leader. A leader who killed his people, killed them for the glory of power. Roderick escaped and went to a land with the promises of freedom and a better life. He went there and believed he would be welcomed, they would see the misery from which he emerged. His belief in human kindness was marred, his new country's embrace was a suffocation. Even though he was free from a tyrannical leader he was kept confined by his new country. In his new life he was a janitor, not a role befitting his brilliance.

There was no freedom in his uniform, the mandatory dress all immigrants had to wear in the city. They were told it was to identify the workers, ensuring a smooth running August. He lived under the rule of segregation long enough to see it even when subtle. Only the immigrants wore the uniform, only the immigrants worked those most menial jobs.

Roderick allowed the wave to wash away thought, wash away the all too familiar feeling of disenfranchisement. Tonight would be a good night; his brother Alexander was coming to be with him.

Alexander in the land of the tyrant was a great tennis player, a hero and hope to the people. With this status Alexander thought he was untouchable. They would not kill someone so loved and admired. Action against him would be in contrast to their loving propaganda. They enjoyed the atrocities most when they were hidden from the public eye. Allowing the citizens to only watch the celebrations.

Alexander spoke in public, imploring them to rise up and take back what was theirs. Always the idealist, he believed great change could come from those so oppressed. Then the police came, the force behind the tyrant. They were there to support a leader giving them so much, they would happily forsake their fellow man. Alexander's celebrity meant his life was safe, for the moment. It is difficult to hide the death of a national hero who shone so bright.

Alexander's life was spared owing to his celebrity, which in itself was owed to his great tennis ability. Their wrath would not go wanting, for his insolence they took his hand. No longer could he grasp the racket, his celebrity would wane with his athletic status. It was only a matter of time before they were free to do what they truly wanted. Alexander fled with his remaining hand, life and devastated reality. He fled to August and his only remaining family.

On the shore watching the lights of the ship grow, Roderick feared how Alexander would receive August. His importance would mean little here. Again the wave took away the worry. He was just happy to have him alive. A life of menial work was better than no life at all.

The lights moved closer still; Roderick pushed out the negative thoughts that were collecting inside him. His apprehensions turned to great joy and excitement. His brother was coming home, to him, to the remainder of his family. It was a time for joy and celebration. The darkness of his thoughts brightened by the ships lights.

There was no luxury in being an immigrant, they did not travel on passenger ships with buffets and colourful drinks with parasols. They did not fly to their final destination like holiday makers. The immigrants travelled on cargo ships in containers. Confined and deprived; misery grew in those smallest spaces. Just as on his own trip, Alexander would receive few amenities and the doors would rarely swing open. With this in mind Roderick brought a touch of home, food his wife had cooked with so much love and excitement.

The ship slowly docked, his excitement rose. The monstrous vessel moved so slowly and with such force. There was a loud creak as the ship came to a halt against the dock. The force of the ship was so great he feared it would never come to a stop.

Roderick watched from out of sight, the harbour patrol

boarded as was customary. They would have to be so quiet, the fear of being discovered would sit unsteady in your stomach. The paper work would be done, the harbour patrol speaking with the captain. They would hand over enough money to quiet their curiosity.

Time ticked slowly, the tension between harbour patrol and crewman was strong. August, particularly those in the services did not appreciate the diversity the world offered. They held suspicion of all those, the ones who were different.

Boarding and inspection normally lasted an hour. After two past nerves began to grow in Roderick's stomach. If they found him there waiting for the boat he would be arrested. If Alexander was discovered in one of the containers he would be detained and never be allowed the limited freedom of the August. They would ship them off, to the camps where the most undesirables were kept. The stories from the camps fuelled the deep fear in the immigrant population. August was far from home in distance and spirit.

Roderick's negative disposition fed on those thoughts. They would not go away, they had manifested and grew from his long journey. His fears fed on the atrocities, those of his old and new homes. The darkness that Roderick could not escape, it existed on all those moments. It was a partner waiting beside him, until he saw the patrolmen walking off the boat. Jovial, as they would be going home to warmth and a full stomach, the captains gift in their pockets.

The harbour patrol went to the next vessel, their next interrogation. They treated those who brought what was essential to the survival of August with such disrespect. As an island nation, it could not survive without the resources the rest of the world sold. Without the lower nations of the world, August would wither.

Roderick was happy; the nerves began to settle in his stomach as the patrolmen moved further away. The risk still existed; you were never free as an immigrant in August, he knew this all too well.

From the darkness of the ship he saw people walking. At first their movements were slow and foreign. As more came out, their confidence and speed grew.

The immigrants were crying as they emerged. Sadness for the country they left behind and happiness for the country they were walking towards. Hope is a powerful emotion, it influenced so much of human history, the good and bad.

Roderick came out from his hiding spot. He approached the ship with an excited caution. Amongst the crowd he saw Alexander, their eyes meeting for the first time in eight long years. They could feel the pull of family, the sense of certainty the closest to you holds. Tears of happiness welled in their eyes, his little brother was safe. Roderick's eyes would not hold the tears back and he cried such happiness, the drops striking the top of the container, Plop, plop, plop.

Alexander was crying as well. He was happy to see his big brother, the man who he looked up too. The man who gave him a sense of direction for much of his life. The two men who stood only meters from each other always held a close bond. The eight long years apart were the hardest either had experienced. It was hard for the loneliness of each other and also for the occurrences that bookmarked those long years.

Alexander stepped onto the ramp leading to the pier and stopped. He looked up into the sky and breathed deep. Hope was what he felt, a great sense of it. Alexander had hope for the future and a pain in his arm from the past.

Alexander was stuck in his spot, apprehension and disbelief took hold. The brothers' eyes held each other. Their love so evident, covering the distance between them. With that feeling in his heart Roderick walked towards the boat clutching the container. Perhaps he brought it as a peace offering; the disagreements of the homeland he hoped were behind them.

Alexander walked down the plank; other passengers walked around him, friends he made on the journey. The group was half way down the plank when there was a noise, like a firework too close. A shout came from the ship, a deeply distressed call. It screamed for those around to run, run fast something was wrong. The strength of the message stopped Roderick for just a moment, Alexander turned his attention back to the ship.

There was an explosion and the boat shook violently. Containers began to fall all around them. More screams, the passengers were still aboard. The ones on the plank attempted to run. If they were fast they would have moved two steps, after such a time at sea they were not. Another explosion, this time much stronger, hotter, the flame engulfed the ship. The pressure threw the plank from its rests and the passengers were sent overboard.

Roderick was pushed backwards with the force of the explosion and tripped on his feet. He landed on his back still clutching at the container, for a moment unable to register what it all meant. Back on his feet, he ran to the edge of the pier, Alexander, what happened to Alexander? At the edge of the pier he saw 12 passengers in the water. They climbed over each other to scramble up the ladder which clung to the pier. Alexander was nowhere to be seen, he was in the dark water.

Even though Alexander was two years Roderick's junior he was always a better sportsman. From a very young age Alexander dominated, that was with the exception of the water. In the water Alexander felt foreign, "The Rock" he was called by the coach.

Roderick looked once more but could not see Alexander; there was a scream from the ship. One of the crewmen ran to the edge engulfed in flames and jumped into the water. The burning man illuminated the area as he jumped but still no Alexander. Roderick placed the container down and jumped into the water. He was a competent swimmer, in his new community he taught the immigrant children how to swim. With the fear of being deported always there, it was a key skill if another sea voyage occurred.

The water struck the bottom of Roderick's feet; the cold instantly hugged his body. He surfaced and scanned the area,

10 meters in front of him he saw splashing. Then a head popped up, Alexander. He swam over, pushing the water behind him, clawing at it. His ears focused in on the sound of Alexander, the rest went into the background. He could hear water in Alexander's lungs, he was choking.

Roderick embraced Alexander, not the type he had in mind. He held Alexander's head out of the water. He saw Alexander's eyes roll back, consciousness slipping. They looked at Roderick for a moment and Alexander smiled.

"No" he yelled into the night. He would not allow his brother to die, not now, not in the cold waters surrounding August. Roderick breathed into Alexander's mouth, his chest inflated and deflated just as quickly. He breathed again, and still only deflation. "No, you must breath Alexander," he spoke to him with the authority of a older brother. Like when Alexander was asleep and would not wake for school. He would say *Alexander wake mother has the spoon or mother has cooked eggs.* Alexander would always wake with a hurry. "Alexander you must wake, Theresa has cooked Peiorgi." He breathed again hoping that Alexander's stomach would overcome the weight of the water. His chest deflated again, Roderick's head went to his chest in tears.

Then there was a squeeze, it was soft but Roderick felt it. He breathed two more times, then a cough, water sprayed out of his mouth. Alexander grabbed tight his brother. Alexander caught his breath, looked to his brother and through a raspy voice "where are my Peiorgi?"

Roderick helped his brother to the ladder, and then assisted the remainder who clambered clambered around them. He saw a body floating in the water, foot twitching. He looked up to ensure Alexander was safe on the pier and swam over.

It was the man who jumped from the boat, ignited and screaming. This poor man floated on his back, his eyes drifting in and out of focus. Roderick touched the man and he screamed, awake, his eyes focussed. He coughed as he tried to speak, he had breathed in so much smoke, every breathed caused him pain. "August. Bomb." He coughed again, "Watch ".

Then his coughs did not stop, he moved up and down in the water. Roderick tried to stabilise him, the burned man pushed away. He coughed once more and dipped below the water. He didn't surface again. Roderick paused for a moment, and then swam to the ladder and climbed onto the pier. Roderick's mind engulfed from the nights events.

At the top of the ladder he saw Alexander. He had opened the container and was eating Peiorgi. The people congregated around him, he was a good man, a man of the people and so with them he shared.

The two brothers lost to each other for so long embraced. They cried happiness and exhaustion. "Welcome to August my brother". They hugged again. There was a light from behind, the harbour patrol shouted. The immigrants all scattered, three people were caught, they screamed for leniency but this was August.

Roderick and Alexander ran to safety. Once they were sure no one was trailing them they slowed to a walk and began the trek home. Roderick didn't own a car, immigrants were not allowed licenses and cars were well above their meagre earnings. The trains did not run to the immigrant zone at night as they had no where else to be. So together they walked beside the train line, bumping shoulders, happy for the feeling.

Welcome to August.

CHAPTER THREE

"Madam President, the three immigrants caught have been questioned." William Caulfield entered President Katherine Laurie's office. William preferred to be called Bill by his friends, and Madam President was indeed a close friend.

"Bill no one is around, they're all home like normal people." She smiled at him, "There's no need for the Madam President shtick."

"I apologise your highness," he bowed to her and they laugh. She was happy to have him on her staff. He was a stabilising force during troubling times, and it felt as if she would have plenty of those in her future.

"That's better, you have pleased her highness." They enjoyed the levity for a moment, then both their faces returned to business. "What have you found? Why the explosions?"

"Kate they know nothing of the explosion. I've watched the tapes and its pretty clear they are unaware of what's happening. They were so fearful, crying for the people on the boat who didn't make it off." He stopped, the information he possessed would open a box that would again never be closed. "There were two bombs that didn't go off, they were recovered by the divers. They were Augustan bombs. To suggest the immigrants planted them is preposterous. For starters there were four bombs in total. With that kind of money would you risk an ocean voyage. If you had that kind of money you would buy your way in. So how does a group of poor immigrants afford to fly over bombs only to ship them back. With all the turmoil in their country, they have enough bombs of their own."

Madam President leant back in her chair; the enormity

of what they were saying weighed on her. "Is this the work of the Loyalists?"

"Is this the work of a home grown terrorist organisation who want to keep immigrants out?" He leant forward in his chair placing his notepad on her desk. "The bombs scare some people from coming, more importantly it makes our residents fearful of the immigrants."

"Bill we have to be sure, this might be the link we need to officially declare them a terrorist organisation. We need something more solid than this."

"The authorities have a customs officer in custody. He had an identical bomb in the trunk of his car and a Loyalist tattoo across his shoulders. He could have been planting them on inspection"

"What made them suspicious of him?"

"He was pulled over for speeding and a patrolman searched his car."

"Bill, I am going to speak first thing tomorrow, can you send all the info you have? This is going to be an all nighter, can I count on you?"

Bill leant back in his chair and smiled at Kate. He knew what this information meant and the smile was there to comfort them both. The moment Kate declared the Loyalist a terrorist organisation she would doom herself to fail at the next election. "Kate I don't sleep why would I mind." He paused and leant towards her, "Are you sure you want to do this? Even with all we have collected, publicly calling the Loyalists a terrorist organisation has consequences".

"They have done so much to hurt the people who needed our help the most. If my career is sacrificed to keep people safe then so be it." She was angry; she believed the immigrants needed her. She the opposing force to Charles Terri, her old mentor. "How many were on the ship?"

"We're not sure, the three questioned said about twenty per container and about fifteen containers holding immigrants. The best guess says three hundred people, but that could be higher or lower. After the explosion there was so much chaos, they'll be diving for bodies through tomorrow at least."

"How many got off the boat?"

"We don't know that either, the officers who caught the three said they saw about fifteen flee."

"We are talking about the deaths of two hundred and eighty people. They were here to find a better life. We condemn dictators, but the deaths of those who need help the most happen in august every day. We have to stop them; I will not be made to fear the Loyalists." Madam President slammed her hand on the desk, echoing a gesture that she saw Charles Terri do often. Kate wanted to cry for those who died by her failings, and exact revenge on those who caused it.

From behind the two of them readying for war, Grant Laurie the presidents husband walked in. "Honey, you need to eat." He walked by putting a plate of food on the Presidential desk. Katherine looked up at him and realised she hadn't eaten a thing all day.

"Thank you Grant, it's going to be a late one tonight."

Grant and Bill hugged, they dated in high school and that was how Kate became introduced to Grant. She enjoyed their friendship, the three of them sharing so much history. Through all the good and bad, they were her safety net.

Grant walked over and kissed her on the cheek. He felt awkward displaying affection in front of people. Even in front of close friends, he was a gentleman.

Grant held her hand in his, they were so large. She enjoyed that he made her feel like a partner and a woman. In her role as president she was androgynous, something she never aspired to be. She couldn't be a woman, otherwise the many men would view her as weak. She couldn't be a man because then they would call her a fraud, so she was something in between. Androgynous except for when she was with Grant, he was her tether.

"Gentlemen thank you both." She moved the fork on the plate, spaghetti with little hotdogs cut up. Grant always knew how to cheer her up. "I have a lot of work to get done; tomorrow is going to be a tough day".

"You have my support and anything you need let me know." Bill stood up, waved his hand as he bowed to her. "Your highness I will await your correspondence." Smiles all round as he walked out of her office.

Grant leant against the desk, "Is it the Loyalists?"

"We finally have the evidence we need to shut them down." She ate some spaghetti; the little cut up sausage fell to the plate. "Tomorrow I am going to announce them as a terrorist organisation. You won't need to worry about being the first husband after this."

"Are you sure this is the right thing to do?"

"It needs to be done." Her appetite disappeared again. "When my family came to August, it was to escape the kind of fear that the Loyalist try to grow. They wanted to create a better life. If they were to come today, the treatment they would receive is horrendous. It is for the good of the nation, even if she doesn't know it."

"Charles is going to put a giant cross hair on your back."

"My old mentor has been attacking me more and more of late, this will just add to the noise." Kate turned to her computer screen, the curser ticking at her. "Grant, tell me I'm doing the right thing".

"You're doing what is right at your own peril; you will get sainthood in time." He smiled at her, "I'll leave you to work. Come to bed at some point please."

Grant left the room and she was alone with her thoughts and the computer. She was writing her resignation. She loved the job for the people, it was sad that because of this love she would have to give it all up.

The night previous Kate barely slept. She lay beside Grant knowing history would be made in the morning. It was such a heavy feeling to know all would change on your voice. She read over the speech, over and over, was this really what she wanted to do? Was it really what she wanted to say to the world? When she finally slept dreams didn't come. Kate's brain too exhausted to illuminate the night.

At eight the next morning, there was an announcement sent to the media that the President would be making a speech. The details were deliberately vague, as many of the media and parliament were secretly Loyalists.

The Loyalist movement started in the wake of the 2015 riots, the days and nights where blood painted the streets. Kate remembered them as she looked out from her office. She had just taken her seat in a tough fought election. The pictures displayed on the screens terrified her. What had she gotten herself into if these were the citizens she chose to represent?

The riots started as a peaceful demonstration held by the council of compassionate immigration. The group had brought 300 immigrants with them. To demonstrate the conditions these new residents of August were subjected too. The slums at the time were half as congested. Resources dedicated kept it from what it eventually become.

The Loyalists began as an organisation to stop the over legislation the government of the time was practicing. A cause Kate won her election on. Believing the citizens capable of self-governance, for the most part.

The Loyalist's started out proclaiming to stop the nanny state and advocating self-responsibility. This was once a noble organisation. Through the years, the group transformed into a nationalist organisation wanting to exclude *"them"*. An organisation who once promoted a government for the people, began to promote a country where the residents who were born elsewhere were second class citizens. They didn't believe they were deserving of the same types of rights.

Kate watched over ever escalating events, believing there could be a world where both parties could work together. She believed whole heatedly in the premise that there was good in us all. The riots diminished these thoughts, but it took years of attacks to eradicate them completely.

The Loyalists came to the demonstration spewing their hate filled rhetoric, cleverly disguised as patriotism. They placed blame on the immigrants, their slums were their problem not August. After all we gave them food and shelter. The immigrants were a strain on the economy; they took from the good citizens.

Tensions rose, the Loyalist got closer and with more passion. Not being there it was hard to say who actually threw the first punch but it sparked a riot. The some 600 people engulfed to thousands.

The riots lasted two nights and three days. Riot police called in to calm the situation had little effect, especially as the ranks housed many loyalists. The riots moved from place to place, making it almost impossible to quash. Pundits said the events of that day started the eventual backlash. Kate thought it was more correct to say this incident was the straw that broke the camel's back. The anti-immigration rhetoric from the Loyalists had long been propagated, what once was a whisper was now a shout. The anger and hostility felt towards the immigrants had bubbled for some time.

The media had its biased footage, showing the immigrants three on one against a citizen. They showed the immigrants breaking windows of shops and lighting fires. The unspoken conversations about unwelcome guests were now spoken about with the harshness the Loyalists cultivate. Articles written after the riots exclaimed this was how the immigrants showed their ungrateful nature.

Kate thought it was preposterous that such hostility was levelled at a group of people who fled for fear of death. That the citizens of her much loved country could treat those in need like this saddened her. It was this day that her motivations truly took hold.   The saddest part of the whole affair was that the Loyalist had won public opinion. Their numbers grew, becoming more powerful and affecting all levels of government. Though they would never openly proclaim their membership, their strength became palpable. It allowed them to infiltrate and pollute the country from inside the very mechanism meant to keep it clean.

Legislation took away rights from non-citizens. Laws that would have never been passed were now easily walked through. Bipartisan support tied the president's hands. The leader of the Loyalist's was never identified and many rumours spread to who this person could be. The immigrants after the riots were forced to live in more cramped quarters, less funding provided. Their income potential was eliminated by a citizen first hiring law. It was truly sad that it had come to this, that all were no longer equal.

The room got louder as Kate looked out into the awaiting mob of reporters. She had butterflies in her stomach, but her veneer was always strong. She was androgynous, a powerful butterfly. Bill took the podium, introducing Madam President. The photographers had their cameras up. Reporters had their questions at the ready. They were always there and happy to take her down, it was the nature of the beast.

Kate turned to Grant; he had taken the day off from his lectures. He wanted to support her on a day as important as this. He kissed her on the cheek and she walked out.

Madame President took to the podium; she could hide her shaking hands behind it. "Thank you all for coming." She paused as she remembered who she was. Her steel came back to her. "There has been a very disturbing incident last night on the North docks. A container ship carrying immigrants seeking help was attacked by explosion. I'm saddened to say that we suspect in excess of three hundred people were killed in the explosions."

A reporter from the middle of the room stood forward. He was one of the nameless faces who came and went in the gallery. "How many have you let into the country? It seems to me that this was a ploy."

Madam President looked in his direction. "When we open the floor to questions you will have your opportunity. Until then I expect that you will listen carefully and show the people who died the respect that they deserve." Her gaze held on him for a moment, he was silent.

"Many years have past since the riots; it has been much time for us to mend old wounds. The immigrants deserve a respect that has evaded them and your question belittles their suffering."

A pause, allowing herself to calm before she continued. "One of the people responsible for the explosion was detained a short distance from the scene. He had another bomb in his possession, identical to those used." The next passage was the most important. Madame President looked to the back of the room; Bill stood there as a friendly face.

"The man held is a member of the Loyalist movement. It is believed that this group has begun to engage in terrorist tactics. I have informed our national police to engage a full investigation of the group and as of this moment, the Loyalist movement is being held in a state of suspicion. They will no longer be able to practice as an organisation, that is until the investigation is completed."

There was silence in the room, everyone knew what this meant. Those who were not Loyalists stood in shock. Those who were members stood enraged, vying for her blood. "This has not been an easy decision. We can no longer stand by and let these acts be ignored. Let it be clear, if you terrorise a member of the August regardless of their origin of birth you will be brought to justice."

Bill began to walk back to the presidential office. The speech was over and those important words had been said, the Loyalists were no longer to congregate. They would still work in the background but this attention would slow any further attacks they hoped. Madame President stood there and tried to answer questions but Kate wanted to run. The unruly behaviour of the reporters escalated and she turned and walked off stage. She was relieved to be in the quiet of her office. She put her face in her hands, holding off reality. Her staff stood around her. What would she do next?

Bill walked in, "People this would be the perfect time for you all to be working. I'm sure there will be some backlash from this." They turned and walked out, all silent and fearful of the workload and risk that had been placed on them. "Madame President we have to go to Parliament. I think this may come up in question time." She laughed, and they walked out of her office.

CHAPTER FOUR

A loud thud echoed through the Terri household as Charles slammed his fists into the desk. His blood surging, these explosions would not be witnessed by his public. The house keeper dusting in the corner jumped. With all her strength, she resists turning around, the staff deeply afraid of him. As a naturalised citizen she was aware of the distaste he had towards her kind. It was his wife who hired her, it is his wife who buffers the staff.

"Leave your cleaning." He boomed in her direction. The house keeper moves as fast and quietly out of his office as she can. Charles Terri watching her walk out of the room and down the hallway. Her dark skin disgusted him, it is a reminder of her station in life. His attention back to the television, the media conference wrapped up and reporters throwing to commentators. Madame President, Kate, had just started a war which he would not let her win. His fists came down one more time, the redness redeveloping. Mr Terri was the true leader of August. She forgot his power and influence.

Mr Terri stands and paces his vast office, the clicking on the floor boards providing the background to his thinking. The wood was expensive, flown in and milled from the forests in the North. There was not an inch of this room which did not come from his island nation. His friends of wealth flew materials in from across the world, this was a travesty of the rich.

The commentators began to speculate about how the Loyalists would respond. Would this be the tipping point for the leader of the organisation to step forward? If the government ever found out about his involvement with the Loyalists it could end his media career. If this investigation uncovered their final solution it would throw all their plans into chaos.

Mr Terri's phone rang and Tony Trottel glowed on the display. He answered and shared with him his anger. "How was he identified?"

"He is loyal, he won't say a word." Tony had done some horrendous things in his life. Even with all he had done, he was still deeply afraid of the things Charles Terri was willing to do.

"I am confident he won't talk. The moment you have an opportunity, you will kill him." Charles Terri could feel Tony's fear through the phone.

"He is a good man, he is still useful."

"Are you questioning me?" Charles Terri's voice rose as his chest came out and head went high.

"No, I just..."

"You were just doing as I told you". There was a silence, Charles Terri's calm commands brought a chill to Tony. "How did they find him?"

"He was pulled over for speeding and they found one of our bombs in his possession."

"Incompetent fucking idiots." He said this with a now quiet calm, more terrifying than the booming voice. "Tell me when it's done."

The receiver went down and Charles Terri walked back to his chair. He fell deep into it and allowed himself to surrender to his thoughts. Charles Terri remembered the riots Madam President spoke of. Those riots caused him to stand up and formally take leadership of the Loyalists. It was a profoundly sad day for him.

Charles Terri was there on the street, he saw the barbarity the immigrants enacted. Their violence was projected towards the very citizens they proclaimed to want membership with. Their complete lack of respect for the law angered him. They started the fighting, they verbally attacked the citizens. The citizens reacted, as they should. As a patriotic countryman it was your duty.

Charles Terri was there in support of his only daughter Rachel. He had stopped on the way to get them both ice cream as the weather topped 30. He walked in her direction and stopped for a moment. Enjoying his ice cream as he watched her, so proud of her conviction.

She was a kind and loving soul, she took in all manner of creature to care for. She was working for the group supporting the immigrants. It was more than a job to her, it was her life's calling, the thing she was born to do. Charles Terri held so much pride that at the young age of 22 she had found her passion. He did not agree with all her political leanings but was happy that she had conviction. He believed that at the seat of every person there was good, a force pulling them to do what was right. Even if their right was different to his own, he respected this. He didn't think they would turn on their own, become violent for the sake of it.

Charles Terri leant against the treasury building, enjoying his ice-cream. Rachel's ran down his hand as he witnessed the environment become hostile in a snap. Citizens came to them, those brave enough voiced their concerns. They disagreed with the policies that those supporting the immigrants proposed. They argued that August was a place where you worked for your citizenship. You were not entitled to it because you sat on a boat. They didn't believe it should be handed out and its worth debased. He believed the same, and was proud that his citizens were courageous enough to speak out.

Then the immigrants and their supporters turned to the juvenile. They swore and sent insults to the citizen's. Charles Terri could see Rachel's face display so much sadness. His shoulders dropped and he felt a weight for her, she worked so hard for this cause and these people were acting like oafs. Charles Terri's senses started to alert him, the immigrants were going to become violent.

The first person to strike was an immigrant, the energy was almost visible. There was quiet all around for a few seconds then the explosion to violence was quick. Charles Terri ran dropping the ice creams; he needed to get to Rachel.

A fathers chief job was protection and he needed to fulfil his duty. He was knocked around in the chaos, struck by an immigrant that looked at him with such hate. The tragedy in all those moments was that he couldn't get to the one person who made him feel tethered to the world. The person who meant more to him than anyone else.

Amongst the violence, the immigrants realised their mistake and tried to retreat like the cowards he came to know them to be. In the mayhem of the stampede he saw Rachel's auburn hair fall beneath the crowd. He furiously pushed against all those in front of him to get to her. He felt a sharpness in the place that made him a father, the place in his gut that knew when she was in pain.

The police sprayed the crowd; people dispersed quickly under the pressure of the hoses. Charles Terri was wet and beaten but he moved on. He was struck again by the hose and fell forward. He looked up and as the people dispersed he saw her lying meters from him. The only death of the day had been Rachel. She was killed under the foot of the people she tried to help.

The pain rose in Charles Terri, he could not sit back and allow people of that calibre be welcomed. He could not leave it to the law makers to decide for his people. Their decisions ended in pain for his citizens. It was in that moment he knew he needed to take to the airwaves with the truth. It was in that moment he knew he needed to lead the people. He would not allow another citizen to be harmed for the good of an immigrant.

Charles Terri walked into the kitchen. He drank water to replenish the perspiration the memory caused. He used to stand at the kitchen window and watch Rachel and his wife pick flowers for the table.

Mr Terri placed the empty glass onto the counter and allowed himself another moment to gaze out, such peace in those memories. From behind him a noise as the cleaner walked into the kitchen. He spun around knocking the glass off the counter. It fell to the floor, a crack running up it. The rage inside was unleashed.

Mr Terri bent down and took the glass in his hand. The cleaner apologised but he couldn't hear her over the blood rushing through his ears. "I told you to leave the cleaning." He said this calmly and without eye contact.

"I'm sorry," she bowed her head. She spoke quietly and in an accent with all the charm of swine squeal. "I'll fix for..."

Mr Terri threw the glass at the wall besides the cleaners head. It shattered and let out a rain of tiny fragments. The cleaner let out a muted scream. He walked past her on the way to his office, growling at her. "Clean that and make sure you are not seen again."

Mr Terri stormed back into the office, angrily sitting in his chair. The phone rang, he leant forward to see Tony's name glowing once again. "Tony, tell me that you have the situation handled."

"They have him in a federal building; the President is putting every resource into ensuring we are unable to get to him."

"Don't we have anyone who is able to act on our behalf?"

"I'm afraid not."

"Tony this is bitterly disappointing." Charles Terri took his letter opener in hand. "We need to bring forward the project. I will not allow them to stop our work; we need to make sure that August is brought back into alignment."

"Charles."

Mr Terri interrupted him, if Tony had been in front of him he would have buried the blade into his abdomen. "You have not gained the right to refer to me by my first name. You have failed at the most basic of tasks."

"Mr Terri," Tony paused to allow him to interrupt if he saw fit. "The project is not ready; it is still in testing. It does not end the subject quickly." Again a pause, "They die slowly and it is very painful. The test subjects have shown a tendency to anger and violence."

"Then shoot them between the eyes if you're scared." Mr Terri dropped the letter opener to his desk. "They have forced our hand." He had such anger in him. "Their suffering is justified."

CHAPTER FIVE

Tony Trottel put his phone back into his jacket pocket and re-
trieved a packet of cigarettes. Charles Terri often brought out
a tremor in him; the voice of the nation could be a tyrant at
times. Tony stood on the street corner watching the people of
August walk by, the people he spent his new life protecting. In
the background a shop played *"if I fell"* by the Beatles, a relic of
the past. Tony turned to the shop keeper showing his displeas-
ure at the non Augustan music.

Tony Trottel crossed the road en route to the train
station, his shoulders bumping with those around him. The
conversation with Mr Terri had not left him. He didn't like disappointing his mentor. He thought about Mr Terri's comment,
that their suffering was justified. He believed they had done so
much wrong to August, they deserved to be put in their place.
He allowed the fire inside himself to ignite, to illuminate the
cause.

A cigarette went to his lips, the last one in the packet.
Tony lit it, the crackling of the burning tobacco soft but Tony
felt it. He took the smoke deep into his lungs and then out
into the cold winter air, the cloud lingered for a moment. He
stepped out of the crowd, drawing deeply on the cigarette. He
watched them again, were they worthy of his sacrifice?

Tony threw the empty cigarette package towards a bin;
it hit the rim and fell to the ground. He looked around and
spotted a cleaner and motioned him over with a clicking of
his fingers. The cleaner walked towards Tony, his head down
and shoulders hunched. Tony clicked again and pointed at the

empty crumpled cigarette container on the floor. The cleaner walked to it, his eyes always on the ground.

Tony stepped on the packet as the cleaner bent over to pick it up. "You do nothing but take from us, the least you could do was say thank you for our trash." The cleaner was confused, he clearly did not have a firm grasp of the language. Tony leant close, the cleaner shrinking into himself. "Say thank you."
The cleaner looked up at Tony, "Thank you" he said in an accent Tony chose not to acknowledge. He took his foot off the crumpled packet and walked away, his fire relit. Their suffering was justified because they caused so much pain in the August.

Tony's phone rang as he stomped the cigarette butt into the ground. He stepped onto the train and walked to the back of the carriage. It was Michael, one of his prison contacts. Michael worked at the federal prison where the man of interest was held. "Michael, the President is getting extremely fed up with our inability to solve the problem at hand."
"I have good news on that front. He has been transported to my prison devision. He is currently in a holding cell. By tonight he will be in my care."
"Are you able to get me in to see him?"
"Yes, but if he dies in our care, it will put us under a very uncomfortable spotlight."
"Are you concerned I will kill him?"
"Yes," the phone went dead for a moment, "he is a good guy. He is stupid but I know he can add value to the organisation."
"I'm afraid I don't agree with your analysis." The lady next to him looked over, trying to hide her prying eyes. He kept her gaze, "Don't worry, I will make his death look like an accident". He smiled to the lady and put the phone back into his pocket. She hurriedly got off at the next stop and he was pleased at his impact.

The train came into his station, he took out a fresh packet of cigarettes from his jacket. Lighting the first one was the most enjoyable. Tony took it in deep as he walked towards the lab.

He was in an industrial zone of the city. In this area muggings were a common occurrence, not by the undesirables but by citizens of August. This type of citizen on citizen violence was deplorable. With all the problems they had with immigrants, the citizens should support one another, not act like those he worked to eradicate.

Tony didn't need to worry; in this neighbourhood he was well known and feared. This was a fact he felt a very strong sense of pride about. He dropped the cigarette butt to the dirt and stood on it before opening a large metal door. With a creak it announced his entrance into the small and unassuming foyer.

Tony walked to the intercom console on the far wall. He pressed the button and after the static subsided he spoke. "It's Tony, let me in."

There was a loud electric buzz as the doors unlocked and swung open. Tony walked into the lab that would cure August of her immigrant problems.

The men inside the lab were under the illusion that their work was used to protect August from warring nations. Their ID's read military, a handy feature obtained by one of the Loyalists who was a high ranking army official. Everything was top secret, so they asked no questions and did not discover their horrible purpose. The funds came from the Loyalist coffers, it was all untraceable, they made sure of this. The building was even zoned as military, so there were no intrusions from the outside world. The Loyalists were indeed a well organised group.

Tony shook the hand of Dr Carl Fleming, the man responsible for engineering the virus that would solve the immigrant problem. He was employed with the understanding that he worked to stop the Asian and European forces. Dr Fleming worked to develop a virus which would hold their warring counterparts at ransom, leaving August to continue in peace. What he did was a necessary evil, destruction for the preservation of their great nation.

Dr Fleming was allowed to believe this mission and why would he question it? He was sought out by General Christian Wilson, a man of valour and popularity. He was given this mission and took it on as a patriotic duty. He was also flattered that his mind was worth so much to August, particularly the amount deposited into his bank account monthly.

"Dr Fleming, some news has come to light which has made it necessary to move your project forward." Tony picked up a flask which he promptly placed down when the red sign baring a skull and cross bones glared up at him. "We need you to produce enough of the virus to disable 200,000 people." Dr Fleming looked at him stunned, "We aren't going to use it are we?"

"Doctor as always, it is being used to stop the Asian and European alliance from trying to invade our northern front. We need to back our threats or they will never come to respect us."

"The virus is not ready; we can't put this into production." Dr Fleming paused, that awful feeling in his stomach retuned. It was there whenever he thought about what his work was capable of doing to another person. "Mr Trottel, you don't understand."

Tony smiled at the doctor; putting a reassuring hand on his shoulders. This softer approach was not in Tony's nature but was essential with a person of such importance and intelligence. His usual persuasion through force would not suffice. "I have read the reports. It is very unlikely to be used. They have forced our hand."

"Mr Trottel I don't think you understand, the reports do not show you the terrible symptoms of the disease."

Dr Fleming walked off, waving for Tony to follow him. They went into an anti-chamber where they were required to put on biological suits. Tony objected but the doctor would not listen. There was a blast of air and the doctor walked hurriedly into the lab. It was the first time Tony had been inside it. The right wall was stacked with cages, filled with rats genetically engineered to be as close to perfect human analogues. There were metal tables down the centre and along the left. The room was filled with scientific equipment Tony was befuddled by.

On the far wall was a table with a reservoir to catch liquid. Tony smiled at the thought of its purpose. This table was used to cut open and explore the insides of a body. The sight of it terrified and excited Tony, reminding him of a life long ago and one he tried to forget. The doctor stood in front of the cages.

"The virus does not work as quickly as we had wanted. In the rats, it kills 20% within the first 10 minutes." The doctor pulled a dead rat from a cage and placed it on one of the table down the middle of the room. "In 30% of rats the disease takes up to four hours to kill the subject." The Doctor pulled another from a cage, this one was bald. The skin was red with welts across its body.

The doctor moved to another cage, he poked it and there was movement. The rat inside ran and hit the front of the cage. Its hissing grew louder, and the movement in the cage grew more erratic. "Mr Trottel, the most terrifying aspect of this agent is that in 50% of cases the disease shuts off the biochemical signals that stop degradation of the body. It attacks the brain and makes the rat increasingly more violent." He tapped the cage and the hissing exploded again. "The flesh degrades while the organs stay relatively preserved and functional, a biproduct of the disease. This essentially creates a type of living corpse. Then when the body cannot handle any further stresses the rat dies shooting the disease into the air."

Tony stood stone faced staring at the cage, "Doctor this is necessary and I have my orders."
"How will the August fight against an army of these?" The doctor stood back and opened the cage. The rat leapt out and fell to the ground. Its two rear legs were missing and flesh was hanging from its body.

It took a moment for the rats eyes to focus. It fixed on Tony and its two front legs began to move feverishly. It ran, jaws chopping, the little creature so fixed on attacking him.

The rat with all the strength it possessed lunged forward; Tony raised his foot and stomped on its head. There was a wet sound, the bone was soft. Tony stood back angrily glaring at the doctor. Then the rat made a sound, its body filled up with gas. The skin could stretch no further, a loud bang and it shot a mist into the air. The doctor looked at Tony, "I am a smart man for two reasons Mr Trottel." He picked up a syringe and walked towards him, "I made the virus smart enough to get around the filtration devices found in the most advanced bio-hazard respirators. As a weapon it is flawless." Tony began to smell something akin to rot, he began to cough. Frantically he tried to get out of the doors but they were sealed shut. "Mr Trottel, the other reason I am a very smart man is that I never make a virus that I cannot cure." He stepped forward and jabbed the syringe into Tony and pressed the plunger down.

Tony ran to the other end of the room, he needed to be away from the smell. The façade of kindness slipped from him. The doctor walked over and looked into his eyes. "The virus has an indicator, if it has taken hold it turns the eyes a blood red. The virus moves quickly through the body. The capillaries are first to succumb to its erratic movement. They rupture and cause bleeding. This is why the eyes turn such a brilliant red, they fill with blood, the very first red flag if you will."
Tony looked at him, burning through his suit. "Are they red?" Tony had such a deep fear.
"No, you are fine." The doctor smiled with an educated smugness.

Tony lunged at the doctor, pushing him against the centre tables. The two dead rats tumbling over the side. "If you ever do anything like this to me again I will kill you. Do you understand me?" The doctor nodded fearful at seeing the true Tony. "You will make the dosage I have requested and as much anti-dote as possible." He let the doctor go, and walked towards the door. "I need a sample of the virus to take with me today and as much of the antidote as you have."
The doctor nodded, the feeling in his stomach all the stronger.

"I will make this batch and then I will be resigning."
"Good doctor, I wouldn't have it any other way."

Tony took a military vehicle and drove to the prison. There was an ominous briefcase on the seat beside him. This one dose was intended as an experiment and punishment. Tony waited in his car smoking a cigarette and looking at the giant imposing structure. He knew it well; at one time it was his home.

The cigarette joined the many in the ashtray; the smell of nicotine was strong in the car. With briefcase in hand he walked to the prison entrance where Michael waited. He looked concerned as he waited for Tony, always the jittery fellow. "Michael it's good to see you."
"We have to be quick; they are becoming very suspicious of everyone."
Tony put his hand on Michael's shoulder, "We are doing this for August, and your sacrifices will not go unnoticed."

As the pair waited to see the prisoner Tony took out a syringe. The liquid had a slight red quality aggravating its sense of fear. "Michael I must administer this to you, if I don't you may become sick." There was an ever growing fear in Michael, Fair August played in his mind. Tony noticed the apprehension in him. "It will keep you strong." Michael rolled up his sleeve and Tony injected him.

The prisoners focus moved from man to man, settling on Tony Trottel. The prisoner shook with the little knowledge he had of Tony Trottel. Tony was a menacing creature, he did unspeakable evil. The more frightening fact was he took his orders directly from the Loyalist President. "Good evening Robert".
"Tony I'm sorry, it was poor luck."
"It was stupidity Robert, pure and simple." Tony lit a cigarette, sucked it deep and then blew the smoke into the terrified mans face. "You are a danger, you know too much and they have some persuasive methods of information retrieval."
"I will never speak, I am a proud Loyalist, you have to believe

me."

Tony stood and walked to Michael who watched from the corner of the room. He sucked on the cigarette once again, the smoke billowing up. "Michael, if there was a biological contagion released in this room how long before it was locked down".

"This facility was retrofitted with anti-terrorist sensors, after the infiltration of the Europeans attempting to get to their political prisoners. As soon as the sensor catches a trace of a pathogen it will lock down."

Tony turned his attention back to Robert, the cigarette bright red as a puff of smoke came back out. "Robert how lucky do you think you are?"

"Not too lucky after this incident but I can change that. Please don't kill me." It sounded course as he said it.

"Well, I don't think you can change luck." He butted the cigarette on the table. The bright silver canister coming out of the bag grabbed the attention of the room. "Your death will do a great deal of good for August." He said it with such a cold calm that Robert took a moment to register the words. He stood out of his seat and stepped back.

Tony walked to him, his right hand moved firmly around Roberts neck. "The harder you make this, the more of your family I will personally kill." Again the cold calm of his speech took the impact away for just a moment. "Sit down."

Robert obeyed his orders, ever the good soldier. Tony pressed a button on the side of the canister and a mist came out. "Breathe deeply Robert". He followed Tony's instruction, he took in as much of the mist as he could, and then the mist disappeared from the air.

Robert looked to Tony, confused about the canister and afraid for his family. Then a cough. It got worse quickly, his body began to convulse. "What have you done to me?"

"Robert you are lucky it would appear, your death will come quickly."

Robert came out of his chair once again and fell back

into the wall. His face hitting it with force as his arms were unable to support his weight. The curious thing was that his skin did not act in its normal elastic fashion. It held the imprint of the wall. Robert looked to the two men asking for their help. Tony stood with an unconscious gleeful look, happy that the pathogen was working. Michael stood in horror.

"You see Michael, had I not given you the injection this would be your fate." Tony walked over to Robert. He was now slumped in the corner, trying to gulp down air. Tony picked him up, propping him against the wall. "Aren't you glad this isn't your fate?" He said with menace, staring into Michael's eyes.

With a flash of arms Tony punched Robert in the face; flesh flew away and adhered to the wall. There was a non human groan. There was a change in Roberts demeanour, he lunged at Tony but his legs were uneasy and he tumbled before reaching his target. The groan got louder and more persistent, with what motor function he had left he dragged himself towards Tony. He looked just like the rat and Tony treated him as such. With one swift stomp the life went out of him, the red streaked across the floor. Michael let out a cry from behind. The body lay still for a moment and then it began to inflate.

Tony stopped in front of Michael. "You don't want this to be you do you?" Michael shook his head in horror. "When they ask, you don't know what happened, are we clear?" Again all he could muster was the movement of his head. Tony slapped his face, "good boy, now you stay here".

Tony walked out of the room and turned to look through the window. There was something deep inside him that longed for these moments of horror. That thing delighted in knowing this would be the fate of the immigrants. It delighted him knowing he would cause their pain.

Tony took out a cigarette and lit it. He had time for one deep drag and then there was a pop. A red mist enveloped the room. The doors locked and a siren sounded. Michael ran to the window begging to be let out, Tony could not oblige and even if he could he would have taken more joy from the horror on his face. "They will incinerate this room with me in it. You have to help me." Tony stood silent, sucking on the cigarette. The protocol called for incineration if a pathogen breached the first bladder which he knew it would. Before anyone arrived he saw the flames ignite. Michael screamed loudly, the heat of the fire charred him quickly.

Tony dropped the cigarette and walked down the hallway. He knew the men would respond in hazmat suits, this bought him two minutes. This was long enough to be lost in this place. His two loose ends were all tied up.

Tony walked out calmly from prison. The potential emergency was contained by the flames. The prison had not gone into compete lock down, that would have been inconvenient. He sat in his car and called Mr Terri. "I took care of it, there are no witnesses."

"It is good to see that you are still useful". The phone went dead.

CHAPTER SIX

It had been three days since Alexander arrived in August. For much of it he slept, the journey took a mental and physical toll. The withering of his body was only surpassed by the damage to his spirit. He slept and ate. Alexander was disconnected from what happened to him, disconnected from the lives that were lost that night and the many before. Hope for a better life was why they left, arriving only to find despair. Perhaps those who were lost found a better fate, their suffering gone.

The home Roderick welcomed his brother into was small and crumbling. The building was built long ago when attitudes towards immigrants were much more accommodating. Then the immigrant riots happened and the prejudice which was hidden came out to show its true nature. Funding was cut and all building works suspended. Roderick's apartment was initially designed to occupy four with its one bedroom. With funds cut and new immigrants having to hide their existence, Roderick allowed the apartment to become home to nine. Nine people, all good people, forced to share a tiny space deteriorating by the day.

Nina came out of the kitchen and saw Roderick sitting beside Alexander. She held back tears, they were for the joy of the brothers reunited and for the sadness of her own missing family. She wanted to leave him sit there and be with his brother but they needed food for dinner. The immigrant zone became more dangerous as light gave way to dark. He would never let her go out, always the protector.

"Roderick, we need food for dinner, could you go to the store." Nina had kept her accent much more strongly than Roderick. Maybe it was because as in the home land, she stayed and tended to the house. Perhaps it was her resentment towards August, unlike Roderick she didn't want to be one of them.

Roderick turned to her, she loved him and every time she looked into his eyes she remembered the boy she fell for. Many years had passed since then but still his eyes held hers. "Yes, of course, I believe they were restocking the rations this afternoon." The rations were another way August controlled the immigrants, restricting their diet made them much more pliable. Give them enough to survive, but not enough to live.

Roderick kissed her, it was soft against her cheek. He didn't feel comfortable revealing the fullness of his passion in front of people. It had been so long, there were always people. He walked to the stairs, past the elevator that had its cables cut. The Loyalists, the apparent patriots had cut the cable. Immigrants didn't deserve such luxuries, three were injured in the attack. It was up to the immigrants to heal their own, healthcare was a luxury to rich for the immigrants. Dr Chekov mended them but without proper medical supplies many of them faced a life of invalidism.

Roderick stepped out of the building, twenty stories high and grey like a cloud before the explosion of rain. He had a metal bar in his left hand, with little to eat and so many without jobs, it made people desperate. The immigrants received no benefits and most were illegals so they were not accounted for in the rations. The citizens first hiring policy meant that all but the most demeaning jobs were available, and even those were scarce. Desperate people turn on their own when their survival was in jeopardy, many felt being a thief was better than a beggar.

The store was only a few streets away. The Pravo house was able to subsist on the meagre rations by growing vegetables wherever there was flat earth. Across the roof and down the sides of the building where the light struck. It gave sustenance to the people's body and hope to their souls. It was Roderick who cultivated the idea but the building was responsible for keeping the garden alive.

The store was sparse, the deliveries were few and far between. Roderick picked up some rice and flour. The shop keeper was an immigrant as well, and sat at the store watching the food he couldn't eat. Rations were a tightly controlled commodity. The last shop keeper was caught with more than his allowed amount and was sent to the detention centre off the mainland. No one ever returned.

Roderick gave the shop keeper his ration coupons. He bid farewell to the man who suffered from the pangs of hunger while starring at mounds of food. Stepping out of the front door the wind bit him, it was not as severe as the old country and he was thankful for that. The wind continued to berate him as he walked on. It reminded him of a time when he could make so much power from it, now it was sapping his.

The roads were dark, the street lights long ago turned off as a cost cutting measure. The streets were quiet, no cars on the roads, they weren't allowed a license. This is the reason why when he heard the low rumble it brought fear to Roderick, and the lights striking his eyes stopped him. Cars did not come through the zone, the only exception to this was when soldiers thinned the herd.

The rumble grew louder with Roderick's anticipation, and then it passed. It was a civilian car and this peaked his interest all the more. He didn't allow himself to breathe or turn around but was beginning to allow relief to come over himself. His eyes went to the ground and he began to walk, wanting for home.

Then there was a screech from behind, the smell of rubber in the air. The low rumble got closer. The car mounted the curb behind him and came to a halt. There was a shout of anger from the car, Roderick dropped his bags and ran.

He knocked on the doors of the houses he passed but no one would open. They had been so down trodden they became suspicious of each other.

The men behind him shouted out again, they were

catching up. The next building had a now unused underground car park. In between two gates he squeezed, his shrinking girth for once an asset. Roderick hid in one of the lock up garages with hopes they would leave him. What could he offer them? All he had he dropped in the street. There was a pain in his stomach. If he couldn't bring home the food, his ration was wasted.

The gates began to move, they were trying to get in. Perhaps they would leave if it was too hard. Leave him there cowering like the animal they thought he was and the one he now felt like. There was a voice, "We're coming to get you." The gate rattled and he heard it fall to the ground. This time another voice, "We found your rat hole immigrant. You know you don't belong here, it's time to exterminate the infestation." They laughed, as they banged on the doors to the lock up garages. Cowered in a corner, he hated himself for being so helpless, a man does not cower. In his haste he had dropped his metal bar, completely helpless.

They came to the door he hid behind, his breath stopped. Their feet were visible through the crack between the door and the uneven ground. Their shadows got closer and he moved back, fearing for his life. The door moved up, opening to reveal three men. They stared down at him, he looked up hoping for their pity. This was not given.

The biggest one, in height and girth stepped forward. He picked Roderick up by his shirt, effortlessly like his material body didn't exist. "Immigrant you are not welcome here, you are filth." He threw Roderick to the floor, he slid amongst the dust and dirt that formed clouds around him. "Boys what do we do to immigrants who do nothing but take?"
The men all at once, "We show them their place."
"Where is their place?"
Again all at once, "In the dirt".

The biggest one walked over, swung his foot back and planted his steel capped boot into Roderick's stomach. Roderick shouted out in pain then breathed in deep, the air filled with dust and dirt. "You are not welcome here immigrant". The biggest one stood back and the next walked forward, "Your kind are a leech on our society." He lifted Roderick to his feet, looking into his eyes. He had such hatred for Roderick, hatred because of the place he came from, hatred for the man he didn't know he was.

The fist hitting Roderick's face made him forget about his stomach for a moment. He could feel blood trickling down from the split on his forehead. The blood poured into his left eye. Another hit and he felt a tooth dislodge, the man let him fall to the ground, back to the dirt. The third man walked forward, "You don't belong here, none of you do." He bent down to Roderick and looked into the eye absent of blood. "We are going to drive you out or kill you all. The final solution is coming, you should run." He stood back up and spat down at him.

Roderick saw in these people what August thought of him and immigrants in general. They were as good as filth. Roderick saw the foot for only a moment before it struck his head. His vision was hazy and then black. His last thought was for them to spare his life.

CHAPTER SEVEN

Consciousness came back to Roderick, motionlessness in the filth that settled around him. The building he lay under was originally built on promises to those who were less fortunate. It was a cruel joke by a cruel people, to let them have such hope. His blood was dried on the floor, mixed with the dirt he laid on. His heart was sore for this. Sore because he believed as they did, that he was an intruder in their country. He hoped for more, to be one of them, to be a good Augustan citizen. Hope, it was becoming clear was a citizen right.

Roderick lay there for some time, his body in incredible pain. If he lay still it dulled for the moment. He cried softly, keeping his body as still as it could. The tears rehydrate the blood but it would never clean the dirt from it. He cried.

With a whimper unbecoming of a man he stood. The pain in his abdomen was met with that in his head and mouth. His right upper canine was laying somewhere, becoming part of the filth. Holding his stomach he walked to the opening, slowly one step after another.

On the street, Roderick was grateful for the dark as he made his way in hope of the food he dropped. It was not there, the people here too hungry for politeness. He made his way home, to the wife and brother he persuaded to come to this place. As he walked he was ashamed for the promise of safety he made to them. That the fears of the old country would not follow them here. It was a promise he couldn't keep for himself.

Climbing up the stairs was slow. His shame weighed heavier than the injuries that had been inflicted. Another step would awaken pain again, brighten up which was most dark. Roderick stood at the door afraid. Why did he feel the shame of other peoples actions upon him?

Roderick knocked and heard his wife yell, "Roderick is that you?" his sadness was all the more burdensome with the worry in her voice. He let out a yes or something similar, it was weak. The door opened and the dark hid his condition for a moment. "You have been gone for over two hours, where have you been?"

Roderick stepped out of the darkened hallway and into the dimly lit room. Her eyes along with Alexander's widened. "There were three men who thought I was someone else," ever the protector, Roderick's rattled mind attempted to formulate a story to hide them from his pain. "It looks worse than it is".
Nina stepped forward, embarrassing her husband with the tears that came. "Who were these men?"
"Nina please I don't want to scare the children." He smiled at Mr and Mrs Yolkin, they held their daughter Sophia tightly. The beatings happened in the immigrant zone often and without repercussions. They were fearful as this was another attack to add to the mounting numbers of battered bodies. Another making this month scarier than the last, took a little more hope.

Roderick pushed his way through to the bedroom and Nina asked the people in there to leave. As soon as they saw his state they dropped their heads and left. "Roderick they have been doing this more and more. Who was it?"
Alexander was silently watching them, "Nina it is not of importance, what is done is done. Nothing good will come out of this, no one will pay. We must forget it and carry on."
"We cannot forget this, and we mustn't carry on. That is how the old country became as it was, because we were quiet and let it carry on."
"This is not the old country, we are in August now." His voice raised.
Alexander stood forward and with fear and anger he spoke,

"We are in need and this is how they treat us. August shows us no respect, why do you show them yours?" He didn't allow Roderick to answer, he waved his stump in Roderick's face. "This is what carrying on leads too, my hand and your face. If we run we are substituting one act of oppression for another."

Roderick was solemn, they both stood judging him for his cowardice. No Augustan citizen would stand up for him, if he went to the authorities at the very least they would ignore him and note it. At worse they would beat him further for calling into question an Augustan citizen. "Alexander I give them respect in exchange for my life, for the life of those around us. I don't spend my life on a crusade, I spend it trying to survive."

"How are their lives going to ever be better? They are constantly hungry and fearful?"

"Do not forget that these people would be dead had they not fled."

"From one oppression to the next, that is all you know and you have accepted it. I will not accept this."

"You will loose more than your hand if you continue on this path. They were kind to me, they were warning us. They will kill you if you rise up, what do you plan to do against people as powerful as them?"

"I will fight."

"Then you will loose and your bloodshed will be forgotten."

"I will make them take notice, they cannot treat us like this. They cannot treat you like this." From the powerful roar his voice softened, "Brother, they should not treat you like this, you are a good man." Nina resumed her soft sob, stopped when the argument erupted. "I will make them take note of us."

"Please Alexander, violence will only cause them to return in kind. It will assert the beliefs they hold of us being barbarians. Do not do what you are thinking about, what you did in the home country."

"Brother no amount of hiding will convince them we are worthy. They have made their minds up that we are below them, the only way to change this is to rise above them."

Alexander walked out of the room, Nina brushed Roderick's hair. "Where do we go from here, where is home for us?"
"I don't know anymore." Roderick cried again this time in the safety of his wife's arms. "They have taken my hope and if Alexander acts as he speaks they will take him. Home is something God hides from us." Roderick fell to the mattress and the two of them held each other close. They could hear Alexander in the main room but Roderick was too tired to stop his speech. His anger was warranted but not helpful.

Alexander spoke to all those who sat in the main room saddened that this was now a normality of life. "For too long we as a people have been beaten by the ones who should protect us." His stump waved, many were shocked as this was usually hidden. "My brother who has done so much good, who has so much hope, has been attacked. Attacked by those people because he is an immigrant." Alexander's colour became a deep red, his tone righteous and authoritative. "Tell all that tomorrow night we will meet. Every immigrant, from every country is welcome. Tomorrow we will start the movement towards equality. Tomorrow tell every immigrant you see that we will meet outside of this building. Tonight I will watch over my brother." There was a silence as Alexander's words settled in the minds of those in front of him. "You are all worth more than what August designates to you."

The room was filled with an anger towards a country that constantly pushed them to the ground. The hope of revolution was there, unnatural amongst these immigrants. Hope was a commodity, perhaps the only one left.

CHAPTER EIGHT

Parliament that Thursday was more of a circus than usual. Questions about the investigation into the Loyalists had erupted into a full blown attack on Madame President from the opposition. Both sides were fearful of the backlash from their constituents. Being thrown from office because you appear weak on citizen rights was a real threat to politicians in August. This fear was perhaps second place to that of your financial backers leaving you for another who would better serve their interests.

They all fought to appear to be pro-Loyalist's without commending terrorist activity. Madame President was stone face, strong willed and internally fearful. The leader of the opposition stood and walked to the podium. His party quieted and then hers followed suit. Trevor West had been leader of the opposition for two years, a quarter of Madame President's term. He was the current puppet of her old mentor Charles Terri.

Charles Terri her old mentor, how strange the thought felt in her head. How strange that he allowed her to continue as August President, he must still have some warm feelings towards her. She knew this would not last much longer. She waited for the knife to be inserted, to be twisted till she either fell or bowed to their will.

"It is a terrible travesty, the day a government turns on its people for the act of one lone and may I say mentally damaged man." Trevor West turned to his mute party, "it is an even greater shame that we cannot stop the actions of the woman who sits uncomfortably in the seat of power, abusing both her citizens and that power they bestowed." There was cheering and jeering from all over, Madame president could not tell which side it was coming from. "I now speak to Madame President and her party, your citizens no longer want you. Do what is right and resign your post." Again the noise, she felt her stomach tightening, this was it. This was the end of her tenure, she could feel it in the energy of the place.

There were whispers amongst her party, the plotters began their task. She took to the microphone, "Before I defer you to our defence minister," he too was a Loyalist and because of this was held in the dark for much of the long investigation. In fact he only continued on now because those who plotted deemed his position important. Even if for the moment he was in bed with the enemy. "This investigation has been ongoing for much of the last two years. It is an investigation that should have been started earlier if I am to be honest." She held for the noises of the corruptible, "This investigation did not start because of the actions of one man. The action we have taken is based on the aforementioned evidence amassed through the ongoing investigation. Too many signs point to the organisation having terrorist tendencies." Madame President felt the full force of her stature rise, "If any of you had any integrity you would be asking for this investigation."

There was silence as she called them out. It was reckless but necessary. She must let them know that she is aware of their dealings. If they would bring her down she would go down fighting. She would destroy as many of them who protected such a dangerous and callous group. Their founding principles of justice and safety were now only words to be said. They were more concerned with party and allegiances, than they were with country.

The silence was broken by Trevor West walking to his podium. He looked Madam President in the eye, "If there is such a large amount of evidence why can't it be seen by parliament?" He said this with extreme smugness.

"It is sensitive in nature, indicating high level involvement." She held his gaze, "For what we can share I refer you to the Defence Minister".

Gary Rodger took to the podium and began his briefing. He was uncomfortable, it was clear to those around that the words he spoke were not his own. Madame President looked over and caught the eye of Trevor West, he smiled at her. His smarmy smile, the same one he always gave when he believed he had a leg up. Madame President was sure that he was Charles Terri's new protege, there was a confidence coming with that position. Madame President took out her notepad and wrote on it *I KNOW*. She handed it to a steward who delivered it to Trevor. She didn't let his eyes leave hers until the note was delivered. His face turned to anger upon it. One last glance and he left the room.

Gary Rodger's was closing his briefing, "Every member will be given a pack with all that we can share." He turned to Madame President, "Thank you all." He sat down two seats from her. She could feel the heat coming from his direction. The remainder of the session went as could be expected, an orchestrated argument. There were not clear lines as to who was arguing with who, except for the bold one in front of Madame President. It was curious though that Trevor West had not come back in to gloat on his almost certain upcoming Victory.

The end of the session could not have come quicker. With the Loyalist comprehensive and smartly disguised communications, August wanted what the Loyalist's told them too. They wanted what Mr Terri told them. Most people were followers of his as she had been, Mr Terri was a powerful and convincing man. He is good at hiding those things which would make you cautious. He wants what is best, but what is best is built on so much of his pain.

Madame President wanted to get back to her office. She needed time and privacy to be Kate. It was all collecting on her shoulders, the inevitable was not the desired and at times this was difficult to rectify.

In the hall that transitioned from parliament to the members offices she was met with Trevor West and Charles Terri having a heated conversation. They saw her and turned. "Charles what an unexpected pleasure". She shook his hand and smiled. In the corner of her eye she saw her note crumpled in his hand. "Would you like me to take that for you?" she pointed to his hand, "I have asked them to get more bins in here. Keep August and her capital clean"

"No, thank you. I think it is something I should hold onto." He stuffed it into his pocket, her heart beat rapidly. "I am here on somewhat official business."

"Can we expect you to run for office, I'm sure your viewers would love that."

"No, I couldn't do that". He gave her a laugh, "I'm here for some information on the Loyalist story. It is quite compelling."

"Always considering the ratings." She turned to Trevor West and smiled, "I would be happy to brief you on the information at hand. Trevor missed most of the briefing, I'm not sure what kind of help he could be." She paused, Kate's emotions came through. She saw him as the father figure that he once had been and her voice lost its Presidential presence. "It would be nice to have a coffee again."

The two shared a moment, a silence that perplexed or brought fear to Trevor West. He motioned to speak and got a stern look from Charles Terri that stopped him in his tracks. Mr Terri stepped forward, "Madame President I think speaking to the defence minister would be of great use if you would allow it. Receive the story from both sides of parliament". Madame President gave an accommodating nod. "Kate, I would very much like to catch up, it has been too long." He was silent for a moment and perhaps saddened, those riots took Kate from him as well "All I do is for August I hope you can see that, its for what I believe."

"Well I better let you get back to it." She turned to Trevor, Kate receded and Madame President came back. "I'm sure Trevor has more than enough to tell you.

She left them with an uneasiness, tall in her posture hiding the sadness which ate her. In her office she could breath, Bill came in and sat in front of her. "I saw you talking to Charles, did he have much to say?"

"No, I think he is hurt from my actions."

"As the Loyalist president I bet he is."

"First we don't know that for sure and no it's not that. I was like a daughter to him. The loss of her and then our relationship must have been painful. He was the first person to see me for my potential and not dismiss me for my gender. He was the confidence that was lacking." She leant back and slouched in her chair. "My policies, he sees them as being lax on immigrants. He sees me as putting into place policies that endanger citizens. They endanger his soul because of what happened to his daughter. I have betrayed him on more than a political level."

"He is a tyrant." Bill pause, "A tyrant hell bent on destroying your reputation."

"Tyrants hurt, he is hurting, I could see it in his eyes. His way of combating pain is by punishing me. A hurt tyrant is a most dangerous animal."

"Are you sad for him?"

"I am sad for the father he was to me, I am sad for Charlie. That man that taught and gave me so much. I am angry at Mr Terri and all that he is doing to me. I am angry that he can be two people, so different from each other."

Bill was lost in that thought, lost in his hatred for the man. The man who stood against all that he personally held. "I am sorry for your loss, I really am." He paused to politely separate the sentiment from what he was about to say. "You cannot forget that this man, even if not the Loyalist President, is responsible for the deaths of countless immigrants. His newscasts replicate the small minded opinions that allowed the immigrant funding to be cut. So they live in squalor with so little to eat." His anger came forward with his body and Kate sat up. "How many have died from the conditions that he has broadcasted? How many have died trying to find a better life? He is a tyrant and no matter how kind a tyrant can be they are still a negative force. The deaths of so many people are at his feet, so with respect I cannot feel the pain that you do." Bill's eyes went to the floor, "We need to do something worthwhile before the inevitable."

CHAPTER NINE

Charles Terri watched Kate as she walked to her office, the office he had given her. There were very strong feelings, love and hate isn't that the way? The immigrants took another person from him, they demanded protection at the expense of so many. Kate could have been a great leader, one to rule for so long and with an impact on history. He felt bitter at this, as her former mentor he wanted so much for her. What was he now? Her enemy?

Trevor West waited patiently, he would not lead August. He was weak, a dull man and as a Loyalist was a necessary pawn. "Trevor we need to continue this somewhere much more private." Mr Terri told him, and as usual Trevor obliged. They walked to his office, people smiled as they passed, this was all for show. No one really liked Charles, they feared Mr Terri. Whether it was Mr Terri the broadcaster or president, it made no difference. Kate didn't smile just for fear, she had genuine moments of tenderness to cling too. She smiled for Charles, or Charlie but never Mr Terri.

In Trevor's office they sat opposite each other, "Trevor we are beginning to see a light at the end of the tunnel. Support is swinging in our direction with great swiftness." He leant forward and gazed into Trevor's eyes. "This new period needs some new leadership. That is what we need to talk about."
"I am ready, the polls say it. The people are sick of the President. It is inevitable that we will be in power."
"Yes, that is very good." He leant back never releasing his hold on Trevor. "There are a great many things we need to do that

you are not and will never be privy too. Because of this, it is important we have someone to lead August who is aware of our most deep secrets." Trevor didn't see the knife which would soon be in his back, "I am asking you to step down."

"Are you going to run?" His eyes were wide, such weakness. He could never lead the country with such a lack of conviction.

"No, Tony Trottel will be taking the leadership of the party and country. He is the closest person I have to a second in charge and as such I need him to be in your seat."

"I have to object to this."

"Your objection is noted. That however does not change the plan. It is essential to the final solution, don't let your selfish short sightedness cloud your duty."

Trevor was silent, his anger was clear and growing. "He's not even in the political sphere, no history or experience."

"I am well aware of his credentials." Mr Terri's voice took on a gruffness, "He doesn't need a history of politics. In fact politicians would be much better placed if they did not have such a history." He stood out of the chair, towering over Trevor. "All he needs is for the party to elect him. I can accomplish this, I am here to alert you to your fate. Your vote would be appreciated but it is not necessary. As far as his history is concerned we have our men working to give him a more appropriate one."

"This is a bad move, it will come crashing at your feet."

Mr Terri stopped at the door. "Don't forget who you are talking to. I control both sides of this parliament. I decide who rules. All I ask is relinquish your role of leader but I can see that something more extreme is needed." Mr Terri's posture stood up strong, "I am revoking your Loyalist membership, be sure to keep a low profile from here on out".

Mr Terri walked down the hall, the tyrant in him satisfied. He determined who would run the country, not some piss ant that was put in place as an easy win for Kate at the last election. Who would have thought things would have turned so sharply for her.

The message was very clear to Trevor, leave or be removed. Mr Terri was more than comfortable sacrificing one lamb for the entire herd.

"How is the project coming along?" Charles Terri asked from behind his desk. "I hope that you have progressed further."

"We are progressing much faster now that we've gotten rid of Dr Fleming. His understudy is very proficient and accommodating. We are on track to start full scale production within a few months."

"That will have to do." Charles Terri looked out in front of himself, dismayed by the way his country was allowed to be treated. "We will not let them plunge our country into disarray. I have great things planned for you Tony." There was a pause in his voice, "I want all non critical members to reveal themselves."

"That will mean certain detainment for so many. Is this really something we should be doing?"

"I want them to march on parliament, to inform those self inflated idiots that we will not be treated like this." He held so much passion within his words, "How will they detain 200,000 people? Who will detain them? We have the police force. When they see us, they will fear what they have awoken."

Tony sat in silence, this was an act of treason against the government. This could jeopardise all he had worked for. "This is war Mr Terri, it may unleash more than we may be able to handle."

"They have forced our hand. We were going to be humane and respectful but now we must be strong." Mr Terri walked around the desk and stood in front of Tony like a king over his subject. "We need to move fast. This needs to happen soon."

"It will take two days to get the communication ready and organise the march."

"Two days it is." Charles Terri walked back to his chair, "After this your public duty to me will be over." Tony stood in protest, Mr Terri sat him down with the wave of a hand. "I told you, I have great things for you. After this you will no longer work in the shadows. You have done so much for August I couldn't imagine a better person to run for Augustan president."

Those words compressed the room atop Tony, "Mr Terri I am honoured." All thoughts of his disastrous former life receding the longer he spent with Mr Terri, "I will serve you and August with great dignity." The two shook hands.

"Dignity is what we need right now".

CHAPTER TEN

Dr Carl Fleming knew his suspicions were correct the moment he arrived at his apartment. After his run in with Tony Trottel he stayed at the laboratory to finish some work on the virus and anti-dote. He was a man of his word and wanted to be rid of that man, as well as the situation he found himself in. The laboratory was dark, everyone had gone home to their families. Dr Fleming was distracted as he moved around the space which used to feel so familiar. He loved what he did and was sad to see it finish. In his distracted state he thought a walk was in order and went out to buy cigarettes.

Dr Fleming could no longer be part of something so horrendous. Something that would cause so many people such pain, even if they were August's enemies. When his work was hypothetical, when war seemed unlikely he loved it but reality had set in. The fact that Tony had all but fired him was unimportant.

A smoke, the vice that so many had told him would be his death. He walked back from the corner store, his craving was strong in response to the stress. The new packet opened nicely, the shrink wrapping kept its perfume. He smelt it, his death had such a dense bouquet.

Then he saw them. Something about the way they moved was out of place. The car came down the street at break neck speed, it did not have the caution of the military. It stopped him where he stood, this was not the area to get tangled in someone else's business. It just so happened the screeching car was his business. They jumped out of the vehicles and went to the front door of the building. Dr Fleming was expecting them to break the door down, an explosion maybe. There were four men in civilian clothing. He looked on as four vigilantly broke into a laboratory holding one of the most deadly virus' man had ever encountered.

The expected violence towards the door did not eventuate, it stayed in tack. They entered with a key, walking in with confidence. His heart beat that much quicker, they had to be a part of his organisation. He stuffed the cigarettes into his pocket, the virgin smell would be lost to his panic. Dr Fleming turned and walked, he didn't want to run, he didn't want them to notice him. They came out of the building, he heard them yell "he's not in there". Dr Carl Fleming was the only person expected to be there, Dr Carl Fleming was the target of the organisation he now no longer worked for, Dr Carl Fleming was 'he'.

The shop owner smiled as Dr Fleming walked back into his store. The man had owned it for as long as he had worked at the laboratory. The place he designed a weaponised form of an already deadly virus. The very same laboratory whose ownership came to be questioned in that moment. "Forgot to get something to eat, going to be working late tonight."
The owner smiled to him and then looked back at the television screen. The car came roaring past the store.

A panic broke out, they were after him, the short, bespectacled and slightly pudgy scientist. All he had was his wits and right now he felt like they were less than useful. Panic grew in him, his stomach churned and the room felt unstable. There was a reason the dorky scientist wasn't an action hero. Think, he told himself, what do you do now?

Money, he needed as much money as he could get. He walked to the ATM and withdrew the maximum one thousand dollars. That's all he could have today. They would begin tracing his account, he was sure of it.

Dr Fleming walked to the counter with a packet of chips and handed the man some change. "Thank you" he ignored the panic, "I never asked your name."

"It's Dave," he said this with an accent Dr Fleming could not place. "Have a good night".

Calmly he walked out the door. If Dave was part of this, panic might raise his attention. Surely Dave was not in on it. He looked back at Dave with suspicion as his legs performed the foreign act of speed walking. He hoped deeply that Dave was not part of this. Back to the lab, then to his car. His paranoia was not stronger than the burning in his thighs.

Dr Fleming's focussed on slowing his rapid breath as he sat in his car. Sweaty, he hadn't been in a state like this in years. He began to calm, his brain allowing him to control his thoughts. Perhaps they weren't after him, what would they need from him. He gave them what they wanted, they had enough for their immediate use and Kevin his assistant was now well versed. What more could they want? Kevin, he shouldn't have taught Kevin everything, then they would have needed him alive.

The paranoia was lifting, allowing him to breath the cold air. It allowed him to contemplate his life choices and possible gym membership. He could only be sure if his paranoia was justified by one of two ways, They were at his home or, he was killed by them. On he drove, hoping for the first.

Arriving at his apartment complex, he was sure. Sure that life as he knew it, as he was comfortable with was gone. There were the four men parked opposite the entrance to his apartment building. They didn't know he knew who they were.

No longer could Dr Fleming retire to his apartment, there was now a bounty on his head. He was now on the run, with a car that was traceable and a thousand dollars that would not last him long.

Dr Carl Fleming cried, alone in his car, alone in the world. He found a hidden spot and tried to sleep when he felt far enough away. He preyed before his eyes closed, that they would not find him, he didn't even know who they were. Were they the military or some terrorist organisation? The thought hit him and its absurdity made him laugh, a terrorist organisation just like the Loyalists. Again he laughed, no that was not possible. He was a supporter and knew what they stood for.

Dr Fleming woke to lights, bright lights behind him and a man yelling. It took him a minute to realise where he was, the man yelled, "You're blocking the driveway, I need to get in there."

Carl Fleming took a minute and then waved his apology. The car started and he drove. The freeway stretched on for such a long time, it would allow him space to think. He didn't know where he was going, just away from the city. He passed a sign, immigrant zone. The Loyalist propaganda reminded him of how dangerous they were, that he should hate them. He never hated them, he feared them. He belonged to no one now, not the Loyalists or August. If he showed his face, told anyone his name, he would surly be killed. He was like them now, August was not home. He was like them now, scared for his life. Why should he go there? Because like them he was now one of the unwanted.

CHAPTER ELEVEN

Madame President and Bill held a meeting to discuss their tactical options. The options were less about saving the Presidency and more about how to make a less embarrassing exit. The opposition continued their attack. Telling their constituents that she was more concerned with immigrants than she was with citizens. Not everyone fell for it but a population large enough to swing the balance of support away for her. Her voice was being taken from her, and she felt powerless to stop it.

Bill was in the middle of his plan of attack, to force them to enter into intelligible debate. His optimistic mindset was a relief to her. "Bill we have no way of winning. The more time which passes the more they hate me." She wanted to slam her hands on the desk but thought better of it. "The party are working to oust me, they are too weak to keep to the standards it was founded on. The only way for me to save face would be to put in legislation that will further demonise the immigrants, to prove to them I am loyal."

"Is that worth doing? For an opportunity to stay in power?"

"Bill, I no longer want power."

"What exactly do you want to do?" He was confused by her unusual indecisiveness.

"I want to stand down and force an election. If the people want Trevor to be their leader than who am I to stop them?"

"The President that's who." He was angry at her for wanting to quit like this.

"Bill we are delaying the inevitable. In the last week alone there have been fifteen threats on my life." She looked down and wanted to be Kate once more.

There was a knock at the door, she turned to it. It took all her strength to become Madame President. "Come in, please." The door opened slowly and in walked Trevor West.

"What the fuck are you doing here?" Bill attacked, the sight of Trevor had a physical affect on him. The usually reserved man walk forward in aggression.

"Please, I need to talk to the President."

Madame President stepped in between the two of them, staring each other down. "Bill could you give us a minute." She could see that something was wrong with Trevor, his usual stone arrogance had crumbled.

Bill nodded, making his disapproval known to both Trevor and the President. As he walked out he turned to them, "I'll be right outside." Trevor sat down and Madame President took her place from behind her desk. "What brings you here today? Do you want me to hand over the keys in person?"

"No, its nothing like that." He looked around the office, he became less her fierce opponent and more a scared little child. "Is it safe to talk in here?"

"Of course it is." She observed the unnatural fear gripping him, "What exactly is this impromptu meeting about? As a result of your efforts I have quite a bit of work to get done."

"I think I'm in danger." His gaze jumped from the President, darting around the room. "I have been removed from leadership."

"By who?"

"I cant tell you, it will make me more of a target."

"Trevor let me be frank, if I don't know who we are dealing with I'm not going to be able to help you." She sat forward in her chair.

Trevor looked utterly defeated, they both knew him going to her for help was uncomfortable. "I was asked to step down by the Loyalist President. He has so much control over the party, both our parties," his head was now in his hands. "He wants to put someone in to act more directly on his behalf."

Madame President's chest felt as if it was weightless and being crushed all at the same time. They had suspected involvement but here was the evidence. "Who is he?"

"Katherine please, the Loyalists have killed and will kill to ensure their power is kept." His face dropped before her. "they gave me no option. I have to stand down or be stood down."

"I can provide you and your family protection. If I am to do that I need to know who he is."

With one deep breath the name came out "Charles Terri".

The desk slam Madame President was holding in came out, "are you sure?"

"Yes, I'm sure. I'm afraid he has put a price on my head. You are the only person I was sure not to be a Loyalist. I need your help, I don't know what to do."

There was a strange mix of accomplishment and sadness with the name. "Wait here, I'll get my security detail."

Madame President ran out of her office, Bill sat at the receptionists desk unconvincingly reading the financial section of the paper. "Bill he told me who the Loyalist President is, its Charles." She stood in front of him, her breath and heart rate racing. "You need to get my security detail on this. Make sure you use the team we vetted for Loyalist activity."

Madame President walked back into her office, Trevor turned to her. He seemed so much less of a threat right now. He was an asset. "You need to move me somewhere safe". He said this, and then the words went hollow in his mouth. There was a sound of glass breaking, Trevor fell forward. Madame President stood there stunned, confused by what she had just seen. "Trevor" she yelled, realising the worse when she saw the hole through the back of his shirt, the chair and into the floor.

She ran to him and could feel that life had left him. A scream for help came from her and people flooded the room. Her security guard grabbed her, he pointed to the window and she saw the hole. She was dragged out of the room amongst the screams. All the way out of the door she kept watch of Trevor.

Down to the bunker, she demanded Bill follow her. She was frightened but her inner strength took command. "Bill, they have just raised the stakes." He nodded to her. She turned to the policemen, "You need to notify his family, bring them in for protection." She picked up a phone and then set it back down. "We need to be careful how we handle this. I don't want to kick the vipers nest without an ability to control them." Bill handed her his handkerchief for the sweat on her brow.

The door to the bunker opened and Cecil West walked in with her daughter Rose. There was an awkward silence, the two only ever seeing each other in opposing camps. "Mrs West I am terribly sorry." Cecil's eyes were red from crying, she looked like a woman broken. "This should never have happened."
"Thank you," it escaped her body but her mind was not there.
    Madame President turned to the officer holding the radio, "What is going on? Have they found anyone?"
He looked nervous, "No, they have finished doing sweeps and the surrounding grounds have been locked down."
"When are we able to leave the bunker?"
"When the chief of police gives the all clear ma'am."
    She turned back, Cecil and Rose sat in the corner. They neither moved nor spoke. Madame President and Bill quietly conversed, they had to be veiled. They agreed that it was likely the shooter would go unpunished. They would play the loyalist involvement close to their chest. They agreed that this information should be kept between them until they could properly use it. How or when they could use it was beyond the both of them.
    It was another four hours before they came out of the bunker. Madam President called a meeting of her security chiefs. Cecil and Rose would be taken to a secret residential building and kept under 24 hour guard.
    From over her shoulder she saw Cecil talking to Charles Terri. His somber apologies made her mad beyond belief. She hoped her face didn't deceive her. After he spoke to Cecil he

walked over to Madame President, not a hint of guilt emanating from him. "I am so happy you're OK." He took her hand and she hated that she let him. "We might have our differences but always know you hold a place in my heart."

Kate's head spun, was this his subtle way of telling her she wouldn't be assassinated? Did he know what the subtext really was? "Thank you Charles, I feel the same for you." The smile burnt a scar onto her heart.

"I hear it happened in your office, did he tell you anything which could be of use in finding the person who did this?" The concern he showed was real.

"No, he wanted to discuss a way for me to exit without embarrassment." She let go of his hands. "I hope I will not see this on your program."

"Of course not, I only ask out of concern".

Bill came out of a meeting room ahead and the look on his face spoke chapters. "Madam President, we are ready for you". Kate gave him a smile and turned back to Charles. He took her hands once more, "If you remember anything I am here to be a shoulder. If you need it."

"Thank you Charles."

He leant in and kissed her cheek, the father she always wanted. "Be careful Kate". The enemy she feared.

CHAPTER TWELVE

Roderick watched from the apartment window as Alexander stood in front of a crowd of immigrants. In another life Alexander would have made a great leader, the people followed him so easily. Alexander watched them, his silence allowed the crowd to come closer. The news of the attack on Roderick moved through the community quickly. He was a much respected figure and all were angered by this.

Nina sat beside him, Roderick had just woken up. He slept all through the day, she feared for him and was happy to have him conscious beside her. She wiped a damp cloth over his forehead, taking away the blood and seeing the wounds. It terrified her.

Alexander looked up to the window, Roderick's eyes implored him to stop. To reconsider the actions he was going to take. They could not march in the city, it would make the citizens more intolerant. Alexander was still the idealist even with his hand missing.

Alexander looked back to the crowd and their faces hit him. They were scared, tired and hungry. They were not welcomed by so many, and they looked at him to help them lead a better life. He also feared that this march would cause more harm than good but what else could they do? Alexander could not sit on the sidelines, he couldn't allow them to treat his brother with such contempt and get away with it. He was angry.

"This is August," the crowd gave him their attention. "It should have meant we were in a place of safety." He took in some air, it tasted all the same to him regardless of the country. "Protection for its citizens, help for those in need. That is what we were told. August was supposed to be a utopia that we could all escape too. It is not." He hid his stump as his left hand moved through the air.

"We are again being pushed down, made to be the unfortunate ones. We can no longer stand for this. In the short time I have been here I have seen the one man I have looked up to my entire life be made to bow. My brother was beaten and is afraid to go to the authorities. We did not take him to the hospital because we are not welcome there. We did not take him to the police because they do not care. He lays up there bloodied because he was an immigrant." He pointed to the window and Roderick moved back, his voice raising to a shout. "He is an immigrant like you, like your family. We need to tell them we will not stand for this treatment. That good people should not be treated like this."

A man stepped forward from the crowd, "What are we to do? They are too powerful. If we push their hand it will be returned with force."

"We will march to the steps of their parliament. We will let them know that this is not right, this cannot happen." He looked to the man, "We will do this peacefully and with the dignity that they try and take from us. This is how my brother would want it, with dignity."

The crowd clapped, people came to stand by Alexander. They all chanted "with dignity." Roderick was happy his words made an impact but still felt this would end in pain for those who marched. Nina smiled at him, "Alexander listened, it will be peaceful."

"Nina they will not allow an uprising like this, they will make an example of them".

There was a noise again through the crowd. Alexander yelled, "Dignity will again be ours. We will receive what is right and just. Tomorrow we march, tomorrow we fight for our dignity". The crowd was abuzz, Alexander was hugged by the masses. He was a hero to them, he believed what they had all forgotten. He was a natural leader, but what did he lead them to?

The door to the apartment creaked as Alexander came back in. People commended him for his stance, for the quality of the man. He was the eternal idealist, he was going to start a revolution.

He made his way into the room, Nina saw the look shared by the brothers and walked out. She kissed Alexander on the cheek, "You need to be careful, this is not the home country. They are much smarter at punishing us here." Alexander and Roderick stood together in the room, "Alexander we can not march in with the expectation that they will respect our peaceful intentions"

Blood still stuck to Roderick from the attack, "What should we do, bow to them? We left that kind of tyranny"

"Alexander we are in August now".

The two brothers were silent for a moment, "Roderick I share your worry, it is not with an absence of fear that I do this. We cannot just sit and take this treatment."

"Brother I will support you." Roderick moved forward, "Please promise me you will take care."

"Of course I will." Alexander wiped the blood from Roderick's brow. "We will march tomorrow with the dignity we deserve."

The brothers spoke into the night. Their apartment became a centre for organising the action. All who wanted to participate came and voiced their support. The brothers spoke about plans, Roderick still worried but certain support would be much more important to keeping Alexander safe.

CHAPTER THIRTEEN

Carl Fleming pulled over on the side of the road. He took out his wallet and viewed his identity as it once was. That person was now more of a danger to his safety then a comfort. He took out the cash and dumped the wallet. Plans, he always had them. Neatly laid out clothes the night before, it was the plans which helped him. Not any more.

He was now a stranger in his own country. He thought he could slip into a life amongst the immigrants but was unsure of how to make that happen. He got back into his car and drove. Ten more minutes on the highway and he found his way to the outskirts of the immigrant zone. It was where the city stopped encroaching on nature. He drove down a trail, it lead to a dead end. A place to sit and think.

Carl Fleming needed time to begin the rest of his life and save the last of it.

CHAPTER FOURTEEN

Madame President looked into her office as the men installed new bullet proof glass. It was a necessary precaution after the previous days events. It was never thought necessary this far into the capital complex. They had taken the chair and covered the bullet holes, but the image of him there, lifeless and bleeding would not leave her. In her mind she saw his last breath escaping.

Harold Vick tapped her on the shoulder, her nerves had relaxed and this generated a slow turn from her. Mr Vick was the head of security for the complex, he was an ex-army sergeant and took on this role at the request of Charles Terri. That was at a time when Charles Terri was protecting her not being the agent of her demise. She looked at Mr Vick with suspicion, Charles' appointments, in fact anyone she had seen him talking to was now not to be trusted.

"Madame President, until the work has been completed I really would recommend you stay away from the windows." He was a gentle man, not the type you imagined to be battle hardened.

"How long until I'm able to go back into my office?" She walked into the hall.

"It shouldn't be too long."

"Have you got any new information on the shooting? I don't understand how this person was able to get off the grounds during a lock down. Have we checked the staff?"

"All staff have been checked and every visitor accounted for. We have run a sweep of the premises and found nothing. This person was well trained. They were able to get off the complex within the two minutes between the lockdown order being given and a full lock down being enforced."

Madame President peaked back into her office. The window was now in and the men were cleaning. "It sounds like someone who knows our processes, I want all employees not working yesterday to be questioned. Also anyone that worked here after the new security measures were implemented."

"Yes, Madame President." He nodded to her, "I have increased our personnel for the time being."

"We need to catch who ever is responsible. We cannot show weakness. The citizens watch us to know how to feel. The world is watching us, any weakness and we could have war on our hands."

"Yes, madame President."

The workman came out and faced the two of them, they seemed humbled to be standing there. The older workman spoke to Madame President, "Everything has been installed, it will take an hour for the glue to set."

"Thank you." They smiled to each other and then the men disappeared down the hallway.

"Mr Vick please find those responsible." She walked into her office and sat at her desk. There was a security report sitting in front of her outlining the threats from outside the boundaries of August. The Eurasian forces had seen the instability and were readying their military. "Mr Vick I need to tend to these matters."

"Madame President would you at least wait until the glue is dry?" He said this with a small smile.

"Thank you but I need to get to it."

As he walked out she opened the folder. So much time and energy was spent on the dangers coming from inside the country, enemies outside August saw it as a chance for them to capitalise on the instability. To finally make August fall. The Eurasian forces had manoeuvred there ships to be three hours outside Augustan waters. The luxuries of being an island state were lost with these new technologies their opponents employed. Within three hours there could be war, this frightened Madame President greatly.

Bill walked into Madam Presidents office, she felt the concern as soon as they made eye contact. "There are two hundred thousand people marching to parliament." Madam President put her glasses on the desk, "Who are they?"

"The Loyalists"

"About thirty minutes away."

"We need to lock down the building, Bill we are in trouble." She picked up the phone and called Harold Vick, "Mr Vick I need you in my office now."

Harold Vick came into the room and acknowledged both of them. "Madame President it is a peaceful march and I believe they will be gone soon."

Madam President looked to Bill confused, "You said they were a half an hour away." She turned back to Mr Vick, "How did 200,000 people arrive without my knowledge?"

"Madame President there are no more than 200 immigrants."

"What do you mean 200 immigrants?"

"There are 200 immigrants demonstrating out the front. They arrived in the last five minutes and are demanding to open a dialogue with the government. They want better conditions."

Madame President turned to Bill, "There are 200 immigrants wanting better conditions and 200,000 Loyalists coming this way." The two men looked to her, they were both terrified by the approaching event. "We need the riot squad now, Mr Vick you need to organise transport for these people. If the Loyalist's arrive while they are out the front lord knows what they will do." She looked out her window, it was such a clear day. "You need to move the immigrants, then ensure you have all your men ready for the Loyalists"

He left the room once more, she was now Madame President more than ever. Bill stepped to her, "Kate you need to leave, if they breach the walls you could be in danger."

"I will go to the basement."

"I must insist." He picked up the phone. "The chopper needs to be readied. Within five minutes we need to leave."

"Bill I think it is better if I stay," she sat at her desk in disagreement.

"Kate this isn't about your political career. This isn't about you controlling the situation. 200,000 Loyalists mean that we need to keep you safe." She nodded seeing Trevor West having his last breath. "We can work from the sky".

Madame President and Bill were escorted onto the roof, men in tactical gear flanked them. The helicopter was ready and whirring on the launch pad. They guided her in and as soon as the door closed the engine revved and she felt her stomach sink.

Out of the window she watched the immigrants being shoved into trucks. She was saddened that she needed to treat them like this, but it was for their safety. Down the road the Loyalists came, it was a group bigger than she had ever seen. Upon seeing her citizens amassed like she realised her task was much bigger than she was able to handle. The Loyalists were now August, this realisation struck her as the crowd faded with their elevation into the sky.

There was a call over the radio that the Eurasian ships had entered into a position capable of striking august. They saw these events as a sign of weakness, as a sign of dishevelment. She commanded the navy to intercept and take any action necessary. She had declared war on her enemies and country alike.

CHAPTER FIFTEEN

Alexander stood at the front of the group, two hundred and twenty-three people willing to stand up to the injustice that was August. They were there to demand a better life, to show their new home what they were worth. They were fearful of retaliation but still they marched on. The violence towards immigrants had steadily increased while authorities turning a blind eye. Roderick's treatment was common place now, they were made to feel fear on their streets and the meagre places they were given as shelter. That is why they were on the steps, that is why they stood there looking at Parliament. Roderick sat at home beaten and bloodied believing their actions to hold grave consequence. Praying for Alexander and all those who stood resolute, his fear as strong as his pride.

A man came out of the government building, he looked at the group and stood silent for a moment. "Your demonstration is in violation of the Augustan code of public gathering. You must disperse immediately."

Alexander emerged from the body of the group, he looked the man in the eyes. "We only want a peaceful conversation about our conditions, our right to live a life with dignity." He looked at the group and back to the representative of August, "We have come to ask for your help. Daily our people are being hurt, starved of basic necessities."

The man was stone face, all he knew was bureaucracy, that which worked to slow progress. "Before you can demonstrate you need to fill out form 365B and hand it to your district representative."

"We have no representative." The crowd moved forward behind Alexander, "We come to speak, to open words."

"The form must be filled out and given to your representative, then if it is approved you will be given a permit." The man spoke as if the people in front of him did not exist, did not have the circumstances which would stop them from participating in freedom. "Until you have such a permit this is an illegal demonstration and you must disperse."

The crowd was becoming more disenfranchised with the mans responses. They pushed and Alexander could feel them at his back. It was easy for him to speak of dignity and administrational process. How were you to act in such a way when you weren't allowed even the basic rights of country? What was your obediently peaceful dignity worth?

The man spoke into a radio and then back to the crowd, "Please disperse or we will have no option but to forcibly remove you."

The words struck the crowd harshly and the movement on Alexander's back become much more vigorous. They pushed forward, Alexander turned to them. "Do not let them dictate our intentions. We have come to show them that we are not the people they have demonised. We will peacefully stand here and show them that we are people of character. We cannot be pushed to behave as they deem fit".

The man dressed in a suit worth more than the monthly rations of five families took the radio from his ear and walked back into the building. He left them on the steps.

The doors opened and policemen came out of the building. Alexander was disgusted by this, that they would be treated like criminals. Disgusted that their voices were worth so little. The anger brought forward a want to lash out but he felt the responsibility stopping him. The police walked down the steps, "You must disperse."

"We have come here peacefully, we have come here to speak and we have received no such respect. Isn't it the right of citizens to have a voice."

The policeman who spoke walked forward from his formation, "You are not citizens, you have no rights." He took out his baton and struck Alexander across the shoulder. Alexander fell to the floor, the crowd surged forward. He held his hand out to stop them. "I will not act with the same disgrace that you do." He shouted, his voice shaking with pain. "You may strike us but you will not cause us to become like you".

Alexander stood up, the police officer walked back into formation. The group advanced, their silent forward motion allowed the sound of a helicopter to boom as it went over head. The police radios all came alive, a code was being called that made them all seem very uncomfortable. The garage doors that led to the basement of the government building opened and trucks came out quickly. From behind them came men in riot gear. The police went back into the building and the riot police took over.

"We are here peacefully." The group shouted as the riot police advanced on them. The fear in the group cultivated quickly. "You must get on the trucks now, we are in a state of emergency." The voice came from the speakers atop the trucks. The crowds anger showed itself. They pushed, trying to get up the stairs but the might of the riot police was strong. There was surge after surge which the police countered with their shields. Like cattle they were being herded to the trucks. Alexander felt disgust inside, it hurt, they were no more than animals to August. Rage came to him and he began to push against the men with all his might.

Batons came from over the shields, striking man and woman alike. Spilling the blood of people who had so little left. In the background the speakers blared 'stand down 'and 'get on the trucks'. This was mute to them, their ears were blocked with the outrage of being no more then a herd to this country. One of the men to the left of Alexander took a baton from the police and began to strike back. He yelled into the air. Words were no good here, they fell on deaf ears. They had believed words were their saviour, now it was the stick. From both sides force became the tool of communication. Desperation became all the they felt as people fell around them. They looked and saw blood on each other.

Alexander pushed hard, all his pain and suffering came through his body. He broke the line and fell to the other side. The hole closed quickly and he found himself separated from his people. He turned, maybe if he made it inside, it would allow him some ability to speak. He ran and felt the hands of a police officer catch him and spin him around. Alexander braced for the stick but was met with the eyes of a worried man.

With calmness he spoke, "You need to get them on the trucks." The police officer spoke to Alexander as if he were a person and it stopped his rage for a moment.

"We will not be treated like cattle. We want a voice."

The police officer lifted his visor, his accent changed from Augustan to one Alexander would consider a comrade. "A voice can only be had by the living brother." Alexander was confused, shocked. An immigrant or an Augustan citizen? "There are 200,000 people who want every immigrant dead marching this way. You need to get your people on the trucks or we will see many deaths."

Alexander took the mans hand as they shook with an uneasy respect. He ran back to the crowd, the line opened up and he was pushed through. He shouted but only those around him could hear. "On the trucks, we must go." Alexander pushed forward, and got on the truck. He shouted to them but amongst the commotion few took note. From where he stood he could see the mass of people the officer told him about. There where more people then he had ever seen in one place. A sea of hatred personified coming their way. A fear grew in him, he was given a megaphone. "Get on the truck," he shouted with all that was in his body.

People began to follow his instructions, they heard the importance of his voice. The crowds push moved from the steps of Parliament to the trucks. The police spoke into their radios. There was a revving and the trucks began to move. "No" he screamed as he saw the eight people laying on the ground. No one listened. He saw them being dragged off by the police. He felt a failure in himself so strong.

The crowd looked to him as they were being carted off, they looked to the man that promised a voice. Alexander looked out the back of the truck as they were taken away like cattle. He couldn't make eye contact with them, not yet.

CHAPTER SIXTEEN

There was a divide, as the smooth roads transitioned into the unkempt roads of the immigrant zone. The resources lacking in the upkeep of buildings was also evident in the state of the roads. The line was a physical manifestation of the difference between those who were welcome and those unwelcome. The truck was quiet after the initial questions, why did they abandon?

They abandoned because a citizens life was worth more and an immigrant would be sacrificed if it came to that.

The convoy drove to the centre square and then the trucks stopped. The rear doors opened and the defeated masses walked off. The noise of the trucks drew more immigrants to the square. When the immigrants who stayed behind saw the injured walking tears began to fall. The group was defeated, they dispersed to their homes. They hid from the reality of their place in August.

Alexander walked into the apartment, head hung in defeat. Roderick was waiting for him, he hoped for Alexander to be heard, he had a belief in his brother. A belief that was now missing from Alexander himself.

Roderick approach him and from his eyes could see how the events unfolded. Alexander fell to the floor and looked into the distance.

"Alexander, what happened?"

"They do not want to hear from us, we are sub human to them." His defeat was heavy.

"Alexander I am sorry." A hand on his shoulder, "This is August. They do not welcome us and any defiance to this results in pain." Roderick sat beside his brother, "Alexander was anyone hurt?"

"We left eight people there from what I could see. What will happen to them now?" The question was undirected, as the answer was more difficult then unknowing. They feared it. "The Yolkin's, both of them were left there. We will never see them again will we?"

From behind the two brothers there was a cry. A soft little sound, innocent in its pain. They both turned and saw Nina chase little Sophia out the door. Alexander stood, "This is what our lives are destined to be." He took the little girls doll in his hand. "She will grow and live her life like this. What purpose will she have?"

"Alexander we must believe that times will get better, this will not be our lives forever".

"You didn't see them Roderick, they despise us." He handed the doll to Roderick, "We are not welcome here and our presence is seen as an infestation."

Alexander walked into the other room and Roderick sat alone for a moment. He tried to have a strength of character and a hope for the future. He believed their suffering was for something. Their lives had purpose, the little ones had purpose.

Roderick walked out into the hallway where Nina had Sophia in her arms. Such pain in the little ones eyes. This was that moment in her life that would change everything. This would be the memory that she saw at night. Such a sweet little girl, she deserved more than the bleak hallways and constant fear.

Roderick knelt beside them and handed Sophia the doll. She took it and held it so tight. She wept on it, holding it in place of her parents. She looked up at Roderick. Her parents looked up to him and so it was him she would ask. "Mamma, Pappa, are they going to come back?"

Roderick was stuck by it, he wanted to say yes and it be true. He wanted her to have a happy ending. "I'm sorry my dear." Her face contorted with the soul destroying pain. "We will pray for them."

The tears were there again, he was angry at them all. Angry there was a place that would let this happen. Little Sophia deserved so much, she deserved parents to be there to tuck her in at night. The absence in her life would never be filled. This was the worth the Augustan people placed on the immigrants.

CHAPTER SEVENTEEN

Charles Terri sat in his office watching the immigrants stand on the steps of parliament. His anger that they would choose this day simmered. The news cameras cut between shots of the immigrants and the 200,000 Loyalists. A group of citizens walking to reclaim their country. That was the truth of it all, they had lost their rights to be citizens. The two groups so opposed each other, displaying it in such a similar way.

As the riot police took their place, Tony Trottel walked into the office. It was that moment which sparked the greatest anger in Mr Terri. The immigrant took the baton from the police officer, the camera zoomed in tight as he struck the officer. The crowd grew more violent, their intentions clear. The police pushed back, Charles Terri could already hear the weak willed liberals bashing their tactics already. Tony sat and watched in silence, he appreciated the passion Charles displayed.

"How dare they," it came out of no where and caught Tony off guard. "How dare they come here and act in such a barbaric way?"

"It is their nature." Tony said wanting approval from Mr Terri. He looked at him awe struck. He was the man to turn him into something more than he could ever have been on his own.

"This is why we need to ensure our project comes to fruition. This what we fight for, what we stand against".

Silence fell in the room as they both went back to the television. A reporter came on, talking from the gardens across from the steps of parliament. *"We have some breaking news. Due to the activity we see before us, Madame President has been evacu-*

*ated. We saw the presidential helicopter fly over head only mo-
ments ago."* She paused and brushed the hair from her face, *"We
are going back to live pictures now."*

The camera went back to the immigrants and Mr Terri's
face scowled, there was a distain there which had now become
a reflex. The two of them watched in silence as the immigrants
were loaded onto the trucks, ferrying them away from the
Loyalists who came to stake their claim. Mr Terri thought it ill
of them to assume the Loyalists were built of trouble but was
glad to see the immigrants gone from those most sacred steps.

The trucks began to move and the remaining immigrants were taken into custody, Mr Terri took a sip of his drink.
"They want more, thats what they were there for." His cup left
a ring on his desk, he was careful to place it back down in the
same spot. "What do they give in return? We are not a com-
munist country, we were founded on reward for work done,
it is simple." He stood out of his chair and walked around the
desk to sit in the soft leather couch directly in front of the television. "Now they want us to fund their housing, fund their
food and do it all at the peril of our own people."

"When the change of government occurs, we will ensure this
does not happen. Mr Terri we will reclaim August."

"Very good Tony, it is an important time in our history. It is
now that we must make a stand".

The camera turned to the Loyalist, walking towards
parliament, 200,000 people all as one made Mr Terri incredibly proud. They marched slowly, without menace but with
purpose. They chanted 'We are citizens, not terrorists'. Charles
Terri turned to Tony, "Your first act as President will be to re-
peal this ridiculous investigation".

The thought of standing before the country as president made
Tony smile, "It will be the first paper I sign." They both turned
back to the television as they saw their fellow countrymen
standing for what they believed in. The first few took to the
steps of parliament. "When will my candidacy be announced?"

"Madame Presidents party will have her out by the end of the week." Charles Terri sat forward as a citizen waved the Augustan flag. "It will be shortly after that. We also need time for the tragedy of Trevor West to settle." The citizen on screen folded the flag they marched with, showing it the dignity which had been lacking from the previous demonstration. "His funeral will be in two days, make sure you attend." Tony nodded.

The camera came back to the reporter, *"It is rare to see one demonstration on the steps of parliament, two is history making. As you can see the energy of the two could not be more different".* The camera panned across, showing an immense crowd with an unusual calm. *"The violent nature of the previous group has been replaced with a feeling of resolution."*

"We are here with some members and they have agreed to speak." A man stepped forward, he was the public leader of this demonstration. *"My name is Clayton Smith, I am a Loyalist but foremost I am a citizen of this great country. I work hard to provide for my family. I pay taxes to provide for this country. I have never and will never use violence to prove my passion, to label all of us the same as one lone man degrades our patriotic spirit. The Loyalists are a group that upholds the basic tenants of August."*

"If you could speak to Madame President what would you say to her?"

"We understand that she has left the city for fear of her own people. I would like to say that you have nothing to fear. As our President we all have the upmost respect for the office you hold. We want you to understand that what you are doing is wrong."

"If there was an election held today would you vote for her?"

"I would vote for the person best suited to run the country, and that is not her."

The television was quiet, the two men watching nodded with the man. Both believed that truer words had never been spoken. *"Do you have anything else you would like to say to our viewers?"*

"My name is Clayton Smith, I am a Loyalist, a teacher and most importantly a citizen of August". The person behind him

stepped forward;

"My name is Bradley Green, I am a Loyalist, a mechanic and most importantly a citizen of August". One by one there was a parade of people.

"My name is Carol Beck, I am a Loyalist, a mother and most importantly a citizen of August".

"My name is Paul Abbott, I am a Loyalist, a minister and most importantly a citizen of August".

"My name is Howard Simpson, I am a Loyalist, a police officer and most importantly a citizen of August".

The people stood forward one by one, the camera focussed on them. Charles Terri stood out of his chair with pride. His hand was on his heart, Augustan came out to show the bureaucrats what they were really made of. "This is who we are, we are proud and we are the nation. They can try and demonise us however they feel but nothing will take away the honour from our people." Tony stood beside Charles Terri, "Tony, this is who we work for." Charles Terri turned to Tony, "This is who you shall lead."

The cameras stayed with the people for a few more minutes and then showed more of the peaceful gathering. They showed the shields and batons the police needed to protect themselves from the immigrants being put down. Not one arrest, not one person acted in a way that endorsed the view Madame President had of the Loyalists.

The cameras were held on them until they went to the nightly news. The headlines sat well with Charles Terri; Immigrants riot, Loyalists in Peaceful demonstration, Madame President flees and August under attack by the Eurasian's due to instability shown by the government. Charles Terri was indeed pleased, he showed Tony out and worked on his next address to the people.

CHAPTER EIGHTEEN

Madame President touched down at camp Caesar, it was named after one of the founding fathers of August. He was a rebel who would not lay down, would not die. He fought to victory against the odds and gave so many a better life. She thought herself like Caesar fighting against the odds.

The helicopter had a live feed and Madame President was able to watch the events unfolding. It astounded her to see the news media demonise the immigrants, with such ease and vigour. She couldn't really say she was surprised, it was how it had been for so long. It wore on her, there was a substantial part of her that welcomed her own downfall.

Madame President walked into the building under heavy guard. Though the nature of the Loyalist demonstration was peaceful, her security detail acted as if under hostile circumstances. The PR of the Loyalist's did not reflect the facts handed to her in confidential folders. Once inside they swept the area, the seriousness of the situation came home to her. Even here, in this fortress she was not safe from the reach of the Loyalists.

Madame President sat in her office, the computer displaying the names of known Loyalists. After today the list grew, it was refreshed every minute and every minute brought a new page of names. She could not believe how far reaching the organisation was, how her intel had missed so many. Perhaps it was their secretive nature or perhaps it was sabotage from within. All was not as it seemed, she had known this for some time. She refused to believe their reach, that their might would rival the government. This was a significant mistake.

The sound of another helicopter landing out side brought her away from the screen. The guard at the door told her Grant had arrived. How she needed his support right now. From her actions their safety had been compromised. The only thing to stop this climate of fear was her resignation. She couldn't just leave the fight though, could she?

Grant and Bill walked into her office and she was able to breathe a little easier. She hugged them, her whole body welcoming the touch. They sat on couches and looked at each other, disbelief at the reaction they saw. Bill was first to speak, "The media is having the time of their life right now. They are working to focus the harshest light on you."

"We can't blame them".

"Yes we can and I do." Grant said with the quiet anger that he so rarely showed. "What they are doing is slanderous. How dare they?"

"We handed them this, we should have known the Loyalists would fight back".

"How could we expect this level of organisation?" Bill dropped his head, "Any hope of recovering from this." He stopped and looked at her, "We have six months until the next election, we cannot win".

The three of them knew this was true. They felt as if they were the last three people in the world. The last people willing to stand and demand better. For all their efforts they were hated. It was no longer about the political game, the siren had been sounded. It was now survival, there's and all of the disadvantaged. The most Madame President could hope for was to arrive at the next election with some pride, honour and life.

"We can't sit here and be defeated before it's official." The strength that brought her this far prompted. "We will make a plan, I will speak to the country tomorrow. When we go out we make sure the people of August know why. We will give them the opportunity to do better, even if it is without us."

"Kate I don't want you to be more of a target than you already are. Maybe its time that we conceded and work to give us some hope of life outside of this situation." Bill was uncharacteristically defeatist but as practical as always.

"Bill we need to do this, so it hasn't all been in vein."

Grant stood and put his hand on her shoulder, he was proud to have someone of her character in his life. "I'll get dinner started. You can't fight the hordes on an empty stomach."

"Thank you darling" She turned to Bill, "there is a bottle of wine in that cabinet lets get to work."

Bill took the bottle and poured two glasses, "Kate you astound me with your ability to do good by people who do such horrible things to you."

"It is the job, to be hated for making their life better."

The two of them worked closely, speaking without looking at each other. The two of them were a force.

The group of three sat down to dinner, in that moment they could just be friends. Friends sitting in a secret building, surrounded by military personnel, whose job it was to keep them from being murdered. Sitting there eating lasagne, they were just friends. It was a moment to breath.

That moment did not last, the calm ones never do. They have a way of being disrupted, just when they were about to attain perfection. One of the military men tapped Madame President on the shoulder, "There is an important call for you from the party leader."

"Thank you, I will take it in my office."

The call was expected but not welcomed. Madame President and Bill walked to the room. She knew the party would have a reaction, a new person to fight. Madame President took the call and Bill sat opposite her. A face came up on her screen, Craig Ford. The sight of him was enough to make her angry. He had the look of a man always scheming, you could never quite be sure of his intentions.

"Madame President it is good to see you safe." He smiled,

reptilian. "We find ourselves in quite a predicament. It appears we have a country that hates us immensely."

"Mr Ford they hate me, they have mixed feelings for the rest of the party. That is the nature of politics isn't it?"

"Indeed it is." He went silent for a moment. "This is different you would have to say."

"Yes, it is unfortunately, we can make some ground back if we are smart."

"We can make back some ground, you Madame President will not be able to." There was a fury on Bill's face, he saw it before Kate did.

"What exactly do you mean by that?"

"We are revoking your membership to the party."

Kate was shocked and stared blankly. Bill stood sending the chair to the floor, waking Madame President out of her trance.

"You cannot unseat a President no matter how bad the polls."

"Katherine that is true, unless we choose to forfeit our party seats and force an election."

"The opposition will take the election, it will be a massacre."

Mr Fords tone became harsh, "You brought this on. Your crusade against citizens, it was not on the back of any policy we endorsed. You are more dangerous to this country and party than the opposition."

"You coward, you have rolled over under pressure from the Loyalists."

"The party has voted. We will announce tomorrow." He looked into the camera, his eyes went off the screen. "You have 24 hours Madame President."

The screen went blank. Almost seven years of fighting for what was right and it was taken from them. Bill stood stunned, "We can fight this, they cant do this."

"Yes, they can."

Madame President walked out of the office, she just wanted to be with Grant. The one person who saw her for the person she was. The real person. She hugged him and whispered into his ear, "You don't have to worry about being the first gentleman anymore." Then she cried, tears for today and all those days she had to hold it in.

CHAPTER NINETEEN

Carl Fleming drove through the immigrant zone; the difference was so great. The sky looked unlike he'd seen before. The previous night sleeping in the car allowed him time to think about his future. In the middle of the night, as he struggled against the car seat a name came to him. Ivan Chekov, a brilliant doctor whose work much of Carl's derived from. The last he heard, Dr Chekov had immigrated into August but was lost to the scientific world. It was a shame the citizen first policy existed as he would have made a terrific addition to the scientific community of August.

The car came to life with some hesitation, Carl was ready to start moving forward into the unknown. As he moved through the immigrant zone the state of it shocked him. The buildings were dilapidated beyond repair and many looked to be falling apart. Seeing the horrid conditions Carl felt deceived. Deceived by the media who portrayed the immigrants as having more than enough, more than they deserved. Deceived by the politicians who said we should do less and make the immigrants contribute.

People were on the street but if it wasn't for the slightest movement of the their legs he would have guessed them to be dead. Deceived and ashamed that the country he loved allowed this.

Carl stopped and spoke to a man. He looked to be the same age as Carl but his body drooped. Tattered clothes hung on him, his skin seemed not to belong to his body. "Excuse me," the man ignored him and kept walking forward avoiding even a glimpse at the car. "Excuse me," again he shouted to him and again the same response. "Do you know where Dr Ivan Chekov lives?" The man pointed and then walked down the next alley way he passed.

Carl drove following the directions, looking through the windshield of his luxury sedan. He felt such shame that he spent what these people would never see in a life time. On a car, to show his importance. Three more blocks and he saw *"Lekarz"* painted on the side of a building.

Carl pulled the car to the curb and followed an old lady inside. She looked back at him with suspicion. The longer he was in the immigration zone the more he realised just how scared his country had made these people feel. He walked into an apartment which had *"Lekarz"* written on the door. He was mortified with what he saw. The sick took up all surfaces of the tiny living room. The remainder of the apartment was no different, every flat surface had a body laying on it. Not all of these people breathed, many succumbed to the illnesses that should never take a life in a civilised country. The smell of despair hung.

In the laundry at the back of the apartment he found Dr Chekov. In that tiny room he witnessed a man of such brilliance, treating those dying of illnesses requiring nothing more then a shot. If only they were an hour south. Carl Fleming's trained eye was disgusted, his human heart agitated.

Carl waited outside the room, the door was no longer on its hinge, privacy eluded those inside but still he thought it right to wait. He could not help but steal the occasional glance and listened into the conversation. He heard those words that made him choose to go into research, "I'm sorry there is nothing more we can do." They were sad words no matter who they were spoken to.

The lady that was with Dr Chekov walked out, her face distraught. Dr Chekov looked into the hallway and saw Carl. It was clear that this man did not belong and Dr Chekov's face showed the confusion. "How can I help you sir?"
"Dr Chekov my name is Carl Fleming, I am" he stopped himself.

"I used to be a doctor." He was confused about how to tell his story. Confused about what it was that he was doing here. "Is there somewhere private we could talk?"

"Dr Fleming privacy is not something we are gifted with here." He looked around, "Last winter the cold was so severe. Our energy rations were cut and we needed to burn anything not essential to keep the patients warm."

The shame showed on Carl's face, "Perhaps we could speak here."

Carl sat on the crate before Dr Chekov, he explained that the chairs were considered non essential items as well. Any wood was burnt, the blinds torn down to drape over the dead.

Carl told of what happened to him, the men trying to kill him and his need to flee the city. He left out his secret project, even in exile he was loyal.

"I need somewhere I can stay that will make me invisible." He looked at Dr Chekov. Dr Chekov could easily sell Carl for better equipment and conditions. He wouldn't blame him if he did. "I don't expect to live here for free, I will help with the patients."

"I am an old man, it seems more and more people are coming to me. It is beyond my capabilities." He looked out into the hallway. "I would like to take you on to help these people but it comes with a condition."

"Of course, anything."

"If they come looking for you, you must leave. We have enough struggles without the authorities harassing the people. It may seem cold but we need to look after the sick and injured, they are like this because of the way your government has treated us." The pointed nature of those words struck Carl.

"Of course Dr Chekov, I am indebted to you for my life."

"It will not be an easy life, it is hard here."

"Dr Chekov it is better than no life at all."

"Perhaps" Dr Chekov shook Carl's hand, happy for the help. Terrified of the risk which this man brought.

Dr Chekov showed Carl around the limited facilities.

Carl listened intently and those around him starred. He felt more guilty for his portly figure then he had ever before. The two of them waked into the bathroom, it was cramped and a smell of mildew lingered. Dr Chekov turned to Carl, "This is your office." All Carl could say was thank you and his first patient in twenty-three years walked in, she would die and he would live and the mildew would continue to bloom.

CHAPTER TWENTY

The lights shone on Charles Terri sitting behind his desk. The events of the week were taxing on his great nation of August. They needed him, they needed direction at such a time of indecisiveness. If not handled carefully this period of Augustan history could be catastrophic and a scar on the nation. Charles Terri gave his direction for the good of the nation and her people.

"My fellow citizen's it has been a trying time for our country. It would not be strange to feel we have been attacked by all around us. Our government turning on peaceful citizens, immigrants showing their disrespect and now we hear that we are on the brink of war to the North. Where do we look for guidance?" Charles looked into the camera, his actions may seem evil but his intentions were nothing but good.

"Immediately before we came on air tonight, some news arrived on my desk that worries me greatly. As you all know I am not an advocate of the current government. I do not see eye to eye with Madame Presidents current course of action." The crew were unusually quiet on the floor, there was still. "Madame President's party has chosen to throw her out, largely due to their lack of conviction. This means that within the next month there will be a general election, until then there will be confusion.

"My fellow citizens in any normal circumstance I would not comment on who you should elect for our leader. At this time I cannot stay quiet and wish to inform you of this before I move on.

"It would be a travesty for the current party to return to power. We are looking at a war within and outside our borders, conviction is needed.

"We are now without a President because her party believes they are more important than the citizens of this great country. We are now facing war because they are weak on foreign policy. We have an immigrant problem because they are weak on immigration. When you go to the ballot box vote for the party you believe can truly run this country. I believe in the people of this great nation, what we do we do for August."

PART TWO

CHAPTER ONE

Democracy In August.

"My fellow citizens it is with great pride and concern that I speak with you tonight." The news media stood in front of Charles Terri, their usual jostling absent amidst the tone of the country. "It is with pride that I stand here, able to speak to you. Able to serve the Country which I hold so dear.

"With this duty in mind and with a great sadness I must inform you that President Elect Tony Trottel has been assassinated." He bowed his head and there was an audible shock coming from the assembled media. "It is no secret that I had a great deal of respect for President Elect Trottel, there is a deep sadness I share with our country." Charles Terri paused and looked into the camera. The sadness on his face was genuine, his feeling of fondness true. His anger was sharp.

It had been two months since Madame President was taken from power by her party. The election process was chaotic, reflecting a country in utter despair. All manner of corruption was employed, the candidate for the workers party was chosen to replace Katherine Laurie as a puppet controlled by the party president.

Tony Trottel was a man of the people, he was embraced and his win celebrated. President Trottel's death was felt across all parts of August, hope had been assaulted with him. He gave people hope that August could be brought back to its rightful place. He gave hope that August would be run by a citizen and held strong against the countries who worked to bring it down.

In two months, the conflict on the North seas had intensified significantly. August vessels once in a position of power were now left defending their territory in retreat. Without strong and unified leadership Augustan forces did little more than hold them at bay. This was seen as weakness and more nations joined with opportunism at heart. The once great nation was seen as crumbling and all wanted to join its downfall.

Tony was the unification August needed. His win was a strong message to the world that August was still a strong and courageous nation. The weakness was momentary and they would retaliate with force. His death brought more ships, more fear to the citizens.

"Tony Trottel was a man I knew well. He would not want us to be stuck in fear and sadness. He would want us to continue being the nation he so proudly chose to lead. It is in his memory that I make this announcement.

"After consulting with both parties and all of our Parliament, I have accepted its offer to become interim President. This is the first time in the history of our nation that this extreme action has been taken." A pause to allow the nation to take a breath. "It is with this knowledge that I take on this role. I do so with humility and a patriotic spirit for our great nation. Both parties are in full agreement that we need a leader in this time. It is with a humble pride I accept this duty.

"I want to assure our citizens, although it may appear contrary to our democratic nature, my new role will only exist until we are able to hold another election. At this time I will proudly hand the presidency to the elected person. Leadership is what we need and I will work to provide it. It is strength I hope to bring back to August, it is with the help of every citizen I will do this.

"My Presidency will not be started with the pomp and ceremony which is customary. There is no time, the seriousness of our current situation is much more important. At this very moment the ships of the Eurasian nations have entered zone two of our northern sea. This is the furthest any aggressive force has reached. Based on this knowledge I have instructed our military forces to employ an attack using any force necessary to move these forces outside of our border. My confidence in our military force is absolute and I believe that they will achieve this objective.

"Our current situation comes with some challenges. At present we have apprehended an enemy vessel and have taken charge of it. We have found weapons on board of a biological nature. In their current position these ships would be able to reach our mainland to the North and discharge these terrible affronts to nature.

"Our great scientists have been able to engineer an immunisation for this and it will be distributed to all August citizens starting tomorrow. The tests have shown an effectiveness of 80%, with further work this number will improve to protect every citizen. I implore each citizen to go to an immunisation centre which will be advertised appropriately.

"Through these grave times we will be victorious. We belong to the greatest nation on the planet and in history. The world will once again see this."

President Charles Terri looked to the reporters who were all stunned into silence. "My fellow citizens do not fear, be alert and act. Thank you all".

President Terri walked from behind the podium and into the halls. Away from the prying eyes of the media. His adviser Vincent Daniels approached him, "Sir, the air force is requesting a course of action?"

"Drive them out of our boundaries. When they are in their own waters then we will strike with nuclear force. Give them my instruction to blow them into fucking pieces." Vincent followed President Terri into his office, the aggression customary from the President when in private. "How has the biological weapons worked on the enemy ships?"

"It is disabling them quite quickly and they are retreating."

"Good, let them go home and spread it." President Terri's demeanour changed from the publicly acceptable to the tyrant with privacy to stretch his wings. "How dare they try and take advantage of us in our weakest moment."

President Terri looked through the papers on his desk, "What about the immigrants?"

"Funding has been reduced, the checkpoint is nearing completion." Vincent read off his tablet, his morality leaving him by the minute.

"If they try and get around the checkpoint I want them detained and shipped off to the island facility."

"Yes, Sir."

CHAPTER TWO

The day was warm on Roderick's face, he gazed out the window. The train moved quickly and he enjoyed the warmth. The clicking of the tracks was one of the few things he enjoyed about his daily commute to work. They were packed into a train too old and decrepit for citizen use, safe enough for the immigrants. There had been three derailments in the last month, twenty people dead. August didn't even bat an eye, perhaps breathing a sigh of relief.

The people around him talked, they had forgotten about the protest Alexander had started. They had forgotten about the eight people who were sent to the island. Roderick had not, he had little Sophia to look after. It was a somber joy which Nina and he felt.

For so long they hoped for a child, to be parents but were unlucky. The didn't know which of them had the problem and they were happy that way. There were no fertility tests, August didn't want to promote child birth amongst immigrants. The couple wished for a child to care for, one to love with all they had. Sophia was their chance, if only it happened under less awful circumstances.

There was an argument in front of Roderick that snapped him out of the unusually happy thoughts of home. It calmed down quickly. The situation they found themselves in caused people to display less than civilised actions. Roderick returned to the sun and for the moment could pretend he was laying on the grass, free.

The train came into the final station, outside of the city

and behind the checkpoint. Once off the train they walked to the jobs they had been assigned. Roderick cleaned the streets, keeping them sparkling for a people who thought of him as filth. Roderick was assigned this task much below his abilities but meeting his station.

The crowd quieted as they marched to the check point. Since the new government took over things progressively got worse, immigrants valued even less. The check points were used to separate those with and without papers. The legal and illegals. The legals were sent through to work their menial jobs, and the illegals sent off to the island. The place of no return. It was the reason that Alexander stayed at home, he had no papers. Illegals were no longer allowed to apply to be legalised, they were one further step below.

This new restrictions caused more pressure on the immigrant zone and those who inhabited it. Less people able to work meant less ration money. Less legal people meant less total rations available. All were stretched, all were hungry and many desperate.

Roderick stood at the checkpoint and held up his ID. The guard looked at him and back to the ID, seeing the product not the man. He nodded and Roderick walked through. The fear in him subsided for the moment. Two I.D. stations to the left a man began to yell, "I am legal, please I need to work". The guards did not offer him an explanation, they dragged him into one of the many grey building that dotted the immigrant fence. If an immigrant was brought into one of those structures they would never return home.

The many behind the man began to shout, they knew what this meant. The man pleaded for leniency which was an absurdity in itself. The guards trained their guns on the crowd and the noise stopped. They had no qualms about firing on them, they would enjoy the opportunity.

Roderick kept walking, head down and invisible to those around him. For a moment he felt sorry for the man, that would be Alexander if he ever dared to come into the city.

The building Roderick reported to was on the outskirts of the city. It was a big imposing structure bleak in facade and intention. The building was absent of signage, its use hidden from the citizens. They do not have to see the undesirable nature of their country. City works was the official title of the department operating out of this building. It was where the immigrants collected their equipment. Roderick walked in and lined up with all the other immigrants assigned to the city cleaning division.

A window became free and a lady called next. Her name was Bernese, she had never introduced herself to an immigrant. It was something Roderick overheard but would never say aloud. She was one of the four regulars, they were all older ladies and spoke as if they were dying of boredom. Perhaps they were.

Roderick stood forward and put his ID on the counter. Bernese made eye contact but gave no indication that she had any recognition. They were all the same to her. "You will be working zone 34, do you need a map?"
"No, thank you." Roderick said with a quiet voice. The maps were worth a meat ration, one he could not afford to give. There were four of them living off of two rations now.

A small trap door opened beside Roderick and he took his equipment. The immigrants were not trusted to bring the equipment home, so every morning they went to the building and collected their kit. A roll of garbage bags and gloves that never fit. The door shut firmly and he walked to zone 34.

Roderick thought of Bernese, what was she like in her personal life. How did these people live, what did they eat? He let the thought leave his mind as he waited for the tram to pass. It was the tram that would take him to the heart of zone 34 but immigrants were not allowed on board. He watched it pass, a daily reminder of where he was in life.

Roderick walked around his zone, gloves on, the fingertips sagging. There was more activity then usual in that part of the city. Normally at this time of day people were in there offices, working at whatever they did.

The activity built through the day as people set up stations, Augustan health department logo on the side. Roderick knew it was the health department logo due to the yearly checks to weed out the weak and sick.

Roderick walked past two men and began tidying the area around them. "This is all an over reaction." The man in the blue suit and large dark sunglasses said to his friend over a cup of coffee. "There is no way anyone, especially the Eurasians, would be stupid enough to take us on."

"I'd rather not risk it." The second man said with trepidation in his voice. "Biological weapons scare the shit out of me."

"Look, I'm getting the shot so if it does happen I don't die a horrible death." The man looked over to Roderick "but in reality this is a waste of our tax dollars."

Roderick walked off, uncomfortable with the eye contact. He began to worry, an attack on August. If the immigrants weren't protected what would this do to them?

More and more people came out of their offices and walked into one of the stations. He heard them all speak about biological weapons, the need for this vaccine. Most were fear struck, a lot were angered. They saw it as a disrespect to the nation they loved. None were concerned about the immigrants, none concerned that they would remain unprotected.

The medical stations remained busy throughout the day. It kept people on the streets and dirt followed them. The ill fitting gloves were made to work hard, little holes appearing in them. Roderick was a silent witness throughout the day. He watch people deep in fear, the same people who asserted their superiority. It demonstrated to him that they were more similar then either thought. This brought a greater sadness.

At the end of the day Roderick returned his equipment to the grey building. Bernese saw the state of it and warned him, "If you return equipment in this state again I'll take a ration." Roderick nodded and walked out. Powerless to speak, in

August any excuse was a good one to persecute an immigrant.

Back through the checkpoint, the bleakness of his life apparent. August's feelings towards him clear. The guards held him under suspicion, an immigrant was a criminal in their eyes. The walk back to the train was slow. With what the day presented to him the threat of a biological war weighed. What did it mean that they were immunising the citizens? What would it mean to him and his family?

In the immigrant zone he walked past his home and to Dr Chekov. The doctor specialised in biological science back in the home country. He would have some insight.

Dr Chekov's apartment was crammed with people, the normality of this lost to them. He was a tremendously kind person, he had needlessly lost so many and wanted to spare that fate from these people. Roderick walked through and saw the new doctor. He was not an immigrant and this gave him cause to be concerned. Only those who were wanted for horrible things hid here, in the past those who have hid brought nothing but destruction.

"Doctor do you have a moment to discuss a pressing matter?" Roderick walked into the makeshift office and extended his hand. He had caught Dr Chekov in a rare moment of quiet. The two of them were close friends, both at the top of their respective scientific fields. World renowned and August hated.

"Of course Roderick." He pushed a crate over, "The garden is looking quite good at the moment, you must be happy with it?"

"Yes, it would be nice to have some more sun like today." Roderick looked to the wall, the doctor had hung his qualification. He was proud of these, believing it made his patients trust in him. "Dr Chekov, today in the city they were giving their citizens immunisations, they said there was the possibility of an attack using a biological weapon."

Dr Chekov paused for a moment, remembering the wars of old, the people harmed by things he created. He went to speak but was interrupted by the new doctor. "What colour were they?"

"Roderick, this is Dr Carl Fleming, he is good enough to volunteer with us"

"It is good to meet you." Roderick offered his hand but the doctor was ignorant of this.

"What colour liquid was in the syringe?"

"The people said it was blood red, it scared them. It scared me."

"It should scare you." He ran to the next room and came back with his coat. "If it is what I think then we are in trouble."

"What are you talking about?" Dr Chekov's concern evident.

"I created a virus, it was meant to be used as a deterrent against the Eurasian forces. If they are immunising the population then it means the virus has either breached quarantine or they plan to use it on the population."

"What is it?"

"Doctor I will tell you when I come back. You don't have any laboratory supplies do you?"

"Of course not." He said with some anger, "Where are you going?"

"I need to go into the city, I will explain more when I get back." Dr Fleming walked out, stopped and came back to the two men, "I am sorry doctor, Roderick."

The two men sat there in silence, both terrified.

CHAPTER THREE

Traffic ground to a halt amongst the peak hour traffic. Kate and Bill were en route for a mission of hope. Since leaving office through the aggravated actions of her party, Katherine Laurie had been employed by the UN. Her passion and obstacles were recognised, the person to champion immigrant causes across the world. She had diplomatic connections and a track record of advocating for social change. The Loyalist influences were well known among the UN elite, a force in her country of immense resistance.

Kate moved out of August for the posting, to be amongst the international community. Her work took her across the globe, the best and worst of people on show.

Kate held being stripped of the presidency close to her chest, the pain was greater than she had prepared for. The UN position was a god send at the depths of herself loathing. She had not seen her family or friend in the nearly two months. She kissed them goodbye, telling them her role would take her far for quite some time. She didn't want to admit to them or herself that she needed to be out of the country for fear of her life. With Grant and Bill by her side, she left to begin a life away from her home.

Outside of August they were minor political celebrities, inside they had a dollar value on their heads. The world welcomed them, their ill feelings towards August did not seem to extend to them for the most part, the enemy of my enemy. There were some country's representatives who held her in suspicion. Particularly those whose countries were now at war with her home land. She rose above this, her new task clear.

"Bill how successful do you think this will be?" She was beginning to get cold feet. She needed support from at least three more countries, the Australian Prime minister was the first she hoped to convince. To swing the momentum in their favour, they would also need to convince Britain and the United States. These three would begin to shift support for increased help for displaced people around the world.

"Well, there has been strong messaging in the media to stop immigration, a strengthening of their borders. The current Prime Minister is less than concerned about our cause."

Kate leant forward and spoke to the driver, "Why is the traffic so bad?"

"This is Melbourne on a Monday morning. Sorry Ma'am"

"Thats ok." Kate's voice trailed off and she turned back to Bill, "What is our plan here?"

"Well, we highlight their record of late has been less then stellar and it does jeopardise their position on the world stage."

"We can't be seen as threatening." She thought to herself, "The amount of displaced immigrants will rise. August has successfully convinced people to stay away, favouring a war torn country over an attempt to find help."

"It's getting worse, everyday the news brings a little more shame to our little nation. How can we be the voice of immigrants coming from August?"

"We are not acting on behalf of August. We burnt that bridge. I never thought we would be in this kind of danger from our own people." She paused for a moment, she used to be the leader of such a great country or that's how she chose to remember it. A rational country, how that changed. "How long do we have with the Prime Minister?"

"Prime Minister Arthur White is a busy man, we have a fifteen minute window."

"Fifteen minutes." She looked out and saw the beautiful tree lined street. The tremendous buildings that defied logic and imagination. They were an example of what we are capable of.

"Do we carry so little weight?"

The car turned a corner and they were caught in traffic once again. "They have an election coming up." A pause,"Kate they are campaigning hard against immigration, don't go in there with high hopes."

"Fifteen minutes to make Prime Minister Arthur White change his mind about a key election subject." She laughed, "This will be a good day."

Kate and Bill stepped out of the car at the Windsor Hotel. Beautifully Victorian built, Kate thought these were the most magnificent. This era had a character like no other. She was extremely happy to be meeting there.

Once inside they were met by an aide, he was impeccably dressed with beads of sweat on his forehead. "Mrs Laurie, my name is Garry Palmer, I'm an aid for the Prime Minister. Unfortunately he sends his apologies." He paused and looked Bill up and down. "There has been an emergency and he has been called away."

"When will he be back?" Kate brought back the sternness of Madame President, who was that character now? Madame delegate?

"He will not be back today, he was needed in Canberra." His head shot around and motioned to a lady who was passing by, "This is Carol, she will give you the details to set up a meeting for tomorrow." Carol stepped forward and smiled. "The Prime Minister values your effort and wants to make this meeting happen. Apologies again, I hope to see you tomorrow."

Garry Palmer walked away, Carol and Bill made arrangements. Kate was suspicious of the emergency, dejected from being thought of as unimportant. Bill came over to her, "What should we do now?"

"Let's get a drink."

They walked to the bar, and sat at a table. The waitress smiled to them and took their order. They were quiet for a moment. "Bill is there anywhere that will take these people. Maybe as a species we are not built for compassion."

"We do seem to be hardwired assholes". He paused for her to smile, "People want to take care of their own. You can't fault them for that. What I can fault them for is the harm they do to each other." He sipped his drink, "My father still won't speak to me. When I came out he was horrified, but I couldn't hate him. His whole life he had been told people like me were wrong, contaminated by evil. I don't hate him, I feel sorry for him that he is so closed minded."

"How is this meant to convince me that the world is not just one big group of assholes?"

"He may be close minded but he can change. My mother spoke to me, she was the most hurt. He asked about me after recent events. She said he was almost brought to tears when he thought I had died. The world is full of people who are afraid of change. In the end they all change or die a lonely life."

"You are a good person to think like that."

"Besides my mother was so upset because she walked in on me and your husband making out. So I'm placing the blame on you."

Kate laughed, "Your lucky I don't claw your eyes out."

They enjoyed laughing together, assholes be damned they agreed. They continued to drink, and their jovial nature was interrupted by the news coming on screen.

"Disturbing news from August, there has been a battle on the August's Northern sea. Augustan forces have opened fire on ships in neutral territory surrounding the region. On returning to port all crewman on these ships were put into quarantine. General Harlow of the American navy has said that they were the victims of a biological attack, one which is highly contagious. It is unknown if the disease has migrated off the ship. The world has come out to oppose these actions and has warned that sanctions will be placed."

Kate and Bill looked to each other, "Bill this is bad." Their phones rang and they were back to work. The two of them felt a change of tide, the world shook and would not be the same again.

CHAPTER FOUR

Carl Fleming ran into the room which was now home, fortunate to be the only resident in the space. His status as a doctor amongst the immigrants afforded some small luxuries, perhaps it was also their suspicion that allowed the isolation. He was looking for clothes he could wear into the city, to pass as a citizen. The plan was still being developed, he knew at this point he needed to appear as a citizen.

Carl looked into the mirror and was shocked by what he saw. It had been months since he ran from the country he loved. His face was covered with a dense fur, his hair longer than it had been since university. There was no need for style in the immigrant zone. The man in the mirror would have made him cross the street at one point in his life. The clothes he wore were ill fitting and dirty, homemade from what could be drawn together. He worked indoors yet there was a general uncleanliness.

Hair fell to the floor as Dr Fleming shaved his face. He had become what the country despised, there was a general disdain for his current kind. As he changed from the hair clad immigrant to well groomed citizen he felt a disappointment for the people he came from. By simply changing his style of hair and clothes he would be welcomed. He paused with the razor in hand, he personally was not welcomed but any other citizen would be.

Dr Fleming had been in the immigrant zone for three months. In that time, the difference between citizen and immigrant were fleeting. The longer he spent with them the greater commonality he felt, the less the propaganda stuck. There was a deep shame in him, with that shame he worked to ensure he added to their community. It was a repayment for all his contributions to the Loyalists and their anti immigrant activities.

The scissors in his hand were a shared commodity in the community, there was still pride in this place. Pride was something the Loyalist's tried so hard to prove didn't exist in the immigrant population. There was a great pride in them all. He snipped at his hair, thankful for the instrument. The hair falling to the floor reminded him of his mother, she was a hair dresser and worked from home while he was a child. She taught him about lines and blending, mostly to have someone to talk to as she missed working in a salon. He learnt none of it. Hope was what he was cutting with now.

Dr Fleming reached under the bed and pulled out the clothes that came with him. He kept them there in the hope he would return to the real world unscathed, welcomed back to his old life. He dressed, his clothes now ill fitting, the belt a necessity not fashion piece.

Dr Fleming stepped back in front of the mirror and looked at himself. If he had lost this weight through work rather than starvation he would have been proud. It was now sadness, he was forced to be this person.

Alexander was standing next to Carl's car, the two had not spoken often but both knew of each other. Alexander was the freedom fighter, the chaos to the calm Roderick tried to bring. "Alexander, how can I help you?"

"Roderick told me you created this?" Alexander walked towards Carl, "He also said you left in a hurry. What exactly are you up to? Why are you here?"

"Right now I need to get back to the city. I need to find a way to make the antidote they were injecting into the citizens. Time is of the essence."

Alexander stopped him as he tried to walk around. "Why are you here?"

"I am here to help, to give back to people who don't have a

thing."

"No, you are not here for us. You are here because of you. Why are you here?"

"I need to leave now." He tried to walk around Alexander again, "If you don't let me go you will doom these people to the most horrific of deaths."

"Doctor you have already done that, it was you who made this".

Carl stood in front of Alexander feeling the pain of truth. "I will tell you on the way, get in I could use another set of hands."

"I can't go into the city."

"I'll hide you in the car, they never stop us anyway." He saw the fear on Alexander's face, "It will be dark when we get into the city, no one will see you." The courage came back into Alexander and they got into the car, the distinguished doctor and his immigrant friend.

Alexander sat quietly for the first few minutes, it had been so long since he rode in a car that the luxury caused him to go mute. "Alexander I did create all of this, the disease that I fear they will use against us." Carl remembered a life he once lived. "It was developed to stop invading forces, a threat to match theirs. That's what I was told, it is clear now the stories were all a lie."

"What is it being used for now?"

"I don't know. I fled because they wanted me dead, I knew too much." He looked out the windscreen of the car, knowing soon he would be entering the place that could mean death for the pair of them. "What is important now is that I am able to gather supplies? I can extract the anti-dote from my blood. It will take time to make, so the quicker I start the better."

The two men spoke as they moved in a comfort both had missed. Alexander saw a fear in Carl, it gave him a comfort. He felt comfort in the fact that Carl Fleming was as much an outcast as they were.

The engine of the car stopped and the two of them sat down the side of a supply store. "In my old life, this used to be a very happy place for me." Carl didn't look at Alexander, lost in his head. "It was like Christmas every time I walked through that door."

"What are we going to do here?"

"We are going to break in and get the supplies on this list." Dr Fleming showed the piece of paper to Alexander. "The door around the back doesn't lock properly."

"With all this equipment wont they have an alarm system?"

"Alexander we are going to break the code."

The two men ran to the rear, Alexander had nerves growing in his stomach. The door was unlocked as Dr Fleming had said, "I used to date the manager." He smiled to Alexander and they walked in. Dr Fleming punched in a code at the console, and the beeping stopped.

"How did you know the code" Alexander looked bemused?"

"They have used the same code for the last decade." He pointed to the warn buttons, "Not the greatest security system.

"What would you have done if the code was different?"

"Run I suppose."

Carl turned the lights on and there was a room of silver and glass. Alexander had never seen anything like it in his life. He followed Dr Fleming around with a cart, loading everything that was requested of him. As they walked around Alexander felt useful, like he had real purpose.

Carl turned to Alexander "That's everything, lets go before we arouse suspicion." The two of them hurried to the door, Alexander couldn't believe with what they had in the cart they would make something so important. They walked out and loaded the car, silence in their speed. Then they were off, a plan well hatched. All that needed to be done was to break back into the immigrant zone.

As they approached the checkpoint the tension in the car rose. To the left of the checkpoint there was a commotion. Immigrants clashed with police. The noise rose and confusion was rife. It spilled onto the road and there was a back up.

Carl turned to the back seat, "We might have a problem.

Stay still they are looking in cars." Alexander lay under a blanket as still as he could be. The cars in front slowly crept forward. The officer at the checkpoint shone a light into the car.
"What is all the equipment for?"
"I need to administer tests on the immigrants."
"I need to see some id."
"Of course officer."

Carl reached into the glove box, his id would alert them to his situation. He needed to get out of there, he needed to think. Slowly it came to him, he opened the centre console. "Sorry sergeant, the car is a mess." The officer turned back from the commotion that was now a normality of life.

Carl shot pepper spray at the officer. He held the button down, the liquid covered the mans face. The officer doubled over, reaching for the car door. Carl planted his foot to the floor. "What is going on?" Alexander was ignored. The car got faster and faster, his nerves were at breaking point. He watched the rear view mirror. No lights followed, they had shut down the border. They were more concerned with people breaking out.

The two of them drove back to the immigrant zone and met with Roderick and Dr Chekov. "I have the supplies but they know something is happening here."
"How?" a simple yet complicated question from Dr Chekov.
"I will explain later." A visibly shaken Carl Fleming took equipment out of the car and handed it to the men. "This needs to be taken somewhere hidden." He paused and caught the box before it hit the ground. "They know I am here, or that someone is here. I need to be hidden. They will come for me."
"We have just the place". Dr Chekov led the men to an underground bunker they had worked on for so long. They set up the equipment and Dr Carl Fleming worked through the night. Only the men who were there that night knew of its location. They brought him food, they watched him work. It was a sight, a man doing what he was put on earth to do.

CHAPTER FIVE

Roderick and Dr Chekov sat in his office absent of a door. They discussed the bunker that was once built to house immigrants most at risk, now a lab tasked with saving the population. Dr Fleming worked feverishly throughout the night, his guilt spurring him on as his malnourished body shut down.

The events of the night previous had caused a great angst amongst those who knew. Dr Carl Fleming came back in such a rush and with such fear. Alexander told the story of their escape from the guards. A feeling of doom settled in their stomachs. August would not allow this transgression to go unpunished. Sacrifices would be enforced, this a good a reason as any. How much more could they sacrifice to keep the doctor safe? How much did they need to sacrifice to keep them safe, in the event that they were attacked by a virus which horrified them in story.

"Dr Chekov we need him safe, he needs to remain hidden if we are to protect ourselves." Roderick looked out into the main room, down a hallway filled with bodies. "Conditions have only gotten worse, your rooms filled with more people. If that virus hits us we will be facing a kind of reckoning we cannot comprehend."

"What do we do when they come for him?"

"We will hide him, we will ensure they cannot stop his work." Roderick was torn, the risk sitting in the bunker was so great. He made this contentious decision for the people, he was not elected but took on the responsibility wholly. He had a great doubt about this decision. All he could be certain of was that they all faced a future of immense pain and suffering regardless of the virus.

The two men stood and walked around the people who lay on the floor so close to death. "Doctor, if what he says is true, we will watch these people die unable to help. Sacrifice is needed no matter how painful." The words were to reassure the doctor, all it did was reaffirm their path of suffering.

"Roderick I am worried, there is only so much more we can do." A man at their feet released a breath, they both new that it was the last he would ever take. Dr Chekov knelt down and performed the sign of the cross. No one cried, there was acceptance in his end. "We need to minimise their pain, our pain." One of the doctors helpers collected the body, so quick, they were used to the constant death. "I will go down and help Dr Fleming, in my old life we shared the same speciality. He mentioned reading one of my papers and being motivated to go into the field. Can you imagine that?"

Roderick could, Dr Chekov was a mentor and great inspiration for him. His tireless work to help others as he suffered. No longer was his mind valued by his adopted country, he was an immigrant and unhireable in that capacity.

The two men parted ways, Dr Chekov going to assist Dr Fleming. Roderick walked to the station to board his train. It took him to a job which was so menial and degrading the food it brought was all that stopped him from laying in bed all day. As he walked he spoke to the people who were there every morning. He smiled, did not allude to the terror they potentially faced. He could not give them the burden of fear that weighed so heavily on him.

Roderick stood on the platform, the wind whirred fiercely and he dug his hands into the clothes that began to fall apart. The trains were never on schedule, but today they were later than usual. The people on the platform with him began to multiply as multiple trains did not come. There was grumbling amongst the people, the irregularity brought out a fear.

After an hour of waiting the immigrants were met by a

military regiment. They were an ominous force, the men who worked in the immigrant zone were specially bred and trained to not feel a shred of compassion. They pushed the crowd from the platform and everyone stood in silence for some time.

"There will be no trains today." A voice boomed form the group who pointed rifles at them, "Return to your homes. You will not be working today". The regiment stepped forward in unison, pushing the group of immigrants backwards. They continued with another step herding the immigrants back to their homes. There was an anger in the crowd which was quickly suppressed by the machine walking towards them. The might of the military broke the spirit of the immigrants and they walked back to their homes.

"This is not right, how will I feed my family?" Felix Griffin said to Roderick as they walked. "They are up to something you mark my word". His steps got more forceful against the ground.

"Felix they are always up to something," he kept to himself the horrible reality. "We will feed our families, we will find a way. The harvest is coming in strong this year, we will share what ever we can".

"Thank you Roderick, you are a very kind man."

The two of them continued back home, to uncertainty and fear. Roderick spoke with people along the way, they felt deep fear today. He tried to reassure them but felt deeply disingenuous.

Alexander came running into the apartment, he had been out working the crops. Unable to go into the city for fear of being sent to the island, he worked hard where he could. Roderick was sitting with Nina, discussing what had happened, what he thought it meant for the people. The haste and fear in Alexander's face stopped them mid sentence.

"The military are doing a building by building sweep. They are taking anyone without papers." He tried to catch his breath, the fear in his body stealing it from him. "They are

searching everyone, there are thousands of soldiers Roderick."
The fear in his voice made Roderick feel like the older brother
again, protecting the little one. "You have to hide."
"We cannot all hide."
"Alexander right now we cannot think of everyone." He placed
a hand on Alexander's shoulder, "You need to hide."

Alexander ran to the top of the building, he would hide
in the garden bed. They had dug tiny caves into the side of the
garden beds for situations like this. They were a secret only few
knew. Nina began to shake, externalising the fear Roderick had
on the inside. "Roderick what do we do?" She looked him in the
eyes, "What if they take people?"
"They will, they are doing this for a purpose."
A voice boomed from the front of the building, "Residents
come down with your papers." Then an alarm began to sound
in the building.

The two of them joined the many in the building walking down. They clutched their papers, it was all that stopped
them from going down to the next level of hell. Soldiers
walked up the stairs as the people came down. They went into
every apartment and forced the inhabitants out. The absence
of compassion in the soldiers came forward as they beat people
into submission. Beat them into moving, beat them because
that is what they deserved.

Standing in front of the building they were forced to
walk in a line. Ten men checked the papers. Nina, Sophia and
Roderick held tight to each other. Roderick resisted with all
his strength to look back at the roof. The man checked Nina
and Sophia's papers first, he starred at her then waved them
through. Roderick held his papers up, the man put a hand on
him and pushed him towards a van. Nina scream and pushed
for him, an officer pointed a gun at her, "Move along".
"Nina go, I will be OK". Roderick yelled out with all the strength
in his body. With tears streaming down her eyes she moved
with the group of people. Sophia clutching her hand tightly.

Roderick was brought into a van and handcuffed to a

chair, his confusion evident, his papers legitimate. An officer walked in, not wearing the riot gear the others wore with pride. "Roderick Pravo, you have quite a story to tell."

"I am not sure what you want to know?" He said trying to suppress the immense fear.

"I want to know where Dr Carl Fleming is?" The officer sat across from him.

"I don't know who that is." Roderick's heart beat in his chest.

"You people are nothing but liars." He stood up tall, "You are also cowards. Do you know how many of your people told us about you and your friends. You protect the citizen, you are a liar. Tell me where he is, I am an impatient man."

"I am sorry I do not know."

"Very well." He called out "Bring him in".

Alexander was escorted in, hand cuffed and bloodied. His left eye swollen so badly he could no longer see through it. "This is your brother correct?" Roderick nodded, "I am sure you have heard of the island. I am sure you know that your brother doesn't have any paperwork."

Roderick kept quiet, he was sacrificing his brother for the greater good. Alexander spoke through his bloodied face, "Keep them safe, I love you brother". His heart broke, his soul crushed. He watched Alexander carried out, to his certain death.

CHAPTER SIX

Alexander fell out the back of a truck that moved many immigrants from the boats to the island facility. One hundred people fell with Alexander, most unconscious. They were all illegals in some respect, all taken in raids. As soon as they were taken off the boat they were pushed to walk past a line of doctors. Then as they stood, the doctor split them into groups. Those who looked healthy and those like Alexander who looked closer to death.

Water hit Alexander across the shoulder, pushing him forward. The pressure was immense, his frail body had not had the nourishment to withstand the battering. There was a spray from around him as the hose moved from person to person. The group who were deemed to be sick immigrants moved towards the gates before them.

Around him people fell and the hose hit them. Many fell out of consciousness and were woken by water. Alexander stood and stared at the gates in front of him, waiting for what ever horror was next. As his consciousness came and went he heard snippets of the guards speaking. "How many of these tests are they going to do, what more can they learn."
"There are plenty more sick immigrants to dispose of, better than us having to kill them."
"You growing a soft spot for them?"
"No!" The accusation made the guard angry. He looked to Alexander, "What are you looking at you filthy piece of shit?" He lifted his gun to Alexander's head. Alexander could barely see it as his eyes were almost closed over because of the beating he sustained. With the little vision he did have it was clear what

they meant to do, and he wish for it take him away from the pain.

"Put your gun away, don't waste your bullets."

There was a buzz and the gates opened. The water came on again and they were pushed into the yard. The grass on it was rough, brown except from where the immigrants were herded through with the hose.

Alexander walked far enough in from the gate so that the hose would not touch him. He fell under the hot sun and waited for the end. The people around him coughed, they were sick and injured, the most undesirable. August allowed them no comforts, torturing them until their deaths, experimenting on them. Alexander didn't even think about what the experiment was, he just hoped it would bring the end.

A man sat beside Alexander and offered his hand. Alexander offered his stump and the man put his hand down. "We will be ok my friend. They may act like barbarians but they will show us some mercy."

"What makes you think that?" Alexander said this head in the dirt.

"It is in our human nature."

"I don't think these people are human." Alexander slowly sat, the sun heating his head. "They are only here to torture us. We will die and they will be happy, this my friend is a taste of the hell that waits for us."

The man stood and stumbled away from Alexander, Alexander rolled back onto his side. His thoughts went to Roderick, the last he saw him Roderick was on the floor beaten. The only fear Alexander had was that Roderick was on the island as well. He didn't have the strength to look, didn't have the strength of spirit to see him in there.

The sun did not stay in the sky for long and night started to fall. They were kept in the yard to sleep, like cattle. Every now and then he would hear a sob, someone would die of what ever sickness condemned them to the yard. Alexander thought of Roderick and the life they shared. Family was the only thing in the end that kept him alive. It pained him the thought of Roderick in a place like this. He loved his brother and felt he deserved so much more.

The buzz of the gate rang through the quiet yard. Alexander lay on his side with the gate in sight. He could see the man being escorted in. The man had a chain around his neck, his skin looked like it was wax melting off a candle. He screamed and the yard looked for a moment. Then their collective strength wained and any attention disappeared.

The man at the gate yelled out loud. The two guards dropped the chains and disappeared behind the gate. The man looked enraged, lunging at those around him. He fell to the floor. Alexander watched, the man attacking the person he fell on. He didn't even look at his victim, it was unfocussed violence. The rage in him exploded with a scream and he buried his face into a chest that had stopped moving some time ago. He lifted his head and had taken flesh from the corpse.

The man stood again lacking proper control of his body. He got closer and Alexander could see that this thing was without eyes. The rage in him was not directed it was rage born in man. He got closer to Alexander and fell to his knees. He tried to stand but had left the lower part of his legs behind.

The man crawled, whenever he felt a body he would strike, tear at its flesh. The next mouthful of flesh was spat out with a tooth lodged in it. He continued to pull himself along getting closer to Alexander. Resigned to a death at the hands of this thing Alexander lay still. He watched with the realisation that this was the experiment.

Five meters from Alexander it let out the loudest scream yet. Then it was still, deathly silent. Alexander watched it inflate, it was unlike anything he had seen before. The skin was brought to its limit and then a pop. A mist rose and covered the yard. It was heavy and sat a couple of meters off the ground. Alexander breathed it in, the smell made his stomach churn though it had nothing to release.

Alexander felt something come from inside. A cough

was followed by blood. The blood came quickly from his coughs and then it came out of his skin. His skin lost whatever it was that previously held it together. He felt a rage grow inside, it engulfed everything until it was everything.

Alexander's body walked forward, screaming and slashing at those in front of him. Many of them died as soon as the virus entered their bodies. Alexander took three steps and then dug his teeth into the man who offered his hand. He came away with the better part of the mans neck. He drew back, blood dripping down his face. They screamed at each other, Alexander fell to the floor from a lady bitting into his leg, another scream.

Alexander bit at the air, trying to grab any who walked by him. Then came the loudest scream, his body giving up to the virus. His body inflated to its extremes and then popped a red mist into the air. Those around him popped as well. All one hundred and thirty-two people were dead within fifteen minutes. A deep red fog hung in the air.

Doctor Brian Walter walked into his supervisors office. "Jim, the sick ones show little to no resistance."
"Yes, but the strong ones are exhibiting greater resistance than we thought. The longest so far is four days and he shows no signs of dying." Dr Jim Nelson sat down behind his desk, "Brian we need to work out how to kill these ones. People bitten by a subject alive for longer than 72 hours can transmit to an inoculated person. Its mutation in the live body is unlike anything we have seen."
"If there is an outbreak we need to destroy anyone who is infected."
Dr Nelson looked into his monitor, it was a live feed into the cells that held their 72 hour plus subjects. "Can you please write your report, this needs to be given to General Christian Wilson immediately.

CHAPTER SEVEN

President Charles Terri arrived at the facility, his advisor ran through his schedule for the day. "Stop, I don't need to know every detail. Give me the speech I need to deliver tonight." He took the pages and scanned them quickly. "Keep me abreast of what the UN plans to do about our alleged misconduct. Cancel the remainder of my meetings. Put one of the ministers on it if it's important."

"Yes, sir, I'll make the arrangements now."

"Thank you," the car door opened. "Vincent I think you should sit this one out."

"Yes, sir".

President Terri got out of the car and shook Dr Jim Nelson's hand. "Dr Nelson thank you for taking the time out to brief me."

"It's an honour to President Terri."

"Please call me Charles." He followed the doctor into the facility, "Becoming President has been an interesting ride. One of the down falls is that people have forgotten my first name." The two shared a laugh, "More people do laugh at my jokes though."

The two of them went into a board room and sat down. "President Terri," he caught himself. "Charles, the virus is showing some unusual characteristics."

"Doctor that is why I am here." He looked around the room, "Our hand is being forced. The international community is accusing us of inventing this despicable agent to justify a war. If they do indeed decide to inflict full scale war I would like to be prepared. I would like our citizens to be protected."

"Yes, of course. That makes the human trials all the more important." The door opened and Dr Brian Walter walked in, "I'd like to introduce Dr Brian Walter, he is partnering me in these trials."

"President Terri it is an honour," the men stand and shake hands.

"Perhaps it would be better to go on the tour as we speak." President Terri nods and follows the men.

Dr Walter scanned the group through a door and then began to speak. "The virus in the documentation I was handed worked in a fairly predictable way. This was in the rat subjects. It was clear that roughly 20% died within 20 minutes, 30% in four hours and 50% survive indefinitely as a sort of living corpse." President Terri followed around a corner as Dr Walter spoke. "The last group basically broke down, till the body could not cope and the virus terminated the rat.

"It was predictable in that the virus had a common path. In humans we are seeing something different but following a path nonetheless." The three men stopped in front of a window. "We can predict based on how sick a person is, roughly the time it will take for the virus to kill that person. Taking a look at the anti-bodies in their blood and a few more markers we can tell that this man in front of us is due to expire."

The men stood and watched the man, he was laying the floor and began to convulse. His skin looked to have dislodged from the body. For ten minutes the three men watched the convulsing man. Then all movement stopped, the body began to inflate. Then the body popped, the three men all jumped backwards as the red mist filled the room. "We have not found a filter that can scrub out the virus so we need to use fire." The room ignited and the men continued down the hall.

"That man was predicted to expire in 3 hours and 42 minutes. We were thirteen minutes off." Dr Walter smiled at his brilliance. "This is a fantastic skill to have, this ability to predict the time of expiry has it uses.

"This calculation is effective until we get into the realm of 48 hours. Unlike the rats where they deteriorate the longer the virus is active, the human virus changes at about this time. Its form is markedly different. Charles, at the 48 hour point the virus goes dormant and the degradation stops. The body is in a state of slumber. The subject looks dead but there are weak signals of life." They stopped in front of a window and looked in. There was a woman, skin hanging, blood covered but peacefully standing.

"At roughly the 72 hour point the body and virus wakes. Their breathing becomes rapid and their rage is silent until they are close enough to a living person to strike. The virus seems to repair the brain and reprogram it to be a walking distributor of the virus. The body resumes it's healing function but it only diverts enough energy to keep it functional.

"The most concerning element of this metamorphosis is that the virus changes its structure so the existing inoculants are useless. We have been attempting to create an antivirus but in each case of this metamorphosis, the virus comes out the other end looking different. If there is any transmission of bodily fluids the virus will infect its new host."

"The new host displays all the symptoms of the original infection" Dr Walter speaking to President Terri but avoiding eye contact. "But they are immune to the inoculant. If they die after the 72 hour mark and send up a cloud, all around will be infected."

"How do we protect ourselves from this?" President Charles Terri stared at the sleeping woman. "How do we protect our citizens?"

"Charles, the only way we have been able to stop them is by incinerating the body" The woman in front of them woke and stared at the three men. She had a lustful look in her eyes. "I would recommend if there are any bodies that display this they are destroyed immediately."

The two Doctors walked President Terri to his car, they promised a comprehensive briefing. What he saw in there shook him, but he was still firm on his mission of reclaiming his country at all costs. Virus or not, August would be brought back to her rightful citizens.

In the car Vincent Daniels worked on his laptop. "Sir, they raided the immigrant zone but were unable to find Dr Fleming."

"Tell them to continue searching. I don't care if they need to kill every last one of them." He said this all with an absence of emotion. "His creation is beyond anyones capability. Only he knows how to manipulate it. I will not have him ruining what we have worked so hard for."

"Yes, Sir, I will send the notification for future raids. What shall we tell the citizens about the absence of immigrants in the city?"

"Tell them that they have rioted and we are working to have the situation under control"

"Yes, Sir".

"Vincent there is something I need you do for me. It is of the upmost importance." President Terri waved the driver to go. "We need a bill that will give me absolute control as soon as a war breaks out. Indecision will rip our country apart."

"Of course sir. I will do it first thing."

"Vincent, there is a war coming, it will be the fire from which our country rises." Charles Terri thoughts were of the woman starring at him. It was a moment steeped in horror, a view of the future. "We will rise."

CHAPTER EIGHT

Amidst the chaos of August using biological weapons on UN aligned countries, Kate had become incredibly busy. President Charles Terri had refused to communicate and all eyes turned to her. Former president and their best hope at reopening a conversation. She was lost in all this, her current position was on behalf of the UN not August.

"Bill what's the latest on the ship which returned?" She was in her hotel room, paperwork across the floor. She was trying to understand their current situation.

"Everyone onboard was infected, the virus cant be contained." He pulled out a paper, on it was a report with the UN insignia. "The virus is able to move through all filters and air scrubbers. The most advanced technologies available have only slowed the virus. They have towed the ship out to sea and have it anchored until they can work out how to proceed."

"So there is a floating infectious ship in the middle of the ocean."

"Yes, but there are also reports of the virus jumping to land." Bill put the paper on the desk in front of him and sat. "It is a plague we cannot stop. If the preliminary reports are correct there could be a 30% infectious rate within the month."

Kate paced, tapping a pen on her lips as she often did when under pressure. All thoughts of talking to the Australian Prime Minister went from her conscious mind. Responsibility had been placed on Kate for the actions of her country. "How did he do it? How has he created and weaponised it in such a short amount of time?"

"Kate, we were naive to think the Loyalists were just another home grown terrorist organisation. We know Charles Terri was their leader, they could have been working on this for years under our noses."

"Why go to war?"

"It makes him appear to be a strong leader, one who will protect his people. And if in that war a few hundred thousand immigrants are killed, who will notice?"

"Do you really think he is that evil?" She kept pacing and didn't wait for his answer. "We need to get as many immigrants out of August as possible."

There was a knock at the door and Kate opened it to room service. Lunch was welcomed, she felt her body weaken. "Bill we have to do something."

"Kate, what can we do?"

Kate's phone vibrated on the desk, she was happy to see that it was Grant. "Hi Darling, have you been following the news?"

"Yes, that is what I have called about." His voice was serious, not the lightness she hoped he would bring her. "Do you remember my friend Mary Bedford"

"Yes, she was the one who worked on immigrant welfare."

"Yes, she has just called me in tears. They have locked her and her organisation out of the immigrant zone. The checkpoints have been closed and people are unable to freely move in and out of the zone." He took a breath, clearly distraught by his conversation. "She said the last time she was there, funding cuts had meant people were dying of starvation." He took a deep breath, "They are doing raids weekly. The immigrants who don't have papers or resist are taken to an island in the West; a military base."

"Grant the island used to be a detention centre, a source in the military has said they are testing the weapon there."

"Kate they have inoculated all the citizens against what they broadcast as a weapon. They are saying the UN authorised its nations to use it. They have left the immigrants unvaccinated, even though by all accounts they have large stores of it."

"Grant I think they are going to do something terrible." She turned to Bill, "Grant I will call you later, I need to try and help in some way."

Kate put her phone down and slumped. "Bill they are going to kill the immigrants. We need to do something."
"What can we do?"
"Get the Secretary-General on the line, I need to speak to her."

Kate walked into the bathroom and splashed water on her face. She could feel thousands of souls screaming for help. Thousands of people who were separated from a horrendous death by only time. Thousands of people who she as President fought for, fought to have welcomed to her country. Now they were to be put to death, all in the name of misguided nationalism.

Bill called to her, "The Secretary-General is on the line" Kate came out of the bathroom and fixed her hair. She nodded to Bill and the screen came on.
"Secretary General, I apologise for keeping you." Kate smiled to her, the two had never met face to face but spoke on a regular occasion. She liked her, but was frustrated by the lack of resources she could offer.
"Katherine, it was nice to have a moment of quiet amongst what has been going on. What was it that you needed to talk to me about, Bill expressed some urgency."
"Secretary General, I have just been made aware of intentions by the Augustan government, to attack the immigrant population. They have given a vaccine to all citizens and built a wall to stop anyone, citizen or immigrant from moving into the city. I fear it is only a matter of time before they are eradicated."
"Katherine we have been made aware of this information, it is deeply distressing. I know you would want us to move against them but we simply do not have the ability."
"Then we are condemning these people to death."
"The nations of the world are preparing for one of the worst wars we have ever seen. Focus has gone to their own shores, especially after the attack on Eurasia."
"So we sit back and do nothing. We are going to watch these

innocent people die?"

"Katherine you must believe this isn't an easy situation for me." She paused, someone spoke to her. "Katherine a strike has just been approved on August for their use of biological weapons."

Kate felt a jolt in her that assaulted her soul. "Secretary-General how do we have the resources to attack?"

"It is a necessity, an act like this cannot go unpunished."

"I agree but a strike will be all that is required for Charles Terri to put in place what ever plan he has been working on."

"Katherine he must be removed from power. This strike is to destabilise his hold on power. Once he no longer has control, we will act to remove him and replace him with a temporary head of state."

"This is a bad idea. With respect, this will result in so much more death."

"Katherine, we would like you to take control of the country once we have him out. We need to know that you are on board." She paused, acknowledging the shock in Kate. "Katherine once you are in power, you will be able to help these people. It is the only way we can do this."

Kate's shock rendered her speechless, for a moment the fates of those people most in need rested on her shoulders. "I reluctantly accept this plan. If you are able to get Charles Terri out then I will step in. I must put it on the record though, this is highly likely to escalate the matter. This is like shaking the vipers nest and hoping they will sleep."

Again someone spoke off camera, "Katherine, I will send official communication to you shortly. Please know that I would not have endorsed this unless I thought it had a chance to work." She turned off camera again, "Kate I have to go we have just been told the virus has surfaced in Toulon."

The screen went dead and Kate turned to Bill, "Can you believe this. It is a mistake to escalate the war against him."

"What else can they do?"

She knew there was no answer that would adequately describe the impossible. They were heading into an unwinable situation. There was no way out of this that would spare the lives of millions of people. There was just a growing bleakness.

"Bill at the very least let's try and find who created the anti-dote, perhaps they will help us." She walked to the window. She was so far away from the world in Melbourne, she felt helpless to their suffering.
"I will contact any sources I have on the ground." He opened his laptop, "Kate to be honest, even if we find the person, it's unlikely we will be able to get to them."
Kate nodded and they went to work. She looked down the barrel of potentially being the Augustan President once more. She was conflicted about the plan, it was like being brought back into a bad dream.

CHAPTER NINE

"Vincent get in here now." President Charles Terri was furious at the news of the UN in talks with it's allied nations to attack. "The gaul of them, the world police. They have less than half the nations supporting them and they dare dictate to me what we can and can't do."

"Yes, Sir." Vincent avoided eye contact with the President, to avoid the immense fury often sitting just below the surface. "Sir, the UN Secretary-General would like to speak with you. Should I set that up?"

"Yes, as soon as possible Vincent." President Terri's attention went out in front of him. Starring at what was not there, focussing his anger.

"Who shall I include in the meeting Sir?"

"I will handle this myself." President Terri spun away from Vincent in his chair. "Vincent how is the bill coming along?"

"I have finalised it sir." He placed the folder on the large and imposing desk. It was much larger than the work dictated, but much smaller than the ego behind it.

"Thank you Vincent, I would like you to schedule a meeting with Craig Ford and Jerome Moffat to push this through." He looked at the bill, he was a terrifying man when displeased with work presented to him. Vincent hoped it was up to his standard. "Good work Vincent, if your work stays like this you will have a bright future."

"Thank you sir, I will prepare your meetings shortly."

President Charles Terri went through the bill with a fine tooth comb, this needed perfection. The bill proclaimed in the event of war total power would be transferred to the president. This ownership of power would be in effect as long as there was a threat on sovereign land.

President Charles Terri was angered the UN would dare threaten him. He knew this would be the event that allowed him to seize power from the woefully indecisive politicians. He was what the country needed, a man of strength and courage. To make decisions which would secure their safety and preserve the ideals of August. He made decisions that were for the betterment of the country, not himself. His intentions were pure and he had no malice in his heart.

President Charles Terri watched the news channels cover the risk of war. He believed the situation was under control. He pushed the enemy ships out of Augustan waters, he kept them safe. The inoculation of the populace was another example of his protective nature. He watched his rating numbers rise. They were the highest in his nations history, he was proud to be doing what his people deemed necessary. Many called him the iron patriot, strength in his love of his great nation. It reminded him of an old super hero he would read about as a child. The stuff of imagination, he turned his imagination into a reality. That was his strength.

"Sir the Secretary-General will be on the line in moments." Vincent walked into the office and stood before President Charles Terri. "Would you like to take the call in here or the conference room?"

"Here will be fine." The anger from earlier had subsided and his calm returned. "Vincent have you scheduled the meeting with the Party Presidents?"

"Yes, Sir. They will follow this meeting."

"Perfect, Vincent I would like you to stay for this."

"Of course sir."

Vincent closed the door to the presidential office. He took a seat at the right of President Terri. There was a sound from the computer and Vincent answered the call. A screen descended from the ceiling. "Secretary-General thank you for your time."

"The pleasantries displayed by my young aid are not an indication of the those shared by myself." President Terri took over with force most are not accustomed to. "Secretary-General we have reports that you are moving to strike my country. This action is an abomination to the ideals that your organisation claims to uphold."

"President Terri, we have already gained approval, I hope to obtain your cooperation. We would like to avoid any unnecessary blood shed."

"You dare call me threatening to attack and demand a ransom?"

"President Terri, the world cannot stand by while a nation develops and uses biological weapons of this nature. The world needs to take a stand, to ensure the suffering inflicted does not continue."

"The UN is not the world, you have shown nothing but weakness and that is why you suffer a membership withdrawal." President Terri stared at the Secretary-General, "What are your demands?"

"We demand that you cease your biological weapons program and hand the remaining over to us. We can then negotiate a way to resolve this very dangerous situation."

"Anything else?"

"We would like your help with the anti-dote to this disease. We are experiencing some significant casualties."

President Charles Terri had the face of a tyrant come to him. What they were asking was for August to be weak, unable to protect itself. He knew for a fact that many other countries were developing weaponry of the sort. He would not allow his great country to be left vulnerable. "Secretary-General we respectfully rescind our membership, it is because of your lack of foresight that we are unable to continue to align with the UN. Your demands leave us dangerously vulnerable. We will not be able to commit to your demands."

"You are condemning millions of people to a horrible death. I cannot believe that a man of your stature would allow this."

President Charles Terri sat tall in his chair and stared down the Secretary-General. "If you strike my country, you will see the full vengeance of my stature. Do not underestimate me or this great nation. We are a formidable enemy to make."

"We do not want to create a disharmony between us, we need you to work with us for the safety of all citizens of the world."

"Maria get your bunker in order."

President Terri ended the call and there was silence in the room. War had been enacted, it was only a matter of time. "Get Craig Ford and Jerome Moffat here now." President Terri shouted walking from his desk and looked out the window. "I want you to have the armed forces at the ready. If they strike I want the solution in place. We will use their illegal attack for the betterment of all Augustan citizens."

"Craig, Jerome thank you for taking the time to meet with me." The two party presidents felt uncomfortable about being in a room together, working as one. After Tony Trottel was killed the Loyalist's moved into the parliament and officially took power. They had members on both sides of the floor and demanded themselves to be heard. Unlike publicly reported it was not them who instated Charles Terri as President, they refused the motion. Both of the men quickly found themselves out of favour with their party majority and bowed to the pressure.

To save their jobs and place in society, the two would do most anything. It had not been the first time this motion had been enacted. Twice in the history of August the two parties put forward a man to lead until one could be elected. They never stayed in power as long as Charles Terri. They were caretakers installed due to untimely deaths. Within week they handed back the presidency to uphold democracy.

The two men felt the normal wheels of democracy grind to a halt. They were uncomfortable about it but unable to stop it from happening. They had lost control, they had given up control. It was a Loyalist democracy now, all who opposed disappeared to the Island.

"I have just been on call with Secretary-General Maria Singh of the United Nations. They are talking about preparing a strike against us because we are defending our boundaries." President Charles Terri herded them onto the couches, "We cannot stand by and bow to this kind of thuggery."

"Surely they cannot expect us to give up our right of protection." Jerome Moffat sat forward, worried for his country.

"They do." Vincent Daniels walked in and sat to the side of the men. "They have asked for all our K class and higher weaponry to be surrendered on punishment of military strike."

The two men were in shock, "If we surrender those weapons we would be defenceless." Craig Ford was astounded.

"Gentlemen it is for that reason that I have informed them we are unable to meet their request. They have informed me they will attack to warn us." He looked to Vincent and saw the very important folder on his lap. "Situations have evolved in a way we hoped to avoid. We will be at war soon. It is with this in mind that I have prepared a bill to ensure we are able to defend ourselves."

Vincent stood and gave the two men a folder each. They read through the document and both of them felt their worst fears being affirmed. "This will give you absolute power." Jerome stood, "We cannot bring this to parliament. It flies in the face of our strongly held democracy."

"Gentlemen this bill is only to be enacted in a time of war, it ensures that our government will keep running without the need for every decision to go through parliament."

"It ensures you will be in complete control."

"Gentlemen it is not the time for argument." President Terri stood to meet Jerome Moffat's stance and Craig Ford joined them. "This bill will ensure our safety. Gentlemen I hope I do not have to remind you of the support I hold. This country will not be rendered weak by your inability to do what is right. We are in a crisis." President Terri's voice raised in intensity, "You will do as I say."

Craig Ford and Jerome Moffat were mute by the sinking realisation that the man before them would be the most powerful person in Augustan history. In the likely event of war the parliament would dissolve and Charles Terri would be given complete executive control. "Gentleman thank you for your time, as you can imagine I need to go into a meeting with the heads of our military." As the men walked out the door he called to them, "This needs to be passed today."

Charles Terri sat with the heads of the Augustan military, they discussed their strategy for the likelihood of war. Vincent passed President Terri a note; *the bill passed with only two dissenting votes.* President Terri smiled, he was now able to do what he always wanted and that was to protect his much beloved country.

The men spoke of strategy, of how to retaliate so the world would realise their might. They would not be bullied, they would not bow to the UN or any country's demands of them. Discussions moved to the solution, if war was to happen. Under the cover of enemy fire they would release the virus, eradicating a resource hog that could not be sustained in wartime.

The men spoke into the night, they moved the necessary capabilities into position. This would send a sign to the world that they would be ready and willing to retaliate. The world was scared and they would take advantage of this.

It was in the night that Vincent came to President Terri. He could not sleep with all that was happening weighing on him. The responsibility was heavy and it was one he proudly wore.

President Terri was in his study contemplating what was to happen when Vincent walked in. "Sir we have been warned that enemy planes have entered our air space." Vincent was out of breath, "The military is retaliating, they have told me that the city will be attacked at any moment."

Vincent's words caused silence in the room, the two men were still. Then the explosion, it felt as if it was on top of them. The ground shook and threw them to the floor. The Presidents security detail took him and rushed to the bunker. The noise was intense, it demanded all around.

President Terri shouted as he stood in the bunker, as his country was bombed, "Retaliate with the full force of our nation." His rage exploded and shocked even himself. "Kill every last fucking soul who dare threaten us, we will destroy them." He threw a chair across the room.

For ten minutes the world shook and then there was silence and war had started. President Charles Terri had complete control. "Vincent disband parliament, issue a message that we are at war." President Terri called through to General Christian Wilson, "Engage the final solution."

CHAPTER TEN

The night was windy and blew at Nina Pravo's hair. She ran quickly, the sirens were on her back. The deep fear which had became an unwelcome guest was there again. The sound reminded her of the raids, the violence that had been so prevalent throughout her life. For so long the sirens directed her through life. They dictated if she could be inside or out. They dictated if she was to be at school or huddled at home. The sirens were a constant reminder of her lack of power.

The night was an ominous backdrop for the sirens. All the immigrants were in their homes, hiding from the destruction that came from the sound. She ran across the centre square and hid in a building. It was the first time since they took Alexander that there were no soldiers. They had gone to protect the citizens. Gone but their memory kept the immigrants in fear.

The sounds of sirens transported her to a time long ago. Before Roderick, when it was her father she clung to. The hurt from these memories never subsided and it attached more firmly to each year that passed. The sirens went quiet, it was in the silence she had the confidence to walk out and ran to the bunker.

Her thoughts went back to the memories, Nina's father was the centre of her life. He was the one her family looked to for guidance. Her respect for him was only out matched by her love. It was in the silence the uniformed men came to the house. They marched to declare victory, it was then the dictator took power. He protected the country and the people gave him their obedience.

A soldier walked into Nina and her family's home, without a sense of the pain he brought as he said those words. "Gustav Kleilar has been killed in the bombings." That was not the first death the soldier had to announce.

Nina opened the door to the bunker, leaving the girl who cried for her father outside in the tumultuous night. "Roderick they are sounding alarms again."

"Nina you can't be here." He took her hands, they were shaking. "If the soldiers see you." Both of them thought of Alexander. The pain was not knowing, the torture was believing the truth. "The soldiers have left." She walked towards the two other men hunched over equipment so foreign to her. In another life she would have wanted to be acquainted with them. "After the alarms started to sound the men left. It is empty outside, everyone is in their homes waiting for bombs to come."

"This is it," Dr Fleming took some of the vials of red liquid from the fridge. "They will use this as a way to send the virus to us. I hoped we would have more time, to produce more of it."

"What we have is a miracle in itself." Dr Chekov looked embarrassed by his surroundings. "To be able to create anything with this equipment."

"It is not enough." Dr Fleming took a syringe and filled it with the red liquid. "We have enough here to provide a dose for all of us in this room and about 5,000 more."

Dr Fleming administered their doses, "We should give the remainder to the children." Dr Fleming injected Nina and laid the syringe down on the table. The four of them were silent, contemplating what it meant to condemn thousands of people to a horrible death. "I will continue to make more, but I don't know how long we will be able to work."

"We must do all we can." Dr Chekov put the vials from the fridge into a box and placed with it as many syringes as would fit. "Nina, I need your assistance administering the inoculant. Roderick you need to stay here and help Dr Fleming. If we are lucky we may have a day."

Dr Chekov and Nina exited the bunker to save and condemn. Carl instructed Roderick on how to help. The door closed and then they felt the earth shake. The two men in the bunker ran, Roderick opened the door and saw a terrified Nina. He looked around but there was no carnage. "It will be ok, help the children. We are the only ones that can protect them now."

Roderick turned to Dr Fleming "what happened?" He was confused by the absence of destruction.

"They have attacked the city." Dr Fleming said. "Someone has attacked August, it is only a matter of time before they use this as a cover. We need to work."

The earth shook once again. Dr Chekov and Nina went to save the children. Roderick and Dr Fleming back into the hole, in an attempt to save all they could. There was another shake, the four of them were now accustomed to the feeling. They had pushed to the back of their mind the impending doom, they had a task that needed all their focus.

CHAPTER ELEVEN

Katherine Laurie with tears in her eyes watched as her country was bombarded by the organisation she now worked for. Bill sat beside her silent and observed the news feed. The world had cut ties with August, in that moment those bombs were the world showing their condemnation. The country now run by a tyrant and mentor. Tears were apt but also made her feel incredibly powerless. The images of people killed by incoming fire, a nation never before at war on its mainland. The fear on citizen faces, like the immigrants.

"Bill how can they do this?" She looked to him with such pain. They were not declaring war on August, they were declaring war on Charles Terri. The UN attacked its people for atrocities the people were unaware of. "This is a black day in the history of peace. We are a part of this mechanism now, we are a part of the mechanism that will cement Charles Terri as a hero in their eyes."

"Kate what could they do? He can't be negotiated with, you know that." He watched closely as his computer ticked over details. "How we have fallen." The truth was painful to them both. "It is now official, there is an embargo on all trade with August, agreed on by even the most marginal states."

Kate answered a knock at the door and Secretary-General Maria Singh walked in. "Maria what are you doing here?" "There has been a cataclysmic threat on the European continent. They have evacuated all they could. I demanded to be brought to you. We need to prepare you for when you are brought back to power and end all of this."

"Maria I warned you that this would be dangerous. How do you plan to get to Charles Terri at a time like this? His security will be tighter than ever."

"His security is stretched, the army is regrouping. It is now or never." Maria took papers from her bag. "We have also gained intel on the virus from people who defected from August."

"Who are they?"

"I am not at liberty to say at this time. They are rightly frightened for their lives." Maria handed Kate pictures of infected people, she had to take in air. Maria went on, "They have told us the man responsible for the virus is one Dr Carl Fleming. Have you heard of him?"

Kate paced tapping her lip with a pen she received as president, thinking of the name, of the so many names that she once knew. "He does sound vaguely familiar."

"I know him." Bill broke from his computer screen. "He was listed with suspicion when we were investigating the Loyalists. We believed he was a member of concern but after vetting him it was determined that he was only a member for social status. He had ideals that contradicted the Loyalists."

"What did he do?" Katherine walked towards Bill.

"Well, he was a government contractor, in the labs. I have his file amongst the documentation we took with us, I'll bring it up," Bill went back to his computer.

"Katherine, we have intel that he was working on the virus. He developed an anti-dote. We need him to help us."

"How sure are you about this?"

"The men we spoke to were confident, that is all we have to go on."

"Do you know where he is?"

"We have been looking for some time, we have located him in the immigrant zone. We are going in to extract him. I wanted to make sure we were not risking the lives of our soldiers on a fools errand. I was hoping you had some more information."

Bill called to them, "Dr Carl Fleming, worked on the project to develop a drug that could suppress illness in soldiers while deployed overseas. He is a virologist, and he reported to General Christian Wilson."

"Kate is it at all possible that this was a front for a more sinister program." Maria looked on with her usual sternness.

"General Christian Wilson was suspected but cleared. If we were wrong about him, which is a possibility, he had the means to organise a front organisation. Especially if he was using Loyalist money." She looked at Bill and then back, "We can't be sure but your intel makes a plausible case."

There was another knock on the door and the three of them turned to it. "Katherine, I would like to introduce you to the man who will be executing the missions." The Secretary-General opened the door, "This is Robert Mander, he is a part of a secret group that does not owe allegiance to any nations military." Robert stood and bowed to the three of them. "He does not belong to a nation, he is apart of the UN's secret military, so what we speak about here is to be kept here."

"Of course, how can we be of assistance."

Robert Mander took the seat he was offered. "Ma'am my team has been tasked with extracting Dr Carl Fleming. We have also been tasked with extracting or ending the life of Charles Terri."

"I am sure that you are highly capable but how do you plan on getting onto Augustan soil? Let alone get out?"

"Ma'am we are able to get in and out undetected, we have done so on your watch." Katherine felt a little anger that subsided on the thought of what they were there for. "We have identified Dr Carl Fleming in the immigrant zone. He is the easy target. What we need help with is Charles Terri, we are able to get to the Presidential building without being discovered. We need your help getting in."

Katherine knew exactly how she could help. "There is a secret passage that is used to get the president out in the event of an emergency. It is only known to top security personal who protect the President." She tuned to Bill, "Can you please print out the emergency evac plan." Back to the two of them, "I am giving you a means to murder the president of my country, to murder a man I knew well. If anything goes wrong and he lives, my usefulness will exhaust itself. I am giving you my life, because if my treachery is found they will kill me regardless of the security you provide."

They went over the plans and the weight on her chest grew. Robert Mander left the Secretary-General and Katherine, they went over the plans to put her into power. She was a traitor and if the plan went well she would be rewarded with power. The bombs kept exploding on TV. The strike severely weakened Augustan forces but they did not understand the lengths their armed forces would go. They all served because they were patriots, the best of the best willing to give their lives. She was ashamed that she was working against them.

CHAPTER TWELVE

"This is a profoundly sad day." Charles Terri held the hand of his wife tight. It was only on this day that he showed such weakness. He showed the uncharacteristic softness before his close friends and family, before his daughters grave. "Every year we are without her, the pain grows and so too does my love. My beloved Rachel was all to me and her passing took something profound from me." He allowed his tears, his wife sobbed and those gathered before them were somber. "It is on this day every year that I remind myself not to dwell on her passing, my pain will consume her memory if I allow it. On this day we celebrate the person that was destined to do so much good in this world. I am sure that she is above us doing all she can to make it a better place."

He remembered her face and the warmth of her. There was always warmth. When she was a new born laying on his chest, the warmth of her little belly on his big one. The look on her face when she was acting mischievous, the smile that froze him and rendered him unable to be angry. The warmth of her soft kiss on his cheek. He would never feel that warmth again. "The sun today smiles on us so we can remember the light she brought. Her memory will always be with us. Thank you all for sharing her memory, thank you for being with us today."

Charles Terri took his seat and the chaplain spoke. He was a broken man, he knew this. Broken from all the pain, he wondered what his daughter would think of him. Would he have been able to make her understand that he was protecting the citizens from feeling the pain he did? Perhaps he would not have taken this path had she been here. He would give it all away to see her once more. He was a patriot, but Rachel was his true devotion, he would have done anything for her happiness.

The ceremony finished and he thanked all those who came, his wife by his side. He forgot how to love her. She looked so like Rachel, the two sharing that softness. He couldn't look at her without pain. "I need to go to work." President Terri's wife was saddened by this. After Rachel's death she wanted to have another child but Charles was in such great pain. "Your brother will take you with him."

President Terri was escorted to his car. Vincent Daniels sat waiting for him. "Sir, I am sorry."

"Thank you, Vincent." He looked out of the window as they drove away, his family and friends disbanded. He took a moment for himself, to try and collect his thoughts. "Vincent has the bill been enacted?"

"Yes sir, parliament has been disbanded and you now have full control of August."

"Is the press waiting?"

"Yes, Sir."

Charles Terri stood in front of the crowd and they quieted for him to speak. "It is with a great deal of sadness." He paused, "No anger, it is with anger that I have to announce to the citizens of August that we are now at war. The UN has been resolute in their intentions to force us to be without weapons that protect our shores. They hoped that we would give up so they could walk into our country and take it.

"I have told them that we are a proud people and we believe in our country. In our right to protect ourselves. They have attacked us with bombs as a punishment for our resistance to their ways. How is this a democratic organisation? They threaten us with biological weapons. It is for this reason that I feel it necessary to declare war and move to protect us. To the men and women of our military, I would like to thank you for the sacrifices you make daily and those you will make with only the safety of our citizens in your heart.

"I have announced to Parliament that we are at war and they have taken the necessary steps to ensure our success. To them I would say thank you. To you the citizens I say god bless.

"We will fight for freedom, for our right to say this is our home, our way. We will protect our way of life and refuse their assertions. We will be victorious, we are August."

The crowd that gathered began to cheer. President Charles Terri waved and stood before them for a moment. They chanted, *we will be victorious, we are August.* He walked off the stage a wartime hero, he felt his rightful history being written. He knew there would be those trying to stop him, to take him from power. He believed his purpose was higher.

"Vincent is the final solution ready to go?" He was walking quickly to his office, to drive the nation to victory.

"Yes, sir."

"Tell the military to engage."

PART THREE

CHAPTER ONE

A Plague In August.

President Charles Terri stood before his people, the cameras, and the God his country worshipped. His country was under attack from the nations of the UN. They were striking as if August was a scourge on the world. The insult would not go unpunished. The final solution, infecting the immigrant population had been very successful.

For two weeks soldiers stood at the checkpoints and ensured that the escalating aggression wasn't let out. The citizen's protection was paramount, the immigrants were kept in their place.

President Charles Terri looked out from the steps of parliament and saw his nation injured. He felt their current suffering would be justified, in the end it would be these citizens who wielded power. August would crush the UN, they would feel the force behind his great nation.

"My fellow citizens," the people gathered to listen to their president, standing to attention. "There is much we have endured, so much pain which the UN has subjected us to. Yet still the great people of our nation hold their pride. Not only are the actions of the UN illegal, they are barbaric. They have lived up to our worst fears." President Charles Terri bowed his head, "They have chosen to engage biological weapons in an attempt to cripple our people. Their use of force, is an attempt to make us bow to them." President Charles Terri's head lifted and he stared into the camera. "Once again they have underestimated us, as a people and a government. From the moment we heard biological weaponry was a possibility, we have been working to protect our citizens. The inoculations provided to all citizens will protect each of you.

"There are those however who could not be inoculated before the UN attacked our country. It is with a great sadness, I must inform the nation that the immigrant zone was targeted and is now in a full and total quarantine lockdown. They have struck our weakest, those who are down trodden. I have not always welcomed them with open arms but this is not the way any person should be treated. This is not war, this is a humanitarian crime and they will be stopped.

"The immigrants are being supported by our aid organisations, trained people are helping. I can imagine that many of you have the urge to help, it is after all in our caring nature. I must ask that you do not, it is dangerous and there has been enough suffering had by us all.

"I would like to thank you all for the support you show your country and your fellow citizen. We will be victorious, we are August."

There was cheering and President Charles Terri looked out over his people. He allowed them to show their support. He allowed them to feel patriotism so strong in their heart. He was the face of resistance, to the UN, to immigrants and to an August so many feared it would become. He waved to the crowd, the cameras would capture the support. All those throughout the country, citizens would see a man who commanded a nation in absolute.

President Terri walked into parliament building. After immense noise the quiet was intrusive to his thoughts. Vincent Daniels gave President Terri a towel, the heat causing perspiration. "Sir the immigrants are pushing against the wall, the army is reporting that without reinforcements it is only time before they burst through."

"Why aren't they dying, they are the weak? The reports said

it should have rapidly wiped them out. Now we are being attacked by the UN and these infected parasites."

"Sir, they have reported many more cases of immigrants lasting longer than 72 hours, they don't know why this is."

"Great, the men who ran the experiments don't know why this is happening. How much fucking money did we spend for them to tell us they don't know? Tell them to find out." The anger was clear in his voice and it made Vincent recoil.

"Sir, they have also said the longer they last past the 72 hour mark, their aggression levels will heightened. If they pass the virus on from this point, there seems to be no incubation period. They are aggressive and will attack all around them within minutes. The inoculation is useless against these people."

"So you are telling me we have created unstoppable fucking zombies?" Vincent Daniels didn't respond, it was an embarrassment. "How do we stop them?"

"The brain stem needs to be severed, if their body is attacked it does nothing more than slow them down. We still have the problem of them exploding and infecting all around them. The best way to prevent this is fire, it seems to be the only thing that kills the virus."

"If they break through the barrier it will be disastrous, we need to stop them." The president thought for a moment, "I want the army to go into the immigrant zone and burn them all."

"Yes, sir."

"Vincent they need to be exterminated, if the barrier breaks there will be no stopping them."

The two of them arrived at the Presidents office, "Vincent, instruct the army to move on the zone as quickly as possible. The men that we send in can't come back, there is too much risk. Am I understood?"

"Sir, we will send our most patriotic men, they will die proudly for their country."

The President walked into his office, closing the door behind him. He needed a moment alone before he went into a meeting with the heads of his military. They were planning for the next strike, the next push against the UN. He walked to his desk and sat, closing his eyes to think. He opened his eyes to a gun barrel and a man in tactical gear. "Do not make a sound or I will have no choice but to end your life. Nod if you understand."

President Terri nodded.

CHAPTER TWO

Private Christopher Jonson was on his second week of deployment. He had been in the army for a year and this was his first posting. He sat watching the gate, watching the people on the other side make every effort to break down the quarantine barrier. Even as he came to the same place and watched the same activity day after day, he was still horrified by them. He never would have imagined the UN would spread such a disease, show such disregard for these people.

He watched their attacks on the gate. Their flesh hung like melting wax, when they lashed out at each other it came off like putty. The noises they made were unlike any he had heard a human emanate. In his twenty-one years on earth, he had never seen such horrors. Everything about them was unlike anything he had ever experience. It terrified him, they were the unknown.

Private Jonson's gun was permanently trained on the barrier, they had orders not to shoot but the urge was there. He had only seen one die, the body inflating scared him. The pop that showered the area in red, froze him in place, he never thought humans were this cruel.

Private Jonson felt a small amount of safety from the inoculation, but still he was fearful. The barrier shook violently, he was ordered to engage only if there was a breach, he prayed this didn't happen. For now he watched the gate shake with the aggression of those who wanted nothing more than to attack.

The people riddled with the virus reminded him of the

undead he watched in movies. As a boy and into his teens, he had an obsession with all things monstrous. He now wished he listened to his mother and watched something a little more Christian. The images from those movies played in his mind, the thought of one of them burying their teeth into a fleshy part of him.

The barrier shook again and then silence. This was not uncommon, for them to all of a sudden be still. There was a roar up into the sky and the shaking came back. His gun still trained, always trained.

There was an odd movement from the section of the gate in front of Private Jonson. The group of infected opened up, they made space for a little boy who was no more than five. With his little legs pounding the ground he ran to the gate and hit it with full force. His momentum stopped by the impact. With head raised, he released a guttural scream. He looked so much like Private Jonson's imagined his two year old son would at that age.

Private Jonson's gun became unsure in his hand, he could not hold the sights on the little boy. Even a boy infected with a virus so horrendous was still a boy. The adults around him seemed to give him distance. It put Private Jonson on higher alert. Then one of the men behind the boy took him by the left arm and leg. He began to spin, as fast as he could he spun.

Then with a guttural moan the man flung the boy to the top of the barrier. With a scream that cut through all activity, he flew through the air. The scream came not from fear, but anger.

As he came over the top of the gate, his little legs hit the bar and he spun to the ground. There was a thud at the bottom, still with his gun in hand Private Jonson looked on with horror.

The boy lay still on the ground, on the uninfected side of the gate. Private Jonson didn't know whether to hope the boy had survived or was dead. He was answered as the boy rose. His little eyes red, his head hanging from his shoulders. The boys right leg was shattered, he hopped in Private Jonson's direction. What was once such purity now had the stench of disease emanating from it?

The boy continued to advance with his slow hop, the head limply swinging each time his foot hit the ground. Little grunts escaping every now and then but for the most part he was silent. He locked onto the boy through the sight of his gun. The silence froze him, he watched the boy get closer through the cross hairs.

Private Jonson didn't hear his Sergeant ordering for him to shoot. He was deaf to the world, only hearing the boys occasional grunt. "Shoot him" there was real fear in the Sergeants voice. He had been privy to reports the front line soldiers were not. He knew that their was a great chance the boy was a *72*, he knew what it would mean if they were infected.

"Shoot him," Private Jonson could not hear him, the boy was so little. His wife would be holding their son right now. In a few years he would be just like this boy. Innocent but for what the world heaped on them. The tears fell down Private Jonson's face, could he shoot the boy, could he shoot his son if it came to that.

The men around him had retreated as per protocol. The area was now quarantined, they could not risk the infection being released to the general population. A siren went off, the Sergeant had ran back to his post and hit the button that was adorned with a big orange sign saying 'breech'.

The sirens finally woke Private Jonson, reality came back with tiny hops. The boys attention fixated, the groans were a quiet reminder. With a soft squeeze and a feeling of loss, a bullet was sent to the boy. The gunshot rang out louder than the sirens, it pinpointed the act of barbarity.

The bullet struck the boy, his little body recoiling violently. The disease had taken hold of the little boy, it ate away at his human structures. The skull no longer containing the amount of bone necessary.

The areas around the boy was now showered in his flesh

and blood. Private Jonson dropped his gun, his training was worth nothing sitting there in the filth. The humanity of the situation brought the handgun to his mouth. He could not live to see his little boy suffer like this. He could not live for this to be a life made normal.

The quarantine team took him by the shoulders and stripped him of his clothes. The gun was thrown in the heap. They threw all the infected material into bright orange bags. Private Jonson ran to get his gun, the naked and crying man was out matched by the highly trained team.

They set up a hazmat shower and scrubbed him, getting every last infected cell. They hoped he would be safe, they would try and save every last citizen. From over the top of the shower he could see the little boy inflate, before he could pop the team burnt him till there was only ash. Then they burned the surrounding area. They took no chances. They did not stop till all was black.

Private Jonson woke in a cell, concrete walls and a toilet in the corner. His skin itched and he couldn't stop scratching. It moved under his hand unlike it had before. All over his body it itched, it felt as if it was coming away. The door opened and a man in a hazmat suit walked in. Private Jonson stood to attention until his legs gave way and he fell back to the bed.

"What has happened to me?" He directed all his considerable anger towards the man. "I am supposed to be inoculated".

"I am afraid the infection has mutated and is able to infect the inoculated. We are trying some new medication to purge it from your system."

"It's not working," he pulled at his skin. He could feel a clear distinction between the skin and muscle. "You have to try harder". He attempted to say something else but his voice emitted only barks. The words began to disappear from his mind, the message was lost. All he could feel was anger.

The man in the hazmat suit stepped out of the room.

He turned to the man who observed. "The drugs were ineffect-ive, he is transitioning." Christopher could only feel a burning rage. He ran to the window, he wanted to break through it. He banged on it, he knew in one moment he could not get through and then in the next the concept of a window was foreign to him. He banged on it to get to the men, thats what was import-ant. The men were his focus, he would not have been able to articulate why even if his voice continued to work. All that was important was to attack them, the rage was them.

On his back there was a heat he was ignorant to, he continued to attack the window. Blood smeared on it, his skin tearing. The heat ate away at his body, he fell to the floor. Right up until the moment he felt no more anger, he used his disfig-ured body to attack them. Then he was nothing, the intensity turned his body to ash within minutes. That was all that was left of many. Ash and a family who would never know their true suffering.

CHAPTER THREE

The soldier held a gun to the head of August. A travesty that would not go unpunished if President Terri could help it. "Charles Terri, you are under arrest for crimes against humanity."

"You have no authority here", he said in defiance. "If you do this, you will feel the full force of our military. You will regret this day."

"Charles Terri I have been instructed to extract you." The soldier turned to his men, "Move out."

"Who do you think you are?" Charles Terri stood and the men raised their guns to him. With his most presidential tone he spoke at them, "You are trespassing and I will not stand for this."

The door to the office opened and Vincent Daniels walked in, "Sir, apologies for disrupting you." He saw the men and shouted out for guards. He turned to run and the solder standing closest shot him in the back. He fell to the floor, the bullet went into his chest cavity and stopped its movement. The soldier dragged him back into the room and saw the August military personal approaching. The door closed, "Sir we have been compromised."

The man in front of Charles Terri put plastic ties around the Presidents wrists, "We need to move" If they took him alive they could show him abdicating, a more peaceful situation. They pushed President Charles Terri, he resisted and then felt the end of the gun in his back. They moved to the tunnel. The door to the office flew open, shrouds of wood flying into the room. With three pops the two men who entered first fell to the ground.

The three soldiers and the president of August went to the back of the presidential office. They pushed the book case and the entrance to the tunnel opened.

In the tunnel they moved as quickly as Charles Terri would allow. "You will not get me out of the country, you will be killed for this," The men ignored him, this was not the first time they had forcibly extracted a head of state. The missions they were responsible for never officially occurred, they were ghosts in the world.

There was a noise ahead of them. The soldier in front of Charles Terri turned, "There is someone at the end of the tunnel."

"Of course there is, the presidential escape route is only known to the President. I knew that traitorous snake would be in league with the UN. Did you not think I would neutralise all her information."

"Sir, we are boxed in here."

"Yes, you are, there are many men waiting for you. If you release me now your death may not be such a foregone conclusion."

There was a crack of light ahead, then the distinct sound of metal rolling down the tunnel. President Terri turned to his captures. I have been inoculated from the disease. The very painful and soul destroying disease. My guess would be that you have not. "There was a small explosion and then they felt a mist on them. "Boys you will be very interesting subjects for our study."

The calmness of President Terri terrified the three men. The doors opened from both ends and the military began to advance on them. They opened fire at the advancing men. The lead shouted to his men, "Take out the president."

The disease began infecting and the sound began to invade. Back to back they fought the oncoming military, then weakness overtook them. The confusion set in. They lost the president in the haze that ate at their minds.

The two soldiers in front of the president were hit and fell to the ground. Charles Terri looked into the red eyes of his would be capture's, "You underestimated our abilities. You will pay for that. I am going to allow this virus to eat you, to poison your very soul. I will let it consume who you are and then I will send you back to your family to infect them." The soldier convulsed on the floor, the pain was quick. President Charles Terri walked to the men in front of him. Saved with the proof that he was true to his position and destiny.

Then there were two pops and Charles Terri fell to the ground. The bullets like with Vincent Daniels, entered his back. President Terri looked up at the soldier, kneeling before him, holding onto his jacket. The man traumatised at seeing the president like this. "Make sure the people know that our former President was responsible for this treason." He blacked out with the loss of blood.

One of the Presidents soldiers slumped against the wall, the second bullet had entered his skull and blown out the back of it. The virus still hung in the tunnel, slowly settling on the walls and floor. "Burn it out," the call came from the top of the tunnel. All the men evacuated, and an intense heat engulfed it.

The men in hazmat suits stood watch over the flame. They had become more of a fixture in the new August as time marched on. The inoculant, whilst highly successful and its efficiency rising was not absolute. People popped up across the country and they took care of them, discreetly. The 72 were their greatest priority and threat. These men safeguarded August from complete disintegration.

CHAPTER FOUR

The three men tasked with extracting Dr. Carl Fleming had worked together numerous times. They shared many memories and events that separated them from normal society. The three of the them could speak to no one but each other about the extraordinary events in their lives. All this considered, they never knew each others real names, their families or any detail, not pertinent to their roles. Their work became their life and the world they went back to was a hollow existence to endure.

They sat in the back of a red cross truck; Mike, Harry and Charlotte. The truck was their way in, the only way any outsider was able to breach Augustan boarders. President Charles Terri agreed to allow aid workers into the country. This would show that it wasn't the despicable place the UN reported. He managed them, allowed them to go where he wanted. He kept a small enclave of immigrants in the South, alive and well to show off to their people. They knew the truth and this was the reason that every person in the vehicle was nervous.

They had two aid workers with them, one driving the truck and the other to assist. Neither of them would sit in the back with them. The weapons radiated unease. The fact that they were aiding a military force went against their ideals.

The road was bumpy, the three soldiers in the rear sat in quiet. They had been briefed, they knew their roles. In civilian clothes they sat beside an arsenal and tactical gear in bags of rice. They could pass as aid workers if they were stopped, delivering food to the less fortunate.

Unauthorised persons were banned from going to the true immigrant zone, for their own protection. The government distributed the message that the disease had ravaged those that were in the Northern immigrant zone. The red cross truck came to the immigrant zone from the rear, away from the city. This point had fewer guards patrolling. It fenced off the forests at the rear, very few people, immigrant or otherwise went there.

The two UN workers saw lights coming from up ahead. The driver Mohammed turned to the three soldiers in back. "There is a vehicle coming." The only vehicles that were anywhere near the immigrant zone were the military. The three soldiers sat in silence, guns concealed under their seats. If they needed to, they would competently use them to neutralise the threat.

The lights came up quickly. The two red cross workers were getting more nervous by the second. The silence of their cargo worried them further. The patrol was now no more than 10 seconds away. Everyone seemed to breathe in unison, then they all stopped together.

The patrol car roared past at a speed, never even acknowledging them. Out the back of the truck the three soldiers watched it drive away. They were happy, they wouldn't need to kill another person.

The rice spilled out as it was tossed from the now stationary truck. They emptied it onto the side of the road. The red cross workers waved after the three had taken their cargo, it was a wave of courtesy. They were happy to drive away.

The three soldiers changed into their tactical gear, the grains of rice became uncomfortably stuck to the inside. They put their gas masks on and prepared to scale the great fence. The three of them paused for a moment to consider what they were about to do. This time could be used to consider what they were to do, or to say a prayer. Each time they shared this silence they could be walking to the end of their lives.

Scaling the fence was not a challenge, the barbed wire was covered by the rice bags, thicker than the usual economy packaging. The three pairs of feet hit the ground and they began their trek through the trees. Silence from all three and their radios. In a complex and demanding world they were invisible to all but each other.

It took no longer than ten minutes for them to reach the main immigrant area. The edge of the trees led into open areas. The buildings were built in such a way to create communal spaces. When August valued the welfare of the immigrants, these areas were meant to be used to build community. They were now pockets of danger.

Charlotte looked down at the screen on her wrist. They had dropped a GPS marker on the bunker during a fly over. Charlotte pointed them in the direction and they moved to the closest building. They used the shadows to disguise themselves. They moved swiftly with a silence almost inhuman.

A group of infected immigrants moved in the direction of the group. Without speaking the three moved into the doorway of a building. There were six infected people, they walked together but did not interact. The soldiers watched them through a window. The violence they showed towards the uninfected was not shared between them. The greatest shock was the profound sadness they all embodied. The aggression was a part of the disease, something in them that was still human displayed the sadness.

The group of infected moved on and the three continued under the guidance of Charlotte. The depth of poverty they saw in this place was counter to the wealth that the cities shared. This was not a new poverty, this was ingrained. Building to building they moved undisturbed. Then as they crossed a courtyard they came face to face with four infected adults. They moved to the nearest doorway and a little girl came screaming out of it.

There was a pause from all sides, the infected looked at them. They tried to understand their presence. The one closest, the biggest man, made attempts to speak. His voice didn't allow what his brain wanted to say. These were 72's, the disease rebuilding the body. The voice would never come back but perhaps the thoughts hadn't completely gone. The aggression was immense, they watched themselves do heinous things. They were trapped in a body unable to affect change.

The man made another attempt to speak, all that escaped was a beastly growl. The remainder joined him, the anger was so infectious. The soldiers stood back to back. The weapons in hand were equiped with silencers and made popping sounds. Four quick pops and the bodies began to inflate. Then the cloud of red. This seemed to draw more towards them. The fifth pop inflated the little girl. All three felt their humanity shrink back at this act.

What the soldiers were interpreting as an attack, the infected saw as trying to protect themselves. Six more pops before they reached the next building, more came from around the corner. They walked through the buildings shinning their spotlight in the darkness. There was no one in this building. They looked out the window and a confused mass stood there. It was a tense moment before they disbanded. These creatures were quick to anger but also quick to forget, their grunts dissipating into the air.

The disease ate away at their brain. They lost memories quickly which aided the three soldiers quietly hiding in the building. They were surprised by how the aggression went as quickly as it came.

As the last of the infected moved on the soldiers began to move out. Charlotte came around a door and was met with an infected male. This one also angered quickly, she raised her fire arm. His arms were surprisingly quick. He grabbed her and pulled her close. She got two shots off into his stomach but it was not enough to stop him. The pain escalated the anger he was displaying. He bit down on her neck through the balaclava, his teeth finding their way to skin, to find a stream of blood.

Mike was the next through the door, and saw the infected biting down. Charlotte did not scream, she was a soldier to the end. Mike shot the infected through the top of its head. It dropped to the floor. Harry walked around the corner, "Charlotte has been bitten."

Harry raised his gun, "Charlotte you need to take off your glasses."

She lifted them up, the two men spotted the red and there were two pops. Neither knew who killed her. They took the GPS and left the building.

It took them less than three minutes to reach the door of the underground bunker. Mike attempted to open it while Harry watched his back, he scanned for any infected coming towards them. It was clear, an empty wasteland that held a certain calm. An infected woman came from around the corner, and Harry shot her in the head. She lay on the ground, Harry watched her as she inflated. The shirt that she wore burst its buttons; popping off one by one. Then the belly exploded. The red mist hung in the air and with a gust of wind it coated them.

The two soldiers pushed their gas masks against their faces as the red enveloped their environment. Mike signalled to Harry as the door clicked open. He spun around and the two moved into the bunker with their guns pointed.

They walked down a hallway into the first room and encountered a man. Harry yelled out, "Get on your knees and put your hands on your head." It wasn't Dr Fleming. They moved through the bunker, and saw an older man and a lady. Again Harry shouted, "Get on your knees".

Then they turned and saw the man in a makeshift laboratory. "Dr Fleming we need you to come with us."

CHAPTER FIVE

The infected often banged on the door and the noise Roderick heard remained unnoticed. They followed them back to the bunker after those in the bunker went foraging for food. The infected persons memories were poor but still occasionally they would bang at the door trying to get in. Then it changed and Roderick's ears pricked. The noises Roderick heard were not banging, they were meticulous. Nina and Dr Pravo were asleep while Dr Fleming was in the lab, leaving the bunker silent. The sound was all the more peculiar in the absence of activity.

The clicking at the door stopped and so did Roderick's movement to the door. He stood so still listening for that clicking to start again, was it his imagination? Then it started and he walked a little further. One loud click and the door opened, his fear gripped him, they were in. It felt an instant between the door opening and the men standing in front of him. The one to the right yelled, "Get on your knees and put your hands on your head".

Roderick dropped to his knees and the man on the left put plastic zip ties on him. Then they were gone into the next room. He heard them yelling at Dr Pravo and Nina, he lifted to his feet but toppled without his hands. Carefully this time to his knees, with a concentrated effort he reached his feet. He ran towards the intruding men and found them with guns aimed at Dr Fleming. They said something to him but Roderick could not hear it over the buzzing of adrenalin. He ran into the soldier on the left burying a shoulder into his lower back. He fell on top of the soldier with gun in hand. Before Roderick could do anything further the soldier on the right kicked him onto his back and pointed a gun at his head.

Nina screamed from behind them, the man on the left got to his feet. He turned and pointed his gun at Nina, "Nobody fucking move". There was quiet, a gun became all the more real once it was pointed at you. "We are not here to harm you. We are here on behalf of the UN. We need Dr Fleming to come with us, he is urgently needed.

From under the foot of the soldier Roderick spoke, "We need him here, have you not seen the state of our people?"

"We have the facilities to help his work, we need him. This is not a question."

Dr Fleming stepped forward from behind the glass of the lab, from behind the once portly doctor the two soldiers saw one of the infected individuals alive on the table. "What the fuck are you doing to it?" The gun pointing out his concern. Dr Fleming came to the window, "I will come with you on three conditions. First; you must untie my friends and treat them with dignity, second; you allow me to collect my things and third; you will tell me how you will use my research to help these people."

The men nodded, Dr Fleming walked into the air lock. He undressed and was showered, the medicine that he was developing to treat the 72 hour cases was used in a diluted solution to disinfect anyone that came out of the lab, it was their most powerful hope.

Dr Fleming stepped out and turned to the soldiers, they cut the shackles off of the three terrified survivors and stood on guard. "You can take those masks off, they're useless against the disease. The mask I wear was specially designed. No small feet with these conditions. It aerosolises the new inoculant with each breath." The two soldiers took their masks off as Dr Fleming began to pack a bag. "What are your names?"

The one on the right spoke, "My name is Mike and that is Harry."

"Doctor, their eyes." Roderick was on his feet and moved away from them.

"You have been infected, how long has it been?"

"Since what?"

"Since you were in contact with the blood of an infected." Dr Fleming walked over and examined them, "Did someone explode near you."

"Just before we came through the door." Mike said a little sheepishly.

"Roderick get some of the medicine and a syringe." He turned to Mike, "Did any of it get in the bunker?"

"I don't think so, it settled before I was able to crack the lock."

Roderick came over with two syringes and a vile. "This is going to hurt. I need you to stay perfectly still. Lay on the bed.

Mike and Harry refused to move until they saw the red in each others eyes. They knew the colour would be a risk to the mission.

Roderick handed the supplies to Dr Fleming, Mike was the first. He wanted to scream as the needle slid in between his vertebrae just below the skull. The medicine needed to be injected as close as possible to the brain stem, to halt the disease in its progression. Dr Fleming moved to Harry, the want to scream was in him as well. He had control enough of his body to lay perfectly still.

"You are going to have a stiff neck, one of the compounds has a slight numbing effect." They both rubbed their necks.

"How will you know if it has worked?" Mike was concerned. The sight of them, body mobile but soul trapped terrified him.

"We wont, this has an 80% success rate over the infected that we have experimented on. It pauses the disease, the earlier the better. The only way we know if it worked on you is if you get more aggressive."

"Doctor is it supposed to make my skin itch?" Harry rubbed at his sleeves. His face began to go red. "It's really itchy."

"Are you allergic to any medication?" Dr Fleming pulled up his sleeves.

"No"

"This looks like an allergic reaction wouldn't you say Dr Chekov?"

Dr Chekov offered a second opinion, "It looks like the disease has localised in the skin." He pushed on the skin, "The flesh underneath is normal but the skin is degrading."

Harry stepped back, he took his top off and his whole upper torso was inflamed. "You need to do something." He doubled over in pain. The doctors got him an ice blanket and wrapped it around the red torso. They didn't know exactly what was happening, all they could do was treat the symptoms.

Harry sat on the floor, the coolness took away the sting of his skin. He closed his eyes and looked to be in meditation. Dr Fleming and Dr Chekov watched him, they hoped that this was an unfortunate side affect but both felt it was more than this. "Harry, we need to move you." Dr Fleming tapped him on the shoulder.

"What do you mean move him?" Mike stood in between the doctor and his fellow soldier.

"We don't know what this is. This could be a side effect of the treatment or the disease could be fighting." Dr Fleming leant into Mike, softening his voice. "Which means it may be a matter of minutes or hours before he turns. We need to move him into the lab where we will be safe." Mike with a heaviness nodded.

The room was silent, they all hoped it was a side effect but deep down they felt it was much more sinister. Mike and Dr Fleming lifted Harry by the shoulders. They took the ice blanket from him. On his feet he screamed, "The blanket, I need the blanket. I'm burning up."

The red of his skin came back, it almost glowed under the dim lights. Boils began to raise across his body. They started out small, then they grew. Harry screamed, the pain gripped him and he forgot all his training.

"Get him in the room." Dr Fleming shouted, and Mike began to drag him. The boils on his back reached the point at which the skin could no longer hold together. They began to pop. With each pop Harry shouted into the air, with each pop the room was covered in a fine mist. The mist saturated the area, the uninfected tried to shield themselves but could not avoid breathing it in.

Mike dragged Harry into the lab and dropped him on the floor. Harry looked up, like a person possessed by a demon, "Mike, I am going to disembowel you." He leapt off of the floor and towards Mike. He drew his side arm and shot Harry in the head. He fell back to the floor with a lifeless thud.

Mike came back into the main room, "We need to leave now." His tone was firm and did not allow for questions.
"You have infected them all, I need to help them." Dr Fleming pointed to the three people who were now his family.
"I will kill every last one of them if that makes it easier." He lifted his gun to Nina.
"No" Dr Fleming walked to Dr Chekov. "I have left enough supply for a month. My research notes are in the lab, use it to make more. I will come back to help you I promise."

Dr Fleming put on his back pack, they were all silent. Covered in a disease that will kill them, even if it slows the progress at some stage they will die of it. "You need to inject the medicine, the sooner you do it the better."
"We need to go." Mike pushed Dr Fleming.

Out of the bunker they were met with three of the infected, Mike shot them with no thought. They began their attempt to escape from August.

CHAPTER SIX

"Bill they've called us into an emergency briefing." Kate tapped him on the shoulder. He was working on her potential reappointment speech. They were both uncertain of the validity of the plan, in fact they both thought it wouldn't work. Even so they prepare. If it happened, if they went in with the backing on the international community it was possible they could affect real change. Bill knew Kate held grave concerns, even for the tyrant. Bill couldn't help but hold out hope that somehow it would work, the good winning the battle.

"Has the operation been executed?" Bill looked on hopefully.

"I'm not sure, they are still staying very tight lipped." Bill closed his laptop, she sat beside him. "Something has happened. For good or bad, it will be a moment we remember for the rest of our lives."

The greatness of it rested on them. They could be overthrowing a government, forcibly reinstating Kate as President. "We need to leave now." Kate walked out of the room, even at 3 am she was ready to face the world. "Bill you have to wear pants."

"Its 3 am, this is the time of the day that pants should be optional." Bill got dressed, taking his trusty laptop under arm.

The briefing room was a large conference room, walls covered in screens. The glow broadcasted intensity, people used to war looking concerned. The 30 or so military and political figures sat silent. Maria walked into frame of the main front screen, the look on her face was not one they had hoped she would have. "Good morning all. One half of the mission you were briefed on has been concluded with devastating effect." Maria pointed to a man at the back of their room and a video of the attempted assassination of President Charles Terri began to play. "This morning we enacted the mission coded 'Stanley'. The objective of this mission was to remove Charles Terri from power by any means necessary. This objective has failed. Our three special operation agents were killed. Charles Terri has been injured, his current status is unknown.

The room was silent, the acknowledgement that their best men had failed pressed on them all. The room watched with sadness as the screens showed the men getting ambushed and then their horrific deaths. The room collectively held their breaths as they watched men slowly and painfully die. Deaths that rested squarely on the shoulders of their decisions and intelligence.

Maria waved to the man at the back of the room and the screen went blank. "This is a monumental failure to our objectives. This will strengthen the current Presidents popularity with his people. This next video is with concern to you Katherine," the attention fell on her before a video began to steal the spotlight.

The screen played, it was the speaker of parliament at a press conference. Jack Weald looked solemn, his eyes to the podium before he spoke. "My fellow citizens it is with a sadness I must inform you our President, Charles Terri has been shot. At 6 pm this evening, UN soldiers infiltrated the presidential office and attempted to abduct our head of state. To the credit of our service people this abduction was thwarted. When cornered they took the cowardly option continually shown by the United Nations and shot the President in an attempt to end his life."

There was a pause, the sense of violation could be felt through the lens. The breath of a nation stopped on hearing this news. "I have spoken with the President, while his situation is serious he is stable thanks to our great medical professionals and a god that watches over our nation. He is a strong man and the doctors have said he will make a full recovery. Even when close to death his thoughts are of his people and he wanted to convey this message. Do not let this atrocity fill you with fear, there are many bumps on the road to triumph. We are a strong and dedicated nation, we are August."

The speaker composed himself, and looked into the cameras. "It is to no surprise that the UN is again at the heart of an injustice perpetrated on our soil. The person who made this possible, giving them intel to allow an attempt on the life of our president was ex-president Katherine Laurie. It is with much sadness that this revelation was brought to our attention. Mrs Laurie you have brought shame for your treachery. We will work to bring her to justice."

The speaker thanked the audience and walked back into the building. The room in which Kate sat went cold. Katherine was a traitor to her country, she was now without a home. Maria came back to the screen, "It was a great risk we took, Katherine it was a great sacrifice you made to try and bring peace to a divided world." She paused. Kate had tears in her eyes, there were so many things to cry for. "We have received intelligence that has indicated there is currently a threat on your life. There is a jet waiting to take you to an undisclosed location. Ladies and Gentlemen we are closing the circle on information about the location of Mrs Laurie.

"There is little more that I can tell you. There is currently a mission still ongoing. This will be reported on as soon as the people involved are back on friendly turf. Thank you everyone."

Katherine Laurie sat on a jet with Secretary-General Maria Singh on screen in front of her, "Katherine I will meet you at our offices in New York. We have the strictest security there."
"My people want me dead Maria, I am hated by them."
"I am sorry, it was a risk that we knew could bare fruit."

Kate sat there, Bill and her had not said a word to each other since being rushed to the plane. "Maria you need to ensure that Grant is safe."

"He has been brought into a safe house, he will be moved to meet up with you soon" Maria was silent for a moment. "The second mission is coming to conclusion. Dr Fleming is in the process of being extracted. We are positive of this outcome."

"Maria what do we do now?"

"We ensure your safety and then we work with Dr Fleming to create a cure for this evil disease Charles Terri has unleashed. I am sorry for your loss, I feel a great empathy for you. We cannot forget why we are doing all of this. There have been 200,000 reported cases throughout Europe of this disease striking. That is 200,000 people that we have had to kill and burn. It continues to move, changing to avoid control. Without stopping Charles Terri and finding a cure to this disease we have a disaster greater than any seen before.

"I feel your pain but I also feel the responsibility which sits on all our shoulders to stop this tyrant."

Kate looked out of the window, the truth was cruel, the truth was coming quicker than they could comprehend.

CHAPTER SEVEN

Mike stopped for a moment allowing Dr Fleming to catch his breath. They had been running from the bunker and Dr Fleming was anything but a fit man. "We need to be quick, it's not just the infected that we must worry about."

"I assure you they are the most terrifying thing in here." Dr Fleming mumbled as he caught his breath or had a heart attack, he wasn't sure of which.

"If we get caught by the military we wont just be killed, they will torture us. They do regular fly overs of this area." Mike kept a watch out for any activity, it was quiet for the moment. "Doctor these infected people were created by you. They were not a defect of nature. In my opinion you are the most dangerous thing in here."

Dr Fleming was taken aback for a moment, the reminder that this awfulness was of his doing came to him. He was working so hard to cure the disease he had forgotten it was him who had been its father. "Mike I didn't know what it was to be used for. If I had…"

Mike cut him off and started to walk, "I have been in the military for my whole life. I know the boundaries which we cross, those the people who sit at home would find abhorrent. I know there are things we have to do. This is not one of them, this is a glimpse into your terrifying psyche."

An infected girl stepped out from behind a building. Mike grabbed Dr Fleming and dragged him into a doorway. His hand went up to his mouth, the sign of silence. Mike followed the infected girl through the scope of his gun. The girl was barely of teenage years. She had almond hair and her complexion was fair. Mike followed her, there was a part of his brain that felt sorry for her. A part of his brain that was intensely guilty for the fact that he would kill her without a second thought. A part of his brain that was intensely guilty for all those had been in his sights before.

Mike watched her walk off, she didn't notice them sitting there meters from her. Her body was decaying, the reports they were superhuman was no more true than Bigfoot being real. At one stage of her life she had a future. She turned into a building and disappeared. He scanned the area, he was told so much of how they would be. The truth was they were humans trapped and tortured, not monsters of late night movies.

Dr Fleming placed his hand on Mike's shoulder. "I never thought what I was doing would result in this. I never thought it would be utilised to harm so many people. You will never understand the guilt that sits with me for this."

"Doctor I kill people, that is what my existence here on earth consists of. I used to believe it was only my job." He looked deeply into Dr Fleming's eyes. "It is who I am. I understand guilt." Mike looked out ensuring that the area was clear. "It is not for me to judge what you have done, that responsibility sits with you."

Mike waved and then walked out, back under the night sky. Dr Fleming followed, sticking as close to him as possible. They walked through grounds that used to be a place for the less fortunate. In Dr Flemings past life he never gave much thought to them. To the immigrants who were viewed as a drain on society. So much effort was placed on stopping them. For them to be anywhere but here. He never gave it much thought but then he was forced to escape and hide with them. To become them. Just like so many people it was easy to be apathetic towards evil that stayed fair enough out of sight. He felt such shame as he walked through, to escape to his own freedom.

Dr Fleming and Mike reached the gate, they stayed five meters back in the vegetation. Hiding from the lights that passed by. Mike didn't say a word, he kept his gun up and ready. He swept the area with it. When the military vehicles passed by the gate he sunk down, almost disappearing from Dr Fleming.

Mike took out the device which was their get out of jail free card. It was a satellite beacon, once he pressed the button it would send an electronic message. UN forces were scanning for it, hopefully they were the first to find it. It had one lone button, he pressed it. The LED blinked green three times and then glowed red. Mike dropped it to the ground and crushed it under his foot. The light died under the third blow.

They waited in the brush for 30 minutes. Dr Flemings heart beat was intense and did not subside with the passing moments. He was not used to being put under this type of stress. Mike sat like a statue, Dr Fleming impressed by his ability to control his body. They sat there in silence and Dr Fleming began to pray. He didn't really believe in anything so he wasn't sure of its use. Something in him prompted him to do it.

There was a set of lights coming up to their section of the gate, they turned on and off three times. Mike turned to Dr Fleming, "This is our ride out of here. You're going to have to climb the fence."

"The barbed wire will shred me."

"Not with this" He rustled through the ground cover and pulled out an empty rice bag. "Put this across the top as you go over."

"You realise I used to be an incredibly unfit fat old man. The only thing that has changed is I have been starved recently."

"This is our option, it is either this or you go back in their on your own."

Dr Fleming put the bag over his shoulder. He climbed one foot after the other, left hand over right. His eyes darted to the distance. Mike stayed on the ground, his gun trained on the immigrant zone. The noise beyond the vegetation caught his attention. He took a step forward and saw a group of infected immigrants coming their way. Mike looked to Dr Fleming, their eyes understood the meaning. Then attention went back to the immigrant group, who halted their disjointed steps and watched Dr Fleming. Mike tried to reason their thoughts in that moment. Did they have any?

The group broke from their inactivity and resumed their pace, Mike turned to Dr Fleming. "Get a move on they are getting close." Dr Fleming looked down their frenzied movements struck such a fear in his heart. Mike came out of the vegetation and the group paid their attention to him. They moved forward, bumping into each other, some fell but the group moved forward. Mike looked back and Dr Fleming was at the top of the gate.

Mike ran and scaled the gate himself. The speed was in contrast to Dr Fleming, the monstrous gate was barely an obstacle. On the other side he looked back. They seemed to stop again. They focussed on the gate and walked back into the immigrant zone.

The red cross workers stayed in their truck. The two men jumped in the back. Mike closed the canvas on the rear and they took off.

"Why did they stop?" Mike asked a hyperventilating Dr Fleming.
"There are somethings that seem to stay in the mind of these creatures." He took a deep breath. "The gate for the immigrants is a symbol of great despair. It is hardwired into their being. It is such a barrier to them that the disease cannot eradicate the memory. "
Mike sat back, "Does that mean the person may be in there?"
"Once someone is infected they will never be the same. The person is lost, the base instinct can remain."

Five minutes into their trip, they saw a light through the breaks in the canvas. The driver, who didn't want to introduce himself for fear of what they were doing, turned around. "There is a truck coming up on us fast."
Mike was quiet, he put the gun on his lap. "Act as if we aren't

here, I'll handle it."

The truck caught up to them, flashing lights for them to pull over. The driver turned around, "What do I do, they want me to pull over?"

"Pull over." Mike said with a soldier's calm. He sat still and looked over at a sweating Dr Fleming. The doctor leant forward to say something, Mike nodded his head no.

The truck come to a stop, Mike got up from his seat. He knelt with the gun pointing out the back of the truck, ready for the canvas flaps to be opened. The two of them in the back could see the shadow of the soldier being projected by the truck headlights. It grew larger as the man walked towards them. He moved left across the lights, inspecting the truck for any irregularity. He crossed once more and walked to the drivers side window.

Mike looked at Dr Fleming, he pointed at the canvas and motioned to unzip it. Dr Fleming paused for a moment until Mike repeated the gesture. The canvas unzipped loudly. It caught the attention of the soldier speaking to the clearly fearful driver.

With the canvas unzipped fully Mike jumped out of the back of the truck. The soldier still sitting in the truck saw him and drew a handgun. Before he could line up his sights Mike put two bullets in him. The first in his chest, his body thrust back with the force. Then the second into his forehead. The two shots were so quick that Dr Fleming took a second to realise that they were separate sounds. Mike ran around the truck before the remaining soldier could recognise what had transpired.

The remaining soldier let a shot out, a reaction more than a purposeful movement. It flew into the night air, Mike shot at the man and hit him in the shoulder. He spun to the floor, blood spurting across the red cross sign. The wounded soldiers gun slid across the road. Mike walked over to the soldier laying on his stomach and kicked him onto his back. The absence of emotion on his face scared the red cross driver. He wanted to run, to escape the clutches of this mad man.

"When will the next truck come by?" Mike asked, gun pointed at the man on the ground. "When will the next patrol vehicle come past?"

"In an hour, please don't kill me."

"How often do you need to radio in?"

"I will tell you if you don't kill me."

"I wont kill you, there is no need for that now."

The soldier on the floor relaxed as much as could be expected with a bullet wound. "We are expected back at the check point in twenty minutes."

"What happens if you don't check in?"

"They will send out another patrol."

"Thank you." Mike said, he turned to the two red cross workers. "Get out of the truck. I need water and rope."

"What for?" The driver asked trying to mask his fear with outrage. Mike turned from him and back to the man on the floor, he put a bullet in his head. The sound of the gun made the red cross worker jump.

Mike splashed water on the blood which sprayed across the truck. He took the rope, "Now I am going to tie you two up. Please go over to their truck and sit down."

"We weren't told about this."

Mike walked up to the man, face to face. Mike was intimidating from a distance, proximity elevated this. Dr Fleming was silent, unsure of what the unpredictable soldier would do. "You have two choices, be tied up or shot. I would like to get this done very soon, a decision is needed quickly."

He turned to the girl who was in the passenger seat and now in tears. She jumped out of the truck and walked to the now dead soldiers vehicle. Mike followed her and tied her up. The driver quickly followed.

"Now when they ask what happened, you tell them you were hijacked, do you understand?"

"You planned this all along didn't you?"

"It was a viable option if something like this were to happen."

"Viable? You killed two people, thats murder."

"They would have killed you without a second thought if they discovered us back here. You are not in some idealistic utopia, there is a very real threat that these people will bring destruction on this earth. This is not an isolated instance of barbarity." He turn to scan the road for company. "We are in a race to be the most barbarous, to be the last one standing in the losers blood." There was a moment of silence. "You were hijacked and they stole your vehicle is that understood?"

"Yes."

Mike walked from the two of them and turned to Dr Fleming, still silenced by his shock. "Get in the cab."

"Are we just leaving them here?"

"Yes, by the time the next patrol comes we will be on a plane." They got in the red cross truck and drove away leaving two corpses and two frightened people. "We have managed to obtain a plane with rights to fly, by the time they realise what we have done we will be in the air." Mike focussed on the road and Dr Fleming on his shaking hands.

Humans are all racing to be the most vicious, victoriously standing in the blood of their enemies.

CHAPTER EIGHT

Judy sat down to breakfast with her two girls, the television was set to the news, as the usual routine. August had been at war for long enough that its coverage had now become normalised. To watch carnage and destruction had become as much a part of breakfast as coffee. The infection had for the most part been contained to the immigrant zone and the government put significant resources into stopping it moving from there.

Judy's girls, Charlize and Christina didn't watch the television. They sat and ate their corn flakes on the couch, watching cartoons. The children of August were oblivious to reality. Rosa came in and said good morning to the three of them. She kissed them all on the cheek as she made her way to the kitchen. In normal circumstances a nanny acting in such a manner would be unacceptable but Rosa was special to them. She had raised Judy as her nanny and when Judy had her own children there was no one she wanted more.

After the death of her husband, Rosa was the support Judy needed. Being the youngest partner, and only female, at her law firm she required a village of support. Luckily for her she had Rosa. She was able to traverse all her life entailed because of Rosa, she was deeply indebted.

There was a break in the usual flow of the morning news. The newscaster stopped mid story and turned to another camera:

"We have just been advised that President Charles Terri has been wounded in an attempt on his life. The speaker has reported the President is in a stable condition and is expected to make a full recovery. No other details have been made available to us. We hope the president makes a speedy recovery."

"Rosa the President's been shot." She stood from her chair, taking her plate and coffee to the sink. "This is really getting out of hand, attacking our President, on our soil. It's cowardly."

"Yes, but there are no rules in war my love."

"I suppose you're right." She finished her coffee and put the mug in the sink. "I worry for the girls, it doesn't seem to be coming to an end."

"We need to endure." Rosa took her hand, "They have said we will come to a resolution soon. We must believe in them."

"Rosa, they are not always the most honest."

"You are cynical because of your work. My dear why would they lie to us?"

"To keep us quiet and compliant. It has been such a tumultuous time for August".

The truth of the statement was stark, understanding just how terrible it had been. The news was good at calming their fears, it was a machine of a very strong government. August needed support, a good citizen did their part.

Judy walked over to the girls and kissed them on the cheek. "Charlize, Christina" they looked up at their mother. "I am going to work, be good for Rosa?"

They answered in unison, "Yes mummy."

"Rosa, I'll be home earlier tonight, I want to spend some time with them while they are on break from school."

"Would you like me to cook something special."

"Everything you cook is special," Judy returned the kiss Rosa gave earlier.

"Brussels sprouts then?" She smiled to Judy as she left.

Judy walked out of the door and into the hallway of the apartment complex. The news the president had been shot stayed with her. It worried her that this could destabilise the government at such an important time. The government was now being centred on the president. She worried for her children, they would grow up as people of war. Their existence would be shaped by something so horrible. She didn't like that her country was at war, her wish would be for it to stop. She did realise its importance, they couldn't let the UN and its nations of thugs treat the people of August this way. Trying to spread a disease so horrific, August needed to strike back.

Judy walked passed a neighbour who lived at the end of the hall. His name was Jerry, an elderly man. She didn't care what people thought, or the money he had, he was crazy. Most people ignored his ravings as eccentric, but they were crack pot conspiracies. His newest was that August was responsible for the disease. Imagine the absurdity of a government attacking its own people.

Jerry walked out, "Good morning Judy."

"Morning Jerry, have you got much on for today?" Her pleasantries were necessary considering he was on the tenants board and she wanted to get a dog for the girls.

"Have you heard the good news?"

"What is that Jerry?" She stopped in front of him. He stood in a silk robe, very expensive and stained with jam.

"The President has been shot, I hope they did the job well."

Judy smiled at him, "I had heard." She stood for a moment and looked at him, a smile was all she could muster. "I best be off, don't want to be late for work."

"Well, you be on your way." Judy walked off ignoring the man, "Remember don't believe everything you see on the news."

She stepped out onto the street and was glad to be away from him. His opinions were offensive, more so that he didn't keep them to himself. She looked down the street and saw a commotion. A man in a hazmat suit walked up to her. "Ma'am you cant come down this way, we have had a containment issue."

"Is it serious?"

"As serious as they all are, but we have it under control."

"Thank you."

Judy looked down the street, there was a scream and

then a flash of flames. These had become more common. Breaches of containment, she knew what the flash of flames meant. The only way to kill the virus was to burn it.

She continued on her way to work, the flash of flames slowly forgotten as her mind went to the tasks at hand. This was now the norm in August.

CHAPTER NINE

Roderick, Nina and Dr Chekov sat in the bunker. The infected banged on the door, continuously and without relent. The medicine to keep themselves from turning had been working but did not stop all symptoms. The red of their eyes terrified each other and they kept their gaze to the floor.

"They will not stop, they keep banging." Nina sat on the end of the bed, they hoped the agitation was not a sign of the virus. "What are we sitting here for anyway?" Her voice held an uncharacteristic anger. "There is no more need for this place or for us. With him gone we have no hope. We are just waiting till we run out of the medicine, till we tear each other apart."

"Nina, it will not get too that. He will come back for us, when he can." Roderick knelt down in front of her. He held her hand but did not look into her eyes.

"How will he come back? He has no power."

"We must have faith."

"Roderick, faith in what?"

She stood up, in such a small space it was hard to have distance. Dr Chekov sat on his bed. He did not speak, lost to his own thoughts of defeat. He believed as she did, all hope had gone with Dr Fleming. His patients were out there, outside the bunker trying to get in. The people he once treated now lost to a disease he did not know how to stop. He was powerless, without direction.

Roderick stood, he did not know why he continued to try. Why did he try and convince them there was hope? They all were of the same mind, hope was no longer reasonable. No longer could he hope for better, a better life was something that was surely a myth. So much of his life was a struggle. So much of his life was spent in hope. Where was the fruition of this? Still something held him to a faith in a better life. That somehow it would get better. Faith that once Dr Fleming conquered the disease, the fighting would be over.

Nina turned to him, "Roderick I have always loved your ability to hope for the future. To persevere when all seemed lost. These are the things which have made me stick by your side. These are the things that make my love for you grow." She leant against the wall, "It is over now. We have fought our battle and we are like caged animals. Death is in here my love, death is out there. The only distinction is how long we allow ourselves to suffer in an attempt to outrun the inevitable".

"She is speaking truth" Dr Chekov's voice echoed through the bunker. "We are waiting for the inevitable."
"We must wait. Doctor, while there is even the faintest glimmer of hope, we must wait." Roderick looked to the front of the bunker. "We will wait till we run out of the medicine. That is when hope is lost. When the last of it is gone we will open the door. Give them what they continue to bang on the door for." Roderick's voice raised; Nina was now crying, for fear and for love. "Till then we will hope".

The banging on the door continued. Outside of it a hoard had gathered, twenty or so. One or two joined them every now and then. The group, disease infested, their brains taken by something so alien. They tried to break through the door for reasons unknown to them. Their bodies no longer their own.

Many fell and were trampled, their loss unnoticed. The door was now the focus of the group. One more joined and their push got stronger. Bang ... ... Bang ... ... How long before it all came crashing down?

CHAPTER TEN

Charles Terri lay in his hospital bed, seething at the actions of the UN. Most strongly at the indignity this showed, the UN so forcefully undermining his authority. His wife sat beside him, keeping watch from the moment he was brought in. She had fallen asleep waiting for him to regain consciousness. Charles sat in silence, plotting what he would do to those who showed disrespect. The attempt by the UN was despicable and he would make them pay. The pain in his abdomen dulled by the drip in his arm, the pain in his mind was not.

The moment the bullet entered his body replayed in his mind. Normally he was not a superstitious man, nor did he fear death. In that moment both were apparent. As his blood drained from him, as his life slipped away he made a pact with God. If his life was spared, he would protect the people of August from those who threatened their way of life. Charles Terri would ensure the will of He who is greater was done through him. He took his waking moments as proof of this purpose, the divinity of his role.

Charles Terri's wife woke, her eyes widened at his animation. She took his hand in hers. "Charles I was so worried. They thought you would die, I don't know what I would have done." She began to cry, her lack of faith irritated him. "I am so happy you are alive."

"Lauren, God would not take me yet." He let go of her hand. "It is clear to me now that my path is the righteous one. They tried to take my life, like it was theirs to own. I will ensure they do not corrupt this world any further. I will demolish them, and all those who stand in our way." His body tensed with passion, the pain grew but he wore this with pride.

"Charles this needs to stop. There are people, good citizens, starving because of this war. Your life was nearly taken because of this war."

"This war is right, it is what needs to be done."

"It is no longer right, it is just about pain now." Lauren showed the deep pain of the nation on her face. "Rachel would not have wanted this, she would be so ashamed."

Charles sat up, the pain grew intolerable and he cried out. His formidable gaze fell on her, "Don't you dare use her memory to manipulate me."

"It is the truth Charles, this pain and suffering it would sadden her greatly."

The guard at the door on hearing the president in pain, entered. Charles held his hand up. "It is no longer about her, it is about our great nation."

"This all started with her, this suffering is in her name." She yelled at him now, no longer addressing the president, but reprimanding her husband.

"It started with her, justice for her" He twisted off the bed, there was a red circle on his gown that grew more quickly with his movement. "It is more than that now."

"What could be more than our daughter?"

Charles stepped in front of his wife, the anger that allowed him to carry out atrocities overtaking him. Charles slapped his wife, the sound made the guard behind him jump. "Don't you twist my words. Nothing is more important than her. She was my world, it is the depths humans are willing to plunge which has brought this. This is about our nation, doing what is right. If you had loved our daughter, as I did you would understand." Charles turned with a stumble and the guard came over to help him. "You are nothing to me, you dare try and tell me what to do. I am the President of this country, I do not need your council. You are a prop to all of this, you will be remembered as my wife and nothing more. Do not forget that you are expendable. Just like all the others too stupid to see the truth."

Lauren sat back in shock. Never had he spoken to her like that she thought. Then the memories came back to her. The times she had to hide the bruises, 'I knocked it on a handle'. The visits to the emergency room. No one would believe the great Charles Terri was a wife beater. It was beyond belief that he kept his family in as much fear as he now kept the country. The memories gathered in her mind. Perhaps it was his weakened state or the fact that he had stolen her daughters memory. Stole it to justify such horribleness.

She slapped him back, "Your daughter would be ashamed of the man you have become. She was ashamed of the man you were. She saw the marks on me. She was smart, she knew her father was nothing more than a wife beater." Charles Terri sat on the bed in silence. This challenged his version of history and shocked him. "Why do you think she worked for the immigrants? If it was against everything you believed. She wanted you to know how much she despised you."

"Shut your fucking mouth you whore." He roared.

"You can call me what you like, I am a good person trapped by evil." She said this through gritted teeth, the control lost long ago returned.

Charles raised to his feet, "God has ordained what I am to do, how dare you accuse me of such lies."

"If you speak to God ask him about your daughter and the level with which she hates you."

Lauren turned from Charles and walked to the door. There was a loud bang, she felt her chest and her fingers came away with blood.

Charles Terri had taken the gun from the guard. He hobbled over to her as she was taking her last breaths. "You will be in the very depths of hell." He shot her once more.

Ten people were in the room at this point; guards, doctors and all manner of administrative staff. Ten people who gathered to protect the President and nation, instead witnessing the death of the First Lady. They were all silent, stunned by the action. He walked back to his bed and with help laid down. "Someone clean that up." He pointed to the corpse of his wife. "Please, can someone call the doctor, I am bleeding badly." He breathed in as the people around him began to move. He handed the gun to the guard, "Son can you speak to General Christian Wilson. Tell him to get the heads of military together. I want a briefing in an hour." The guard nodded terrified. Charles Terri laid back, he was on the right path.

CHAPTER ELEVEN

Dr Fleming and Mike were silent in the truck as they drove towards the awaiting plane. It was easy to ignore what it meant to be a soldier when it wasn't staring you in the face. Death had a funny way of causing those around it to focus on the truth. Dr Fleming had seen so much death in his career, and was the architect behind so much more. Death was always kept in the shadows, he was never the one to pull the trigger, instead he designed the gun.

Dr Fleming couldn't tell if Mike was worried, if they were captured they would be put to death. The soldier was stone faced, focussed. Would it make Dr Fleming feel better if he was worried? Would that make him human? A human who killed without thought. When Dr Fleming thought about the people who caused such horrors they weren't human to him. It helped him contextualise the suffering people went through. The bump in the night couldn't be human, it had to be a monster.

As they moved away from the immigrant zone, he thought of the people he met. Those people he failed. He wasn't able to save them, they became overrun by the disease so quickly. The memories were daggers in his mind, trying to fight what he created. He was the Dr Frankenstein to so many monsters

Dr Fleming was uncharacteristically shocked, they hadn't died as easily as his tests would indicate. When the infection began to infect the immigrants he remembered marvelling at the fact that only 10% of them died in the first 72 hours. Then the changes happened and they became something else all together.

For those 72 hours they were sick, worsening to the point where they were confused for dead. There was such sadness, he tried so hard. They were able to inoculate many, who kept their health. Then 72 hours elapsed. Those who were not able to receive the inoculation were meant to die. How could he predict that quirk of nature.

They began to revive, like a miracle their health returned. With it came the aggression directed at anyone who came near. The disease ate away at their brain. They acted less and less like the people they had once been. Many attacked their children, babies torn apart. Their inability to speak allowed the most terrifying screams to emanate.

When the first died, that is when the ferocity of the disease showed itself. The disease had been able to change itself and work around the inoculation, turning those who should have been protected. The balance of the infected tipped and the three of them went to the bunker to find a cure for the changing beast. They prayed for the pocket of survivors to the east of the North fence.

The longer the disease was in the body, the less the person inside seemed to exist. The disease became who they were, a machine to kill and spread. They began to take people to experiment on, he looked into the eyes of the thing he created. The thing he was the father and mother of, and in those moments he knew real shame.

The truck came to a stop outside the gates of a military airport. Dr Fleming became worried, "Mike if you are from the UN how have you gotten so many contacts within the Augustan military."

"Dr Fleming our sources are confidential."

"It makes me feel very uncomfortable."

"Dr Fleming you are the cause of this. This disease is your doing, the events your responsibility. Uncomfortable is a cross you might have to bare."

"I never knew what they would use it for." Dr Fleming tried to defend once again.

"When I kill a man I often don't know why. The bullet is still my responsibility." The gates opened and they drove to a shed. "Get out."

They walked into the shed, inside was a black bomber. Its size was shocking. It took a moment and then its use became evident. "This is one of the planes that spread the disease." Dr Fleming stood bewildered.

"Exactly, their existent is unofficial and that works for us. If one the planes are spotted in Augustan territory they are expected to keep radio silence and are not to be recorded."

"Won't they question why one is up in the air now?"

"Let's hope not."

Mike walked to the pilot standing next to the plane, they shook hands. The engine started and Dr Fleming was pushed on board. The noise was tremendous, Dr Fleming once again began to worry.

The plane started to move, coming out of the shed. It rolled onto the runway as the sun began to rise. The plane revved and with that they began to take off. It was bumpy, the plane felt like it wanted to stay earth bound. Then like magic, he felt his stomach drop, the plane rose into the air. Further and further up. He looked out the window, the higher they climbed the less he could see the destruction. The less he was able to see the war that was engulfing his nation.

They flew to the sun, the feeling Dr Fleming had was one of sadness. Again his gaze went to the window and wished he could see his friends again. He left them, surely they would die on their own. What could they do? His guilt was so immense, he was the monster in all of this. The further they rose, the more guilt gripped him. He broke down and cried for the horrors he created and the friends they consumed. They would be dead before long.

Dr Fleming looked out the window and saw the open ocean.

He could hear the pilot and Mike speak through the ill fitting headset. The message quickly becoming clear through their military speak. The pilot's worried tone cut through the calm, "There is a patrol fighter coming up on our rear."

"They will let us go, its protocol." Mike didn't sound so confident anymore.

Then like the angel of death whispering into his ear, "Identify yourself, you have 30 seconds."

"Don't answer them, we must maintain radio silence." Mike's voice was stable.

There was gun fire, Dr Fleming jumped. His heart began to spasm, his breath became laboured.

The whisper of death came over again, "That was a warning, identify yourself or we will engage."

"How far from the carrier are we?" Mike shouted to the pilot, his voice less stable.

"Fifteen minutes."

"How long will it take to get a fighter here."

"They are in the air, I have sent an alarm. They should be here any second."

"Stall them!"

There was another burst of bullet fire. This time they heard the ting of the bullets puncturing the wing. "They have hit our fuel. We need to land."

There was another burst of fire and the right engine gave out. The plane began to loose altitude. From in front they saw the welcome sight of fighter planes. They flew over top and pushed the Augustan's older models back.

Their plane continued to fall out of the sky, "Can you land this?" Mike's question not alleviating the spasm in the heart of Dr Fleming.

"I will need to. This is going to be bumpy."

"Have you done this before?"

"Stop asking questions, they aren't going to make you feel better." The pilot sweating profusely, clearly fearful. "It will be a piece of cake." He smiled unconvincingly.

Mike looked back at Dr Fleming, "Doc are you still with us."
"Barely." Dr Flemings breaths became harder. "Where is the oxygen?"
Mike threw a bottle to him, he breathed deep.

The plane continued to drop. "Black bird, you are clear of enemy combatants. We have a boat on the way to collect you when you land. Good luck." The pilot did his best to control the plane, lower and lower. Mike not fond of flying at the best of times used all his will power to stay calm.

The water came closer and closer, the blue never more terrifying. "Hold onto something." The pilot yelled. There was a small bump and then the water took hold of the plane. The thump was tremendous. The plane bounced across the water with violent force. The contents of the plane flew around. Mike lost his calm, "Fuck, fuck, fuck!"

They could see parts coming away from the plane, then it slowed. The thumps lessened. The plane came to a stop and sat on the water. The rhythm of the ocean was far from calming. "Told you it would be a piece of cake". The pilot laughed.
"Fuck you man." Mike took a breath in. He looked behind him. "The doctor passed out."

The two conscious men watched as the fighter jets circled like vultures around a meal. They waited for the boat, water at their knees. Mike checked Dr Fleming, "He has a pulse."
"The boats are a minute off, hang tight." The voice crackled over the radio and Mike was thankful to be out of the air. The mission was a disastrous success. He watched over Dr Fleming and allowed thoughts to enter for the men he lost.

CHAPTER TWELVE

Judy sat in her corner office with a view from the 23rd floor. It took twenty years and a few awful deeds to be sitting where she was. Politicians were bribed and businessmen blackmailed, all in the name of a better life. She would have felt bad had this not been the norm. If you didn't play the game you would be swallowed into the depths of oblivion.

Judy's assistant Cathleen came into her office. "Mr Carlton is in the building. He is in the lift now and wants a meeting." She stood to attention, desperately wanting to impress Judy. She had succeeded on many occasions, although the continued effort was appreciated.

"Could you please call Rothschild and move his meeting to this afternoon." Judy stood and put her coat on, "Good of him to give notice. If he wasn't our biggest client I'd tell him to fuck off."

"Should I prepare the meeting room?"

"Yes, thank you Cathleen." Judy walked with her out of the office. "Who has he knocked up this time? 74 years old and jumps on anything with a pulse."

"I might give it a go" Cathleen joked with Judy, her ease of conversation was pleasant in the jargon ridden legal world. "Easier than getting a raise from you."

Cathleen walked to the meeting room to prepare and Judy the elevators. The last two pregnancy's netted the women two million each and an ongoing pension. That man must have a permanent IV of viagra she though to herself.

The elevators opened and out came Harold Carlton. Judy put on her smile, the one which ignored the constant advances. Carlton stumbled out and nearly fell to the floor. He got his footing and leaned on the wall. "Mr Carlton, are you ok." She offered him a hand which he refused.

He walked to an empty desk and sat down. "They are trying to lock me up, you have to stop them." He said through panicked breath.

"Stop who?"

"Them, they are down stairs. They are trying to illegally detain me." He coughed into his hands and she could see the red.

"Why do they want to detain you? What has happened?"

"I'm sick, they want to detain me because I'm sick."

Judy noticed his eyes from behind the sunglasses. She jumped back, "Mr Carlton, didn't you take the shot?"

"It's a scam, they want to infect us."

He continued to cough, the blood began to fall to the floor now. The elevator opened again and two men in hazmat suits came through. "We need to give him the inoculation."

"No" Carlton hissed at the men. "It is a scam, they are injecting us with it. To control us."

The men moved on him and he shouted at them. He pushed a chair at them and began to run. Two more steps were all it took for him to fall to the floor. One more cough of blood and he lay still.

They jabbed the needle into him and stood back. If his heart had stopped it would be useless. Judy turned to the hazmat men, "What is going on?"

"He refused the inoculation, there was an outbreak and he was infected. He has been on the run since."

"Thank fuck he came here." Judy said turning to the old mans body. "I don't think you got him in time."

Everyone looked as his stomach inflated, stretching the old mans once wrinkly skin. The men in the hazmat suits yelled, "Everybody clear out." There was a panic as they all attempted to be as far away as possible. The red mist exploded and filled the office. People screamed, fearful that they would become infected.

Judy turned to the men in the hazmat suits, "What do we do now?"

"We wait. This building is now a quarantine zone" One of the men in the yellow suits began to talk to someone on the radio.

"We have all been inoculated, why do we need to be kept here."

"There is a new strain and we don't know which one he had."

Four more men in hazmat suits came up to the office, they held guns to dissuade anyone thinking of escape. The one who seemed to be in charge of the operation stepped forward, "We will be quarantined for 72 hours. Please make yourselves comfortable."

Judy walked back into her office. The fear began to grow in her. She may never see her children or Rosa again. She picked up the phone to speak with them. She just wanted to hear their voices. The phones were dead, her sense of dread grew.

Judy walked up to the man in charge, "Can we call our loved ones to tell them we wont be home."

"They will be notified," he said this without even acknowledging her existence.

"When? I have children."

"We all have people we would like to be home with. They will be notified in due course. Please go back to your office."

"You can't keep us locked away from the world. You have to let us speak to our families at the very least."

"Ma'am I don't need to do anything I'm not ordered to. My orders are to ensure no one leaves and that is what I am doing."

"You will let me to speak to my family now!" She stood close to him, he was not easily intimidated.

"If you do not go back to your office I will taser you, do you understand?"

Judy turned and walked back to her office, looking at the red smudge where Mr Carlton once was.

That evening Rosa opened the door to a man from the army. His solemn demeanour terrified her. "Ma'am I am sorry to inform you that Judy Davis has been killed."

Tears came to Rosa's eyes, "How did this happen?"
"Ma'am I don't have that information." He turned and left her to tell the children. That night the house was filled with utter despair.

CHAPTER THIRTEEN

Mike stood watch over Dr Fleming, unconscious in the hospital bed. He was tasked with bringing the doctor to the Secretary-General of the United Nations. He would not be stopped until his mission was complete. The doctor currently responsible for the care of Dr Fleming said he had a coronary episode brought on by stress and poor diet. Dr Fleming was cleared to fly once he woke.

The plane on deck was scheduled to fly straight to UN headquarters in New York. In a matter of hours Mike would be debriefed and sent to his next mission. Mike started to think about a change in career for the first time. He had considered it previously but never with any seriousness. What he saw had shaken him, the depths at which people acted abhorred him. The travesties had gotten worse over the years and Mike felt he was dragged along. To effectively perform his job he needed to break personal rules. Recently did this with more regularity and greater barbarity.

Death used to shock him, affect him in the pit of his stomach. When he killed a man it would weigh on him, their faces forever engraved in his mind. Now he was able to do so with little effort and no ill feeling. Their faces had started to disappear, killing a man was no longer shocking.

Mike worried about how long he could divorce this from the civilian world. When would he snap and act with the same feelings he did in war? He had begun to have episodes when he returned home. The most worrying were directed at his neighbour who came to his door drunk. He accused Mike of sleeping with his wife. Without a second thought he took the man by the throat, he would have killed the drunk had his wife not screamed out. He would have killed a civilian and felt no guilt. With what he knew, he could kill many people and they would never know. Surely it was time to quit and get some help.

Mike continued to watch Dr Fleming, the man who had created a disease which would pale to the 348 people he had killed, their faces gone but the number stayed. Dr Fleming was such an unassuming man, you would never guess his body housed such a monster. If he had been on his list earlier, he could have stopped all of this. Death could solve so many problems.

Dr Fleming opened his eyes, taking a minute to contextualise the grey environment. "What happened?" A weakened Dr Fleming asked.

"You had a cardiac episode while we were in the middle of a plane crash."

"I had a heart attack?" Dr Flemings voice was raspy, his throat sore from being intubated.

"Your heart spasmed which caused you to pass out. The doctor said it was caused by stress and general poor health."

"So, I just have to avoid stress and start eating right." He chuckled to himself, Mike didn't join.

"Once you are dressed there is a plane on deck ready to fly. We need to get moving as soon as possible." Mike took a step forward, "The fighters have been able to hold the Augustan forces at bay for the moment. It is only a matter of time before our area is compromised."

"Heart attacks don't get you a rest these days do they."

"Neither do plane crashes." Dr Fleming smiled, he couldn't tell if Mike was making a joke, his face was stone.

Mike gave Dr Fleming some privacy to dress. The navy blue sailors uniform did not suit the doctor's complexation but it was better than the rear exposing gown. It was a difficult process, his energy had been sapped and he was sore form the crash. Dressed he took a moment to think of Roderick, Nina and Dr Chekov. He was resolute in helping them, but did not know how. His was a multi-faceted burden which weighed heavily.

They walked on deck, people saluted them. The plane was ready to take off as soon as they boarded. They took their seats, the captain spoke but Dr Fleming was lost in thought. Mike checked on him, he was thankful for the effort even if it was only out of duty.

The plane rocketed down the runway, the force was unlike anything he had experienced. They were in the air and on their way. Two fighter jets flanked them for the trip. He had become the most important person in the world. The one who could save humanity from his own damnation.

Dr Fleming and Mike were thankful when the plane touched down safely. It was ushered quickly into a hanger. Dr Fleming stayed in his seat until the door opened.

The hanger was sparse, there were the military personal that would become common in his life. At the end of the stairs was a woman impeccably dressed, the first person in civilian garments since his escape.

"Dr Fleming my name is Maria Singh, I am the Secretary-General of the UN. Our organisation has been coordinating the current military effort." She stopped shouting as the plane engines shut down. "Thank you for coming."
"I didn't realise there was a choice involved."
"We needed to use some less conventional means but you do understand the importance of our current situation. Your disease is spreading through the rest of the world. We are containing it as best we can but it seems to be jumping containment lines."
"When can I get to a lab, to begin working?"
"We will bring you there now, you will be briefed on the way." Maria pointed to the hummer parked at the back of the hanger, "Please this way."

Dr Fleming hobbled to the car, Mike did not follow. He felt unsafe without him now. They began speaking at him as soon as the car pulled away. They stopped the information onslaught when he began to described the immigrant zone, the way it was currently and the way he arrived to it. "We didn't know it was that bad." Was the common reaction? It was, perhaps worse than they could understand. There was a considered silence and then they went back to describing the situation at hand.

There was an 8 per cent infection rate throughout Europe, 12 per cent in Asia and higher in Africa but they didn't have accurate numbers. They had some success with inoculants but could not keep up with the rapidly changing disease.

Dr Fleming looked at the structures of the inoculants they had developed. His brain began to work through the problem. This was where he was useful, he was the leader in this domain. It empowered him to be able to fix what they had termed *the apocalyptic disease.*

CHAPTER FOURTEEN

Mike watched as Dr Fleming drove away with the Secretary General. The bumbling doctor proved to him that there was no evil in this world. Good and evil were constructs we forced on the world. Terms meaningless without each other, but otherwise fabricated. The Doctor created the most devastating disease, not just in its affect but its speed of spread. That surely was enough to deem him an evil man. Tyrants of the past would not kill and maim as many people as he did. Yet Mike couldn't hate him, the bit of him that had empathy felt a sadness for him.

Is it true, all villainous men and women had the capacity to inspire a soft emotion if only we spoke to them. The death of a tyrant was the death of a person. Is there justification for the cessation of a life or even the prolonging of one.

The beeping of the horn woke him from deep of thought. He stepped aside and saluted, the next car that passed was for him and he sat quietly in the back. His debrief was the gateway back to the civilian world where he would wait until he was needed to do unspeakable things.

Mike opened the door and the smell of staleness floated. He had not been home in weeks, a house not lived in began to die a slow death. He took a bottle of whiskey and poured himself a drink. The ritual poisoning of himself had started, it dulled the memories so they were less distinct when they attacked in the middle of the night. The fear of those thoughts held tight to the glass.

The bottles volume decreased as did his conscious

mind. In a room bare of sentiment, a place to sit and sleep. His pain was family. He continued to drink and wait for the call which would take him back to the thing that caused him so much pain. He drifted to sleep only to be woken by a little girl, and him shooting her in the head. The rage in her eyes reflecting his world view.

Three days of drinking himself to sleep, then waking and training, passed before he got the call. The demons in him quieted, they were absent when he worked. He saluted General Tobin, and sat in front of his desk.

"It goes without saying the work you did extracting Dr Fleming was exceptional." General Tobin took a page out of the pile that sat on his desk. "Your fellow soldiers sacrifices were the greatest we are asked to make. I am sorry for what happened to them."

"Me too". He looked to the paper, "Is that my next mission".

"No, this is the report from your last psych eval." General Tobin felt uneasy about the issue of the mind. The number of soldiers under his charge who were impacted negatively by their work was a concern he could not command away. "The speed with which your last mission moved didn't allow us to discuss this report. The recommendations are that you take a break."

"With all due respect I would prefer to work."

"Soldier, this isn't a suggestion. I need to stand you down from active duty. Effective Monday you will report to the medical unit."

"Sir, there is no reason for me to be put on psych leave. Men don't come back from that".

"Son, war is a devastating plague. Not just for the civilians but for the soldiers as well. We ask you to do things against your nature." Gerard Tobin felt the draw behind him that held a growing list of soldiers ending their own lives. "This order is not one I give lightly, it's one I give with the weight of past experiences. Do the work, be able to live with what you have done? That is the best we can hope, we are all scarred deeply by our actions. When you are certified well you will always have a position here, it is the least we can do."

"I'll appeal this, I can't go back to the normal world. On mission I affect the evil of the world, out there it imposes itself on me." Mike began to shake, the thoughts invaded.

"That is why you need to go through with this." The general stood, it took a moment for Mike to reflect this. "It is a great burden I continue to give you, assigning you to the missions, assigning you to be damaged." He put out his hand, ignoring military convention. "Please, allow me to help undo some of that damage."

Mike shook the outstretched hand, he knew the damage was real. The invasive thoughts he was powerless to stop. The damage could only be eased when he was on mission. This was a sentence to strip him of an identity which erased all Mike was.

The bottle settled the shaking, allowing calm for at least a moment. The alcohol clouded his memories, confused the lines of war and peace. In one moment travesties occurred in a peaceful country and then it was a war zone based on arbitrary conditions. Those lines where he was allowed to kill or forbidden were unnatural to the order of nature.

Mike ordered a pizza, and continued to drink. The dark settled on him, the ills of what he did and his inability to do them again. He hated to kill but could not live if it was not in his life. He was torn by his memories but never questioned his need to serve.

Mike answered the knock at the door, he was thankful for the food. He didn't see the man in front of him, truth was he was inconsequential to the world Mike existed in. Mike put the pizza down and turned to close the door when he saw his neighbour storming across his front yard.

"You fucking cunt," the explosion of anger didn't raise Mike's heart rate a beat. He turned and walked inside leaving the door open. He took his pizza and set it down on the coffee table. An unarmed man no longer caused him alarm.

Mike stood in front of the coffee table, his job implied a restriction of diet to keep at a peak physical fitness. It had been months since his last indulgence and he wasn't going to allow the drunk to mess with his pizza.

The neighbour came to the door, paused at the threshold with the psychological barrier it imposes. "You think you can come back and fuck my wife?"

"I haven't touched your wife. You should go home, you're making a big mistake."

"You don't fucking listen, well do you? I am going to fuck you up, you think because you're military we should suck your cock."

The saliva flew out of his mouth, Mike watched his sluggish movements. He calculated the quickest way to disable the threat. "Go home, you don't want to do this."

"How the fuck do you know that?" He took an unsteady step forward and was now within arms reach of Mike. He reached behind himself, nearly toppling over and pulled out a gun. Holding it at Mike's head, "I'll tell you what I should do".

Mike's supposed mistress screamed at her husband, "Miles stop!" It took his attention away from Mike for a split second. That was more time than was needed. Mike grabbed the gun with his left hand pointing it to the roof, with his right hand a sharp blow to the elbow which separated his arm into two. Mile's doubled over in pain, Mike put the safety on put it into the band of his pants.

Miles' wife ran horrified, her husband on the floor as she tended to him. Mile's looked up at her and with his left hand gave her an uncoordinated punch to the face. It was forceful enough to knock her off her feet. Mike stepped over and kicked him in the head, at the base of the skull and he was on the floor unconscious.

The wife looked up and her eye was already red. Mike expected appreciation so was off guard for the slap. She tried a second time but this time he was ready, grabbing her hand and twisting it to bring her to her knees. "What the fuck is wrong with you? He beats you and you are mad at me?"

"It's the drink, it's not him." She sobbed, Mike let go of her hand. "He's not a bad person, he takes care of me. Sometimes he drinks to much, he loves me, doesn't want anyone to take me."

"That's not love." Mike was confused by the twisted nature of these two people. His black and white appreciation of life not accepting this complexity.

"If that's not love what is it?"

"That's possession, he views you as his thing."

"I am his, you cunt." Her anger pushed him back a step.

From behind them Miles stirred, he lifted his head and got to his knees. He saw his wife on her knees in front of Mike. "You knock me out and fuck my wife" he screamed at the pair and they turned around.

"No, he tried to make me but I wouldn't," the words from her confused Mike.

Miles got to his feet, holding his arm. "I'm going to kill you."

Miles took an unsteady step and tripped backwards. Tumbling onto and then over the coffee table, taking the pizza with him. He got to his knees and looked over to Mike, pizza smeared across him.

Mike lost the context of his surrounding, that he was in the civilian world was lost. He was looking at an evil man who needed to be taken care of and that's what he did. Before Miles was able to make another threat Mike took the gun out, safety off and put a bullet between his eyes. The head jerked back and then the body fell to the floor.

The wife screamed, "You shot" was all she got out. He turned and put a bullet in her head as well, there was silence. Two bodies bleeding out onto the floor. "All I wanted was to eat my pizza in peace, to make the world a better place." He shouted at them. "But you're not worthy, none of you are. I take on your evils and this is how you respond?" He took his phone out and order a large pizza.

When the delivery driver arrived he opened up the door and took the pizza before it was dropped. The driver was wide eyed, looked at Mike and then ran. Mike closed the door and sat down to eat the pizza he should have had earlier.

The police responded quickly, two pieces of pizza eaten. They were exactly what he was hoping for. They came in and pointed their guns at Mike, him shouting. "This world does not deserve its existence." Then he took the gun, placed it under his chin and pulled the trigger.

CHAPTER FIFTEEN

Charles Terri walked onto the balcony which looked over the city square. He was a hero standing before them. The applause was deafening. It was clear that he was the man the nation wanted, war was but a challenge he would lead his people through. He stood for a moment, the pain in his abdomen intensified the longer he was upright but he stood for the people he lead.

The applause continued as he sat, they were thankful he was alive. "My fellow citizens, it is because of your good wishes I am here. Thankful for your prayers and support, thankful that you would still have me. The UN and its allies work in the background to shape who we are as a people. All we have worked for, the work of our ancestors is at stake.

"When they attacked me they also attacked the office of President and all who have and will occupy it. They have attacked to claim our power for their own. To create instability in our country and weaken us. I am thankful you are all here standing for what makes us great."

There was thunderous applause.

"We are not without those who have traitorous intent. The news that our previous President Katherine Laurie has worked with the UN is true." There was a boo that swept across the crowd gathered for the momentous occasion. "She has lost what it is that makes us Augustan citizens, she has worked to bring the government down to impose her own rule. There is no one who is more disappointed than I. She was a close friend and at a time my student, this failure I take on myself.

"To that end I will work to ensure their efforts are in

vain. I will work to assert our place in the world." President Charles Terri stood , his voice boomed with all the strength he had. "We are August and we will bow to no one." Again there was applause, every man and woman in the crowd cheered with every part of their soul. He took it in, he revelled in the power they gave him. With their cheers on his back he took leave, to speak to the heads of the military. To do what he had promised. Make the rest of the world bow to him.

General Christian Wilson broke through the chatter. "President Terri, it is with respect that I must advise against this course of action. Attacking UN allied countries with the disease will be signing ourselves to a war with greater pain and suffering. We will sign ourselves up to go against the whole world."

"We have allies who see what the UN is trying to do. The UN has sent us down this road to strengthen their power. We must not bow to them."

"Our allies are not well placed to provide support." General Wilson's tone was reserved, President Charles Terri was notoriously bad tempered when disagreed with. "We fight on our own, our resources are stretched already."

"We will move our resources to this effort."

General Frederick Leake interjected, "Sir if we move our resources it is likely that the immigrant population will overrun their bounds. That would be catastrophic."

"Then eradicate that problem. I will not have us sit here and be dictated to. We will not be lead by their demands." President Terri slammed his fists to the desk, his voice elevating to a growl. "We are going to bomb them, it will not take long for them to bow to us. We must sacrifice to ensure our future."

General Wilson spoke up once again, "Sir you have executive control, we will follow your instruction." He looked down, his lack of power alarming. "We are all in agreement that this is the wrong path to take."

"Your concerns are noted, proceed with the plan." Charles Terri said this with his controlled calm returned.

The meeting concluded, the three heads of military left the room. They left to prepare what would be one of the most important times in Augustan history. Charles Terri stayed behind, for a moment he was in silence. The solitude was rare and he was grateful for it. He reflected on the meeting and their lack of belief. Had they not seen the reception in the streets? Did they not see all he did for the country? They had no faith in him, or the citizens of August. They believed they were smarter than the good citizens, they were wrong.

The moment of peace allowed him to read through reports about the immigrant zone. The disease proved his assertions that they were weak people. Weak of body and mind. The disease took them with little resistance. Even before the disease took hold they were attacking each other. Their character was weak and that left a space for the disease to fester.

There were casualties of Augustan citizens, it was a great shame. It was a great shame they were being tested in this manner. In his soul he knew only the truly strong were tested like this. President Charles Terri believed in their resolve, they as a nation would prosper. The true number of the casualties had not been reported, should not be. They didn't need more worry heaped on them.

The quiet was disrupted by Louise Miller, the Presidents new aide. She was handpicked by his staff while unconscious. She was loyal, had been working in the office for some time. She was across all the details of the Terri Presidency and understood what they did was for the good of the country. She was morally strong, doing a morally corrupt job.

"President Terri, the country is hailing your return as inspirational." She stood to his side. "You have never been in better favour with the people."

"Please, sit down." She sat next to the man for whom she held an all encompassing respect for. "I am grateful for their thoughts. Please ensure they know that."

"Of course Sir."

"Ensure that I am given hourly updates from the heads of our military. This operation is too important to fail." He leant towards her, "Our nations survival depends on it. I cannot stress this enough."

"Yes, Sir." She was honoured to be witness to this moment in their history, the making of a legend.

She adjusted herself uncomfortably, "Sir there is one matter that I feel needs some attention."

"Yes?"

"The location of your wife, there have been questions about her whereabouts."

"Do you know what happened?"

"Yes, Sir." She was terrified of the knowledge, what it meant if anyone would find out.

"She was spouting traitorous thoughts. August comes before all else." He was somber, not for his wife's passing but for the problems it could cause. "You must understand because of this, it must never be told." She nodded to him. "Tell the people she was attacked to get to me. That she is in a coma. When the country has the strength to hear it we will tell them she has passed."

"Yes sir"

"She was a good woman who lost her faith. I do not want her remembered that way."

"Yes, sir, I will make the arrangements." She paused for a moment. "If you are up to it there are many matters that could use your attention."

Charles Terri nodded and they went on with running the country. Running a country that was at war. A country that was fighting disease. He went back to doing the thing he was born for.

CHAPTER SIXTEEN

Roderick sat outside the lab and watched Dr Chekov work. Dr Chekov kept busy to avoid thoughts of the inevitable. The banging at the bunker door continued, it was now relegated to the norm and for the most part silent to them. The banging only entered their conscious mind when the rhythm changed. The medicine they injected into each other began to diminish and the red of their eyes became that much more terrifying. They felt it was a certainty that they would die at the hands of each other or the demons at the door. They only had days left, Dr Chekov worked ignorant of these certainties.

Nina sat in quiet contemplation, tears fell down her face occasionally. She didn't share her thoughts, Roderick could only wonder. To see her like this, the love he committed to protect broke his heart. Failure was all he felt. Roderick watched them both, chronicling their last moments, someone had too. No one may hear their story but he would put it to history non the less.

The banging stopped for a moment and the three of them watched the door. Then bang, bang, bang. They went back to their respective roles. They participated in this routine for hours and then when it was time to sleep they lay awake. They thought of their lives and what they could or should have been. They thought of the disrespect at the hands of the world. The old adage of the world flashing before your eyes when you were to die was true. In their case the flashes repeated, over and over they saw the travesty of life. Clarity in the reasons they should end it, and the most compelling did not knock at the door.

Nina walked to Roderick and put her hand on his shoulder, the first time they had touched in days. She had streams of tears, "I keep seeing it, the moment Sophia turned." Roderick hugged her, the pain of gaining and loosing her was immense to the both. "Dr Fleming said the inoculation would help her, protect her against it."

"He wasn't to know that it would behave as it did." Roderick tightened his grip.

"Her eyes were so red, she became one so quickly. Why did it happen? How could they do this to the children, punish us not the little ones?"

Nina recalled the day the children were inoculated. They didn't have enough for them all but she made sure Sophia was safe, she ensured Sophia was in the bunker protected from the outside world. Then they were out for food, Sophia wanted to be outside again. She should have told her to stay behind but her smile melted all resistance. They walked hand in hand, quietly and softly. The infected spent their time at the barrier, battling the soldiers. They were drawn there, Dr Fleming said he thought it was due to their hate, the disease seizing that thought.

For so long August and its people treated them poorly, that kind of systematic treatment burned into the depths of them. When the disease took hold, it was written into the anger potion of the brain. The disease latched onto this, inflated their desire for retribution. He said this was proof that they were still there, he hoped to retrieve them.

They needed to be cautious, but if there was an infected being they were usually alone, looking for food and could be dispatched of easily. They walked hand in hand, it amazed Nina that Sophia could so easily adapt to this new world. She was happy to be with them, happy to see the trees when they left the bunker. Her attitude inspired Nina to hope.

They found the store relatively unscathed. The dry stock was in good order and they began to load it onto a trolley. Rice, flour and grain, they were the luxuries of life. Sophia went into the back room and her scream sent ice through Nina. A an infected teenage boy had hold of her, biting into her shoulder. Sophia screamed, loudly and with a deep fear. Nina took her gun, one that Dr Fleming brought with him, and when the monster looked at her roaring, she shot him in the forehead.

The infected teenage boy dropped to the floor and began to inflate. Nina took Sophia and with trolley in tow they both ran. There was a pop but they did not see the mist, they were far enough away. They ran with fear, Sophia's little legs barely striking the ground as Nina dragged her.

They came into the bunker, "Sophia has been bitten." She took her to Dr Fleming and Dr Chekov who were discussing the red liquid. They took her, "Dear you will be all right, the medicine we gave you will protect you. Let me wash the wound so it doesn't hurt so much." Dr Chekov's gentle demeanour calmed the little girl, her sobs slowed.

She was so tired after the ordeal as was Nina. They both went to bed, and slept arm in arm. They thought it was all right. The inoculation had not failed. They did not suspect the disease to be so cunning.

Nina was woken as Sophia left the bed, it was dark in the bunker as everyone slept. Roderick in the chair allowing Nina and Sophia to cuddle. He was so happy to see Nina be a mother, he was happy to make any sacrifice.

There was something strange about the way Sophia now moved, stiff. Her skin did not reflect in the usual way, it was missing its youthfulness. She whispered to her and she ignored it. Slowly she walked to Roderick with that unnatural gait.

Nina crept out of bed and turned her around. Sophia with blood red eyes screamed at her, tried to bite her hand. Nina jumped back and screamed, it woke Roderick who saw them in a struggle. He took Sophia and threw her across the room, she tumbled against the beds. The doctors woke to Sophia jumping over the upturned beds and running at the two of them. Nina took a glass bottle and smashed it against the little girls head. It put a concave dent in the front of the skull. Sophia fell to the floor and screamed again. She rolled to her stomach and clawed towards them.

Dr Chekov took the pistol he kept with him at all times and shot her, the bullet entering through her eye and exiting with a mess. She stopped, her lifeless little body lay on the cold ground. Nina cried out, bending down over the little girl. She had never felt a pain so intense, never a pain that took away her ability to be happy again.

Sophia's lifeless body lay in Nina's arms the blood falling over her thighs. Then the tiny little belly began to inflate. "In the lab, she will infect us all." Roderick took her from Nina's arms and dragged her through the doors. He shut their only hope of being parents away from them, then her little belly popped. "Nina we need to wash you." It was Dr Chekov she thought, her mind corrupting under the strain. They took her clothes and threw them in the fire. She went into their make-shift hazmat shower. Her tears fell as rapidly as the water. That was the day Dr Fleming discovered the mutation, the day the world darkened a little more.

"Roderick, I struck her. Her beautiful little face." She cried heavily, Dr Chekov stopped and watched. He too felt a great shame for his part in the affair. "She was to be our miracle, but she was taken in the most horrible way."

They hugged each other, silence was more apt than any words that could be uttered. The three in the bunker were still for a moment, then came silence from outside. The banging at the door stopped, they waited but it did not start again. The three of them walked to it and stood there for what seemed like days. After twenty minutes of quiet contemplation Roderick opened the door. They were gone, not a single infected being was there.

Tentatively they walked to the building opposite the bunker entrance. They climbed to the top of it and saw all the infected heading south. Like a swarm of locust they walked in the single direction. The part of them that was infected called them to follow, instead they returned to the bunker and waited.

CHAPTER SEVENTEEN

Bill joined Kate in her office. The expatriate and confirmed traitor were meeting with a security expert in regard to the ever persistent threat on her life. Traitor to her country was truly a horrific title but no less true. She aided in the coup of the leader of her country. She could justify it as much as she liked but traitor was appropriate.

"Mrs Laurie I apologise, the news is of such a poor nature." Bill stood at the doorway, Brian was the current consultant the UN provided. Bill despised Kate being called a traitor, hated it more because Kate would not call them what they were, lies. Taking Charles Terri from power would be the most patriotic thing an Augustan citizen could do.

"Brian thank you for the update. With all circumstances considered it is reassuring to have you here, even if only to deliver bad news." She shook his hand and walked him out.
"Mrs Laurie if there is anything further please don't hesitate to call."
Brian left and Bill took a seat. Kate returned to hers. "What is it?"

"They got Dr Fleming out, he is currently being moved to the lab." Bill leant forward, "He has asked to speak to you."
"Why?" Kate leant back, "Has he got any idea how to tackle this disease? Is he a Loyalist?"
"Kate I don't know, they want you to speak to him" He put the tablet in front of her.
"At least one of the missions was successful." She thought of Charles Terri sitting in the hospital injured. If only things had been different.

"He has returned to office." Bill said with some disgust.

"Charles? Wasn't he shot?"

"Yes, but the great man has risen from the ashes." Bill took the tablet back, "They have made him a myth now. Able to survive an assassination attempt. Works through a bullet wound. All the media we keep getting out of August praises him. They ignore that he is turning the country into a wasteland."

"It is all for August." She stood out of her chair. "He has a way of convincing you of his view. They watch him and he is a god. Even as they have despair at their feet, he convinces them it is character building." Kate stopped her slow pacing at the corner of her desk, "It's easy to fall for."

"Kate, they will see you for who you are in the end. It is only a matter of time before your legacy is vindicated."

"Bill, I would be happy to see August back in its place. Proud, not war torn. How did it come to this? How was I so blind to not see it building under my watch? For all of their failings, I was the one who allowed them to build this base. I allowed them to treat the immigrants like that, I allowed them to work away at their disease." She sat on the edge of the desk, "Bill if I wasn't such a fearful person I would have stopped the Loyalists before they were so strong. We knew that they were gaining momentum and our fear of the polls allowed them to become what they are today. The ruling class." Her weight slumped on the desk, her body showing her despair for the moment.

Kate and Bill sat in an armoured car, Dr Fleming was kept in one of the most secure buildings in New York and probably the world. They sat and waited to be cleared. No one was above suspicion, everybody was an assumed combatant until proved otherwise. Her shame was heavy as they sat waiting to see the man who caused so much death. He was the architect of this disease and the potential downfall of the human race.

It would be expected that a man such as he would be shackled, a prisoner. No, he was a guest. It was clear he was nothing more than a moronic genius, unable to connect cause and effect. Dr Fleming thought he worked for his government, worked for Kate. It was a comedy of errors, he sat as their guest, the architect. She was a respected dignitary, the enabler.

The car moved on and they went into the deep chasm of the building. Down further, the temperature getting cooler. Kate was greeted by a member of the military, she couldn't tell which country he represented, he was a part of the UN's secret force. He led them down a clinical hallway, the walls brilliantly white.

They were met by Maria in a room, a window on the far wall illuminated with artificial light. There he was, the cause of so much destruction. The genius behind what scientists termed the most perfect pathogen. They hoped his genius would also extend to curing perfection. There was glass vials on the table in front of him, filled with a red liquid. He sat behind the table, she was shocked that this was the man, this middle aged every man.

"Katherine thank you for coming." Maria shook her hand and then Bill's. "This is Dr Carl Fleming."
"I imagined him differently. Not like this."
"What do you mean?"
"I imagined him to be more like a bond villain." Kate sat down. She watched him through the window, he was extremely nervous, fidgeted furiously. How could this man, so unremarkable, so pedestrian be the biggest murderer in history?

Maria broke Kate of her gaze, "He brought with him a medicine he developed."
"Why did he want to speak to me?" Her curiosity and fear intertwined.
"He said as an Augustan citizen he had the right to speak to a representative." She moved in her seat, "All Augustan representatives in an official capacity were recalled." Maria stood, "We said he could speak to you."

Kate was guided into the room, she looked back to the mirror and hoped Bill was watching. Dr Fleming stood when she walked in, it made her flinch at first. "President Laurie it is an honour to meet you, I only wish it wasn't under these circumstances."

"Please call me Katherine, my presidency is no longer recognised." She sat opposite him, still amazed he was it.

"I wanted to speak to someone from August to explain what happened, someone who could understand the situation we come from. I was honoured to find out I would be speaking to a President." He thought for a moment, "To yourself."

"What is it you would like to say?"

"I did not create this to kill people. I know it's a deadly disease but I believed I was doing my civic duty. This threat would keep us safe." He shifted in his seat, "I want you to know I am not a monster like them, I wanted no harm to come to the immigrants. They took me in and protected me. I want to apologise for what has become of my creation."

"Your apology is noted." Kate didn't allow him piece of mind. "What are your requirements, what demands need to be met to find a cure?"

"I have no demands, I will work. It was my apology to our people that I need noted." He shifted in his seat again, "I don't believe there will be a true cure, the disease is shifting and becoming hard to pin down. Those vials hold a medicine which will allow us to stop it in its tracks." He leant over the table, "See the red in my eyes, I am infected but have been able to keep it at bay."

Katherine jumped back, she turned to the mirror. "He is infected, you have to get me out of here."

"That medicine is keeping the disease dormant for now. It won't spread in this state, other wise this whole building would be infected." A guard rushed in but Kate asked him to leave. "I can feel my body breaking down. This medicine is the first step to the thing that will control the disease. We can't cure it, but I believe with this we can control it."

"We are running out of time Dr Fleming, the infection is spreading rapidly. If we have no cure millions will be infected."

"If I don't perfect this medicine, the human race will cease to exist in its current capacity."

The realisation was stark, Kate left the room and watched Dr Fleming in the laboratory. An avenue to apologise to his nation was her purpose there. To allow him to unburden himself.

CHAPTER EIGHTEEN

Private Kellan Russell had been stationed on the gate for two weeks now. At first he was terrified of the situation, the infected attempting to tear it down. He didn't believe it would hold them, they were so aggressive, they numbered so many. For his first few days, he was permanently on guard, waiting for the moment they finally broke through. That moment had not eventuated, over the days he relaxed into the situation. Becoming accustomed to the noises.

There were two breaches in the time he was stationed at the gate. They were taken care of easily. There were no reported deaths due to the disease on the gate. They were contained, that gave him peace of mind.

Private Russell patrolled the gate, his gun to his side. Watching man and woman claw at each other to get to the imposing structure. They were animals, he had to resist shooting them in the head. As he walked past he was glad it was them, the immigrants. If anyone should be infected they were the most acceptable choice. He was a proud Loyalist, the immigrants were a blight on his country. The UN striking them with the disease was a gift in reality.

The gates were clear and he returned back to his post. Private Russell had a view of a large stretch and sat dutifully. The noise was the constant, their jostling was the norm. He thought back to before this had happened, when the immigrants were a nuisance not a biohazard. He and his buddies would drive through the immigrant zone, picking out one to beat up. They were sending a message that this was their. They couldn't come here and take what they pleased.

All his friends were in the military. The moment the war broke out they made sure to be put on active duty, it was their patriotic obligation. They observed their sacrifice with pride, Augustan pride. Most of his friends were stationed on the borders, or on ships holding back the nations that were trying to take over. August was at imminent risk of being invaded. Before the war it was from the immigrants, now it was power hungry opportunistic nations.

Private Russell got a drink and sat back down, he watched them push at the gate. They didn't tire, they continued until they collapsed. At the feet of the mob they fell to their demise. Trampled on day and night, they became goo and added to the awfulness. The news reports confirmed what he believed. The disease illuminated their nature. He knew they were all barbarians deep inside.

Private Richards walked up to take the post from Private Russell, "I don't know how you sit here so calmly and watch them. It still freaks me out."

"Once you realise that we are in control, they go back to being the weak immigrants they have always been."

"Did you hear about the latest breach? They say there were casualties."

"We would have heard about that." He stood out of the chair, "You need a little more faith."

"I'll have faith when they're all dead. What are they waiting for anyway?" Private Richards sat down.

"There is always a plan my friend, they just don't let the minions know."

Private Russell waved as he left Private Richards, and he walked back to barracks. He needed a shower and something to eat. His stomach was empty and his body smelled. Then something caught his attention, forgetting the emptiness of his stomach. The sounds stopped.

There were no shouts or yelling, the pushing stopped and the gate was silent. They were perfectly still, they all looked straight ahead. He began to walk back to Private Richards, his radio went off. *They have stopped.* From right across the gate, the same message. "Richards what happened?"

"They just stopped, its the eeriest thing."

"Did anything happen?" Private Russell forgot about walking back to the barracks. "Call into command, ask them to send everyone here."

"Why? they're calm."

"For how long?"

Private Russell walked towards the gate, all looked straight ahead, unfocused. They were dormant, he had a bad feeling. For ten minutes he stood in front of them, not one of them noticing his existence.

Backup came, command agreed with Private Russell. This unusual display required caution, everyone was brought to attention. His sergeant called for him to join the group. Like a good soldier he followed orders.

For two hours they sat and watched, the infected stayed dormant. The sergeant walked up to Private Russell, "Son, we need someone to go down there and check them out. Command wants to know if they are still alive."

"Yes, Sir." He responded without hesitation.

Private Russell walked towards the gate, his gun in hand. He never needed it more. As he got closer, he could see that they were alive, their chests moved with their breath. They breathed in sync, their bodies orchestrated to move together.

Private Russell radioed back, "Sargent they are alive and breathing."

"Right" there was confusion in his voice, "come back and rejoin us."

"Yes, Sir." He turned to rejoin but something out the corner of his eye demanded his attention. Back to the infected, they began to blink. "Sir, they're blinking, I think they're waking..." He was interrupted by the loudest noise he had ever heard humans make.

In unison all the infected roared into the sky. The noise

was so intense it almost knocked Private Russell over. Then from their dormant state they pushed. All together pushing, they were united. Perfectly timed bursts emanated, synchronised waves of aggression.

The radio screamed, *"GET BACK HERE NOW"*. Private Russell ran as fast as his legs could hit the ground. From behind the gate they continued to push. The ground lifted from around the concrete which held the gate in place. Their roars matched their pushes, they were communicating. All down the gate it happened, a communicated push.

Back in formation, his group was instructed to fire. Taking out as many as they could, their roar was louder than the gunfire. The gate kept swaying, further with every push. The ones hit by bullets inflated to explosion. The gate was covered in a red mist, like on a cold winters morning.

One more push and the gate came down. They stood behind the gate line, roaring into the sky and then they went quiet and stood calm.

Together the sound came again and they ran. The platoon pushed forward, Private Russell shot three of them and then one got hold of him. He fell back, the infected man on top of him. He bit down on Private Russell's face, he screamed until it tore out his throat. It stayed on top of Private Russell and watched him die, then it ran.

They all ran, the military at the gate had no hope of stopping them. Their numbers and new found uniformity pushed through. They headed towards the city, the place where so much of their pre-disease indignities occurred. The immigrants were taking August.

CHAPTER NINETEEN

"You need to tell us when we'll be allowed to leave." Judy stood close to the soldier, she was the only one in the office with the courage to speak. "Its been four days, it's far past the 72 hours you told us we would be quarantined."

"You need to go back to your office." He didn't make eye contact with her, he kept his eyes firmly on his men.

"I know my rights." She paused, still his eyes evaded her. "Unless you missed the sign on the door, this is a law firm."

"You have no rights, go into your office and look it up. We are in a state of war, on sovereign land." Judy stood firm, "You have two rights; either you walk back to your office or I have one of my men drag you back there." He looked at her for a moment, "Which would you prefer?"

Judy turned on her heels and walked back to her office. The people in there were scared. It was funny how fear brought people closer, in a physical and emotional sense. They huddled together, looking to her for guidance. She couldn't say to them she was as fearful, it was the truth but that wasn't always the best policy. Instead she stood up to the soldiers.

They had become more belligerent as time went on. They weren't friendly to start with, but now they spoke to her people as if they weren't even people. They cut off all communication with the outside world, no phones or internet. The TV's were kept out of reach. This made her worry, but she would not let the people in her office see. She needed to convince them it would be all right. It was what you did when people were scared.

"What did they say? When can we leave?" Carmen asked

quietly, she was a junior. Her first real job out of school. Her demeanour would not allow her to do anything more than contract work but she was happy with that. She always was the first to ask a question but looked terrified the whole time she was doing it. Her eyes were wide, she was hoping for an answer which allowed her to go home and hide.

"They haven't given me any word." She smiled, "They are being cautious. It is an inconvenience but with the current climate it is the best way to be."

"Why are they cutting us off from the rest of the world?" Bob stood and gave Judy his phone. "They have jammed the signal, this is extreme for being cautious."

"They don't want to cause a panic." She sat on the floor beside them, now was not the time for the formality of her chair. "I don't agree with their approach but it will be over soon of that I am sure."

They sat silent for a little longer, watching the men on the main floor. They were encroaching on her world. It was the longest time she had gone without seeing or speaking with the girls. She was beginning to feel sick with separation. "Judy," Bob called to her softly, most of the group had dozed. "Rita is sick, she has a temperature."

Judy went over and felt her forehead, it burned. "How long has she been like this?"

"I just noticed, I thought she fell asleep." He rested her on the ground and the two of them walked out of the office so they wouldn't wake any more people. "She fell on me, and I felt the heat."

"We need to get some cool cloths to put on her head." Judy was a mother and her instincts were sharp.

Bob walked off, Judy paused in the dimly lit office. Again her thoughts went to her children. The fear she felt the first time Charlotte had a fever. She was a new mother, her husband had stayed at home to look after her. She remembered the moment so profoundly, walking into the house and seeing her husband Ralph nearly in tears. He had Charlotte in his arms, a cloth over her head. "She has a temperature and it wont go down". Instantly her gut became uncomfortable and there was a fear like none she had ever felt.

They raced her to the hospital, Ralph did a god awful speed the whole way there. Judy was in an utter panic as she came through the hospital doors. A nurse came to them, calmed them down. She gave Charlotte some paracetamol, most importantly she gave the parents some reassurance. When the fever broke it was the happiest feeling she ever had.

Judy walked back into her office, Rita sat up as she came in. She turned to Judy, her face still, no emotions. Her eyes were red, the type that brought fear to anyone in this new world. Judy turned out of her office, "We need help in here," the volume was startling to herself.

The soldiers ran in, they took the increasingly agitated Rita out of the office. She struggled with them and fell to the floor. "Let us leave or we will kill every one of you." The normally placid Rita looked up at them with utter hatred. A soldier came from behind the group and lassoed her with a contraption similar to those they caught dogs with. She jumped at him but the device kept her at a distance. Her threats turned into shouts and then growls. The speed of her transition left Judy feeling horrified. Rita stared at Judy as they took her off the floor.

Judy ran to the Soldier in charge, "Where are you taking her?"
"Get back in your fucking office, I'm not going to tell you again." He listened to something in his ear. Judy pushed him to get his attention, with little effort he pushed her to the ground. He spoke into his walkie talkie, "The virus has been dormant for 102 hours." Judy got to her feet, she realised that control was now well out of her grasp. The officer listened again to his ear piece. "Yes, Sir, compromised."Judy walked back to the office, she knew that word did not have a friendly connotation. She looked into the room and saw her scared staff.They were terrified for their lives and her feeling was this was an accurate

summation of the situation.

Judy caught a reflection in the glass of her office door and saw the red in her eyes. In that moment her soul fell to the depths. She knew what compromised meant; she knew what they did to contain those who were compromised. Without a hint of the fear that took hold of her she walked back into the office. She could see the redness coming to the eyes of all those around her, all of those who were now compromised. She sat down, most were sleeping, the others were in quiet contemplation.

Judy closed her eyes and saw her husband's face. To herself and in silence she prayed to be with him when the soldiers came into the office. She prayed to see and feel him again. She said the prayer that for so long after his passing, she ignored. She ignored the prayer because she felt guilty for wanting to leave their world. She felt that saying the prayer was tantamount to abandoning her children. Sitting there, forced to leave the world, she was free to pray. Her husband's face was so clear to her, she had never forgotten it. She prayed to be with her true love.

The solders left their posts and walked to the office. It was silent and only Judy facing out saw them. She took the few moments of their approach to pray for the twins. Her love materialised, the most pure and perfect parts of her. She prayed to God to take care of Rosa and the girls. She prayed to God that they could all be reunited outside of the horror August had become.

The door to the office opened, two of the soldiers entered and lifted their guns. The others didn't even notice them until the rapid gun fire broke through the silence. Judy lifted her hand as she saw the barrel point to her. The bullet tore through her palm and entered her shoulder, spinning her around. Before her face hit the ground, another bullet enter her body. It punctured her left lung and she was unable to breath. She lay on the ground suffocating.

The soldiers stepped out, silence returned to the room.

She heard the soldier that showed such little compassion speak to a man in a Hazmat suit, "Neutralised". Then they walked in.

The fire was like nothing she had felt or thought was possible. She raised her head, the man in the hazmat suit called over the soldier. Their eyes met, there stood a man who had lost his soul. His eyes reflected her pain with no distortion or acknowledgment. All the soldier saw was the disease, red and ferocious. He looked through the site of his gun and saw his duty to August. It was clear and he was resolute. The bullet entered her brain and she dropped to the floor. He stepped out and allowed the men in yellow suits to eradicate the disease. The flames were hot; they were felt across the floor. The curiosity of the hazmat units work gripped the soldier. He stood and starred at the ash. Amazed the human body could be broken down in such a way.

The soldier got word to move out, that the containment line had been broken. He left the ash of those people. He saw a flicker at the window, and walked over. Every horror that had been professed by the naysayers were made real in the street. A horde of infected ran through the city. He gripped his weapon and hung out the window and shot into the crowd. The swarm didn't even notice the bodies falling to their side.

The men went to the windows when they heard the message, "The City has been taken by the disease".
The team looked to him, "Men if we don't get out of here alive, we will take as many of the bastards out with us. We fight for August, we will fight to the death."
In an adrenalin fuelled mania, all the men took a window and began shooting into the horde.

The bullets weren't noticed and their efforts were futile but they fought for August!

CHAPTER TWENTY

President Charles Terri waited for Maria Singh to answer his call. There was a deep resentment in him, a retaliation waiting to be unleashed. August was in disharmony because of her actions, his life threatened on her word. She took in traitors to assist in overthrowing his country. Never had he felt such contempt for another person. Maria was meant to lead the worlds governing body, to perpetrate peace and harmony. She failed miserably at her duty. Worse still she gave countries who wanted nothing more than to see August crumble a deep hope.

President Charles Terri's assistant Louise sat patiently for the Secretary General to answer. She watched the man who scared her so deeply seethe in anticipation. She may questioned the direction he took the country in but never his resolve. She was ready to take note, to witness and transcribe history.

The connection came alive and Secretary General Maria Singh came to the screen. There was a nervousness which Louise felt, this would only feed the anger President Charles Terri was displaying. "Ms Singh, President Charles Terri is ready to take your call." Louise transferred the call and President Charles Terri came alive. The thing in him that struck fear in her came out and stretched its legs.

"Secretary General, it is a shock that you are taking my call." He sat up tall in his chair, pain from the assassination attempt still there, always reminding. "After your attempt on my life I thought your deceitful ways would cause you to abstain from contact."

"Our goal continues to be in the interest of your people." She looked into the screen with hope. "We intend to continue to work to protect the people of your country and the world."

"Can I take your candour as confirmation that it was you who gave the order to end my life?" President Charles Terri let the venom flow freely.

"President Terri, it was our intention to remove you from power. The first choice was to extract you without harm." She looked at him nervous of the message he wanted the world to hear." For what you are doing to your citizens, and those that come to you in need. Your death is much less than your atonement deserves."

"You dare speak to me about what I do to my people." His voice lifted.

Maria interrupted, "I speak of the evil acts you allow and condone. Charles do you justify your use of biological weapons on you own people?" Maria held up pictures of the disease transforming the citizens of the world in the most horrible ways. Louise saw this and shrank back in her chair, the reality of her participation clear in those photos. "Your life ending would have been a service to your people, and the people of the world. Your inability to see the evil in what you do makes you a tyrant."

"You will regret the attempt on my life. You will regret your attempts to destabilise this great nation. It is clear that your full efforts go behind the destruction of my people."

"Our full efforts go behind the destruction of you." Maria starred him down, not holding back any of her words.

"This is a declaration of war Secretary General. You will lift your sanctions against my people. You will remove your warships from our region." President Charles Terri looked down the lens. "We demand to see these reasonable requests enacted or else we will engage you. With the full power of our armed forces, we will strike you down."

"Charles stand down and we will negotiate with your people." Maria sat back, understanding that she was now speaking with someone blind to reality. "If you strike us Charles, you will be engaging in war with the world. We will stop at nothing to prevent you from further assaults on our people."

President Charles Terri held her gaze, he allowed her to see all his rage. This rage much more powerful than any words he could produce.

President Charles Terri was the clear leader of his country, chosen not just by his people but endorsed by God. He would not allow the UN, the organisation that desired to dictate to his people, a chance of control. President Charles Terri was a loyalist; he was a true Augustan citizen. The pain of the few would allow the many to thrive.

"Maria you have 24 hours to comply or we will strike with the full weight of our might." His voice was much calmer, his belief was strong. "You have underestimated us, and our ability." He paused to allow the UN to see his countenance become resolute, "And tell Mrs Laurie that her betrayal will not go unpunished." Charles looked to Louise and she cut the call off. There wasn't a word shared in the room. Charles contemplated his approach, he contemplated making August the power of the world once more.

General Wilson entered the presidential office and interrupted the conversation between President Terri and Louise. "Ma'am I need to speak to the President in private." She looked to President Terri and he nodded to her. She was used to the gesture, it was becoming the normal way for him to communicate.

"General Wilson we need to ready ourselves to strike the UN with all our force in 24 hours." President Charles Terri was calm; he knew his path was righteous.

The general looked on uneasy, "Sir, we have had a major breach from the immigrant zone. The Southern barrier was broken."

"How many infected made it through?"

"All of them, Sir."

"Fuck" the calm broke, "you need to kill them all, I want all attention on protecting our citizens."

"Sir, the city will fall, we need to evacuate as many people as we can." General Wilson's demeanour was matter of fact and this fell harshly on Charles Terri. "Your helicopter has been prepared. I need your authority to announce the evacuation."

President Charles Terri sat in thought, the very things he thought weak were taking his great city. It stung him, confirming that these people needed to be wiped off the planet. "Evacuate our people; I want all armed personnel on this effort." He stood up, the sharp pain hitting him." Then I want the infected obliterated. Every spare fighter is to bomb them. Eradicate this disease, we will not be beaten by filth."

General Wilson nodded; the two men began walking to the helicopter. It was a priority to keep the president safe; he was the strength of August. Louise followed and they walked through the halls with speed. Those around looked on with fear, General Wilson spoke into his radio and the evacuation alarms sounded. The Parliament building became a hive of panic.

At the helicopter President Terri took hold of General Wilson, "The UN wants us to fall. To be weak and surrender." He looked at the helicopter, yelled over the top of it. "Do not give them the benefit of 24 hours; strike with all our fury General. They will fear us and we will be victorious."

General Wilson nodded, the helicopter took off and Charles Terri looked at the streets of his city clogged with infected bodies. The very people that should have been eliminated so long ago. He thought of his once protégé and now willing assassin. He had failed her but would not fail his people. He continued to look on the city with sadness as they flew to the ship that would become his temporary home. A voice came over the radio, "Missiles have launched."

CHAPTER
TWENTY ONE

Kate and Bill were sifting through their documents trying to find any information which would be of use in shutting down Charles Terri and the virus. The Loyalists had buried their trail so deep, there was no longer any light to be seen. "Bill what are we doing?"

"We're trying to stop him, to give the UN some ammunition."

"We have nothing of use. We have spent so many hours combing through this material. They have hidden their work so well." Kate shut her laptop, "We are out of the loop. They're keeping us around as a courtesy." She looked over to her security detail.

"We are better placed than anyone to help them, we know the military. We know where August is weak." Bill was resolute and would not shut his laptop.

"We are working to kill the country that we called home." Kate looked at him, her resolve broken. "If we help them we will destroy August, if we don't August will destroy the world."

"August is not the enemy, the enemy is Charles Terri. We are working to stop that man, the man who unleashed a plague on the world. We have to stop him".

A call came over the radio and the security guard who sat at the door informed them that the Secretary General was on her way. "Kate," Bill attempted to comfort her, his words were lost to the door opening.

The two of them stood as Maria came through. They

moved into the sitting room. "Kate, I have just been on the phone to Charles Terri." Maria's security detail came into the room covering all entry and exit point. The blinds were drawn. "He has become increasingly unstable." She looked concerned, her usual command was weakened. "He has given 24 hours before he will strike."

"What does he want as a ransom?"

"He wants us to lift all sanctions and roll back our military activity."

Bill interrupted, "So he wants us to give up? Doesn't he realise, he doesn't have that kind of power? Has the man grown that delusional?"

Maria responded with calm, "He is a dangerous entity, and is completely out of touch with what is happening in his own country." Maria sat down, "On my way here I was informed of more news. The containment area that was set up to keep the bulk of the infected confined has been breached. Our surveillance has shown they have over run the city." Kate and Bill sat in shock, "There was an attempt to evacuate but all reports suggests this has been overwhelmingly unsuccessful".

Kate turned to Bill and the tears in her eyes conveyed what he felt also. "August has fallen, how are we still at war with them?" Bill's words hit with a deep sadness.

"The military and political leaders have been successfully evacuated. They have missile launching capabilities."

Kate stared at Maria with utter despair, "They have sacrificed their people for a corrupt ideal."

They room was frozen in its knowledge, and then the building moved with a violent motion. The furniture toppled and the sound of glass shattering filled the area. The security detail covered them until the movement stopped. Alarms went off around them; there was a ringing in the air. Maria turned to her men, they were listening to their ear pieces. "What's happened?"

"Ma'am, August has sent out their full arsenal of missiles. We were able to intercept the majority but a few breached. Our

counterparts in other UN locations are reporting the same."
"Put me in touch with command". Maria turned towards Kate, "I need to use your computer".

The call came through, Kate and Bill stood by stunned into inaction. Charles Terri attempted to protect a country utterly torn apart, a country he destroyed. The man on the other end of the video call was dressed in military regalia; his hair was greyed and he had a Southern American drawl.

Maria spoke with angst, "General Schuler what is the current situation?"
"Ma'am eight missiles have hit the United states, four of those New York." He took a piece of paper from a private off screen, "Four of those missiles had explosive payloads and the other four had the virus."
"What about the status of other nations?"
"Ma'am we are in the dark at the moment, we will be reconvening in an hour to discuss retaliation strategy. The United States have returned fire and are moving resources into the area. We are getting reports that our fellow nations are following suit."
Maria looked to Kate and Bill, they were moved to an adjacent room so Maria could speak in private. "What about the people in August, have we any definitive answer as to the level of infection?"
"Ma'am, I'm sorry to say it looks like the infection has not left any person unscathed. If it has, it won't be for long."
Maria responded in contemplation "Thank you General, I will speak to you in an hour."

The call went dead and Maria sat for a moment frozen by events. It was one of those moments that shouldn't exist. One of those times that reality became the absurdity. They were at war with a country without citizens. They were at war with a leader that could not see past his injustices. August had fallen and risen again, as this most horrible beast, one survived by hatred and pain.

Maria walked into the room where Kate and Bill sat,

"Charles Terri has waged war. He has sent Augustan missiles at UN aligned countries." She sat before them. "We have confirmed reports that the virus has spread through August and there are no viable survivors." She allowed them to process this information for a moment. "The missiles that he has sent contained the virus, he has infected millions of people around the world."

"What can we do?" Kate was the first to break through the silence and pain in the room. "How do we stop this taking any more lives?"

"Kate I don't think we can." She looked at Bill, the rare occasion he was silent. "We are going into a meeting to discuss our next steps." Maria stood and walked to the door. "Let's hope Dr Fleming is able to create something to help."

Maria's security detail followed her out of the room. Kate and Bill let the tears fall. "They are going to destroy everything I knew, the people I love." Kate stopped the tears but her sadness was clearly evident. "We have failed our people." The tears came again, for the millions of people who now suffered and for those who would suffer. Kate felt responsible for allowing her country to fall so far. Hate was the true infliction the human race contracted. This disease was just a physical representation of that.

CHAPTER
TWENTY TWO

Dr Carl Fleming worked in a laboratory deep beneath New York City. He was surrounded by a team of twenty scientists, all there to develop a cure. Every member of the team looked at him with contempt; the scientific community shunned those who perpetrated such evil. Dr Fleming would have felt the same had he been in their position.

It was becoming clear that the solution was less of a cure and more a management system. The only success they had was halting the virus. It changed so rapidly they had catalogued twenty-five different strains, all presenting in a different way. Dr Fleming believed a cure was unlikely; a more effective treatment was where they focussed.

Dr Fleming was held in a constant state of suspicion. His lab area was separated from the rest of the team. They did so for quarantine purposes but also for fear that he was still strongly aligned to Loyalist causes. He could not convince them that he was not a threat.

"Dr Lavrovsky" the intercom system made it sound so impersonal when they spoke. Herman Lavrovsky was a brilliant virologist and the only other person able to engineer a treatment to a new strain. He understood Dr Fleming's thought patterns and applied those in a most effective manner. "I have been able to put strains 21 and 24 into dormancy."

"Very good doctor," Dr Lavrovsky's voice was flat. His accent was strong with Russian overtones but held much more complexity. He spent much of his life studying in England, Germany, and France, amongst others. It was a history of his life on every word. "Strain 23 is still not reacting to any compound."

Dr Fleming sat and thought for a moment. All had been conquered but this one strain. The answer evaded him, the disease evolved outside of how he designed it. "Dr Lavrovsky, I think we need to make this version in mass supply. It is the best option we have."

"I agree doctor." He turned his back to the window and sent off the relevant instructions. There were laboratories all over the world ready to produce this life saving liquid.

Dr Fleming stared at images of the virus, strain 23. Its changes were so minor that he could not figure out why it was so difficult to defeat. Its architecture showed such finesse, taking what he created and with nature becoming much more. The team in the room opposite, only acknowledging his existence with short and sharp questions, could not see the virus like he did. They could not see the fine structures were unlike what nature would create. When he first began working on this he was driven not just by patriotism or money. There was a sense of grandeur, a sense that he was stepping outside of the natural world.

There was a tap at the window behind him, he spun and his official contact from the UN stood glaring at him. He had very few friends here; this man was most certainly not one of them. "I have received the report that we have been able to tackle 23 of 24. When will the last one be neutralised?"

"Mr Carville it is not so simple. I believe the drug we have created is our best chance to halt the progression of the disease."

"When will we see a cure?"

"Mr Carville, that will take years, the fact that we are able to manage the disease is a miracle in itself."

Henry Carville walked down the hall, speaking through a phone that hung on the wall. His movements were calm and calculated as he spoke. He shot a look towards Dr Fleming every now and then. He placed the phone back on the receiver and walked back towards Dr Fleming. The bunker began to shake and the main lights shut off, the emergency lighting flooded a green hue. Dr Fleming covered his head as debris fell from the roof.

Mr Carville ran back to the phone. The other scientists were evacuated amongst shattering glass beakers. Dr Fleming sat in his lab, not allowed to leave, not worthy of saving. The shaking only lasted a short period but the evacuation caused a fear much longer. Mr Carville came back to Dr Fleming, "There has been a strike on all UN affiliated countries by August." He looked at the doctor with a seething disgust, "They have sent missiles with the virus. The infection is blanketing parts of the United States and many countries abroad. You better hope this medicine works."

"It will." Dr Fleming stopped for a moment, "What has happened to August?"

"The infected have overrun the city. The military is not equipped to handle it. All officials have been evacuated." Mr Carville began to walk away, "August will be destroyed by your hand." He stopped before exiting the floor, "You will be the biggest mass murderer in history of the world, let that sink in for a moment."

Mr Carville left Dr Fleming alone in his laboratory. All personal were evacuated minus him. Under the green light and in perfect isolation he was able to think. Think of what he had done. The virus stared at him, the creation superior to the creator. The pains of his achievements were clear.

Dr Fleming wrote down his apology. A sincere outpouring of regret, alone he was able to consider all his existence meant to society. He apologised to the people of the world and to his fellow countrymen. He apologised to those who had been infected and those who would be in the future. His usefulness had expired; Dr Lavrovsky was able to continue. His life was nothing more than the embodiment of humanities ability for naïve evil.

Dr Fleming took a piece of glass that had once made up a beaker. Through these instruments he was able to investigate and create. He was able to be consumed by science and be great. No matter the consequence of his science, he was great. Dr Fleming a once chubby man, awkward around his fellow human. That was outside of a laboratory. Inside the laboratory he was king.

Dr Carl Fleming inserted the piece of glass into his neck and the blood came out quickly. It was infected with the evidence of his brilliance. He fell to the floor and watched the red liquid swirl. His death came much quicker and with less pain than his disease would have dictated. The brilliance of this man spilled out, while the world suffered.

CHAPTER TWENTY THREE

Maria came into the bunker with force and a calm panic. Her security detail lagged behind. She didn't make eye contact with Kate or Bill. She was lost in thought. The meeting she had just come out of posed a question that she was fearful of asking. The course of human history was changing and no one seemed to be able to stop it. No one seemed to be in control, the insignificance of their organisations showed.

"Katherine" again her eye contact was lost, "we are discussing the method and timing to handle this situation."

"What are the options?" Kate followed her as she spoke. "What state is August in?"

"It has been lost to the virus, there doesn't seem to be anyone left." She stopped and realised the harshness of her comments. She sat beside Kate and took her hands. "I am sorry; the infected have over run the city. What little intelligence we do have is telling us there are no survivors." She looked to Bill who sat open mouthed. "All officials who could escape did so and are now aboard ships."

A member of Maria Singh's security detail whispered into her ear. "Thank you," she turned back to Kate and Bill. "I came here to let you know that we will strike August. I am unable to tell you when this will be." She let go of Kate's hands, "Our first target will be Augustan vessels that harbour the top elected officials. Then we will make all attempts to clear the virus from the island. This is less of an act of war and more a containment effort."

Maria stood to walk out, "The war has been lost, and we now are trying to contain this virus as best we can." Just like that Kate realised her home was forever lost, to a man, a disease and vengeance.

CHAPTER TWENTY FOUR

The room was silent once they made the decision. All the heads of UN countries sat for this historic meeting. The silence in the room would have been history making enough. All the countries of the world, the big and small joined to seal the fate of August. How exactly do you debate destroying a country, wiping it from the face of the earth?

Maria stood and looked at the people before her, and those represented by screens. One hundred and ninety-six nations all voted. "Our course of action from here is clear." Maria Singh had all attention on her. "August will be considered a contagion state. As per reports from many military sources, it appears the virus has overrun the Island nation. We will use force to exterminate these people." The weight of her words not lost on her. "We will also engage with the remainder of the Augustan military forces until they surrender. It is with much thought and consideration that we take this action."

The stunned people sat immobile, it was painful to be the only one with a voice. "To all the nations of the world we have distributed the anti-viral medication. It is imperative that we start distributing this to our citizens. It is not a cure; it is a way to keep the virus in remission. We will continue to work on a cure.

"What we have seen in the last few years is a change so tremendous that none of us could have anticipated it. We have seen actions that have been repeated many times, yet we sat complicit. If nothing else we must ensure that this is not allowed to reoccur. That the people of the world are not subjected to these actions again by tyrants who we ignore in the hopes they change. This disease is our cross to bear."

Maria stood for a moment longer and watched them stare and then their chatter began. She turned and walked out of the room, to meet with the countries leading the mission. She was about to authorise the eradication of a people.

Secretary General Maria Singh sat in front of the four nations in charge of the joint strike attack. "Gentleman thank you for joining me at such short notice." Their attentions all focussed on her. "My input here is truthfully only for ceremony. It is my duty to authorise your strike against August." She looked at all four men. "I would like to formally recognise the four nations and thank you all for your sacrifices. The Peoples Republic of China, the United States of America, the United Kingdom and the Federal Republic of Germany." The formality of authorising war seemed an attempt at delaying their purpose.

"To your military, we the people of the world say thank you. To your citizens, we the people of the world say thank you. To you four men before me, the decisions and tasks we ask you to carry out will weigh on you for a life time, we the people of the world say thank you."

The four men before Maria nodded; they were there to discuss war. Her presence was expected pageantry. "Gentlemen, I'll leave you to discuss your strategies."

Maria sat back and listened to the discussion, the weapons that would be used, the approximations of destruction. They discussed the remaining Augustan arsenals. They discussed how long they thought it would take to destroy the majority of the infected. They discussed at what point they would put soldiers on the ground to finish the extermination. They also discussed the number of soldiers they expected to lose. All these were so factual, lacking emotion.

She walked back to her office, leaving the military experts to dissect how they would destroy the remaining Augustan military. Alone she let out a sigh and starred into nothing. Her brain stopped and her energy spent. Maria Singh joined the UN to advance the cause of peace, sitting in her office she realised how great of a failure she was.

CHAPTER
TWENTY FIVE

Private Peter Walker had one aspiration in life, to fight for his country. As a proud loyalist and Augustan citizen he felt an obligation to protect those that could not do so themselves. He held a great pride in giving back for all he received. Private Walker was an infantry man and worked hard at every task he was given. His performance and efforts were not missed and he held favour with his senior officers, he was the model soldier.

Private Walker patrolled the streets of the city with four other men. He looked around at the quiet of a once busy metropolis. Never in a million years did he believe he would be fighting against the very people he pledged to protect. His squad was charged with seeking out the uninfected and extracting them from the city.

The hoards of infected immigrants were now in a state of hibernation. Many buildings were packed wall to wall with them. Quiet and barely breathing, they preferred to be close to each other. The only movement visible was their breathing, in unison their chests moved.

There were reports of soldiers going into these building. They were able to walk through the crowd, walk up to them. Their hibernation only broken if one was injured or killed. Then they would wake, in a flurry every infected being would activate. They would attack until the soldiers were killed and then go back to quiet. The patrol team orders were clear, mark the buildings that had the infected in them and rescue any citizens.

There had been much more marking than rescue attempts. Private Walker had not seen one uninfected citizen. Those who had the means to escape were now living off the coast on a flotilla of ships. Those who couldn't now sat silently in those rooms. Private Walker was dismayed at their poor extraction rate.

Many people commented on the reason for their inactivity. The official word was that the virus was killing them. It would only be a matter of time before they were able to come back and take the city. Private Walker thought differently, experienced differently. He believed they sat waiting for new victims, new food. The teams could be no bigger than five; if more than five people went into a room of infected they would wake up. They were saving their energy, until a time that the food outweighed the effort of the group.

This was a theory but the official version didn't make any sense. These things weren't dying, if anything they were stronger. Their bodies were returning to a normality of sorts. Their skin regaining some elasticity, their walk less affected by wasted tissue. Private Walker felt deeply that these things were transforming. The virus understood that a healthy body while more energy expensive, could take much more food in. A healthy body could infect many more people.

Private Walker's squad walked in formation, silent as men could be. They didn't want to be the ones to test the theory of hibernation. Lieutenant Kroger marked another building. It was a little GPS tracker, they could see it on their screens and track their progress. Not a single survivor found, many buildings triggered.

They walked to the end of the block and heard a scream from the train station atop it. That was base camp, it was tagged and cleared out. Lieutenant Kroger turned, "Walker hold your position, I want your sights trained on that exit." He turned to the two other men. "Kumar, Elliot you come with me." They all nodded. The men disappeared across the road and into a doorway. Private Walker was perched behind a mailbox trained on the doorway. He steadied his breath and kept the opening in the centre of his view.

Five minutes of silence and Private Walker focussing on his breath. Then the door burst open. Elliot had a girl in his arms. Lieutenant Kroger came out, turned and fired into the doorway. He was over run by them and disappeared under the movement. Elliot with the girl ran across the road towards Private Walker. Behind them streamed infected citizens. Private Walker took three out; they were coming quicker than he could shoot. Their movements were swarm like, so much chaos but also a great deal of uniformity. His two remaining squad members and the little girl got half way across the street before the swarm descended upon them. It only took moments for the infected to move off their bodies. Their lifeless and mutilated bodies in the middle of the road. The infected all looked up at him, the hoard moved back into the doorway with the lifeless bodies in hand.

Private Walker was frozen, why had they let him live? They saw him, he shot at them. They left him with only a stare. The answer showed itself on his neck, a small breeze of air. The smell hit him and he spun around quickly. An infected woman lunged at him, bitting his forehead. Private Walker kicked backwards and shot her in the head. The body fell to the ground and began to inflate. He knew what that meant. He ran as fast as he could. The pop came from over his shoulder, he did not look back.

Private Walker was three blocks down the street before he slowed. He felt his forehead; he was missing a four centimetre patch of skin. He would be infected; he would turn into one of them. He stumbled down the street and took the cap off a syringe filled with the inoculation. It stung as it went into his leg; he hoped that it would work. It was his only defence.

There was a sound above, fighter jets streaming across the sky. As they moved in formation it was clear that they were not Augustan fighters. There was a crash a few blocks ahead, they had opened fire. He ran against a wall. From all around there was the sound of missiles detonating. Then the building he used for protection pushed forward and he landed on the other side of the street. Dazed he got up just before the wall above collapsed.

The pain was intense. Private Walker was pinned from the waist down and all around him missiles struck Augustan soil. Destroying his country, the one he fought so proudly to protect. For fifteen minutes there were explosions around him.

The silence after the attacks allowed the pain to come through all the stronger. The jets were gone, the missiles no longer fell. The destruction remained.

Private Peter Walker lay under the rubble. The weight of the fallen building shattered his lower body. The pain was immense; he fell in and out of consciousness. His dad told him when he was younger, that to die in battle was the greatest honour to be bestowed on a soldier. It showed your character; it was proof of your dedication.

As Private Walker lay there, in varying states of consciousness his father's words joined him. His father was a proud soldier, and fine example of a man. His father was the person he looked up to. In a way his death would be honouring that image.

Looking skyward he saw the planes again, fast overhead. Then out of the corner of his eye he saw an infected man. It looked in his direction like a dog following a scent. It walked over slowly, part apprehension and part lack of motor function. Another plane, the sound was loud. They were flying low.

The creature seemed unfazed, he kept walking slowly towards Private Walker, he was unarmed and incapacitated. Peter was a sitting duck for the infected man, then another plane. His attention was split between the two events.

The infected man walked up the rubble, tripped over and crawled. He got to Private Walker, looked him in the eyes and buried his face into Private Walker's shoulder. There was flesh in his mouth as he came up. Peter screamed with a deep agony. The creature didn't notice.

Again and again the creature tore chucks from Peter's arm. All the while the planes flew overhead. Peter's arm came out of its socket and into the hands of the creature. It sat in front of Peter, eating the arm like a turkey leg. "You fucking piece of shit." The thing was motionless.

The reality of his situation caused Peter to scream into the air. He began to bleed out, his vision darkening. "I'll see you in hell." Another plane flew overhead; before he blacked out he saw the blast that killed him and the infected man.

Dying in battle was the greatest honour. What honour did this battle bring?

PART FOUR

CHAPTER ONE

August Has Fallen.

Roderick watched his infected bride sleep. The little food once in the bunker had been gone for a week. The lack of sustenance made the three of them lethargic and they slept for much of the time. Roderick's body wanted to join his wife in sleep but he fought his eyes closing. The love for his wife was strong, always a distinguishable force. He wanted to spend every last moment he could with his eyes on her.

The medicine that Dr Fleming left was coming to an end. The three of them would soon have to make the decision of how to end their lives. They would not allow the virus to take each other. Roderick would end his beautiful brides life before the virus could. He watched and loved her. Loved her enough to kill her.

At night some of the infected would come back and disappear into the buildings. Then early in the morning they would walk back into the city. They did not need the cover of darkness, they had control of the city and country.

They had all but forgotten about the bunker. Now and then they would bang on the door. Only for a short time and then they would be gone. Roderick would watch them come back into the immigrant zone. He was amazed that they went back to the buildings. Roderick was sure there was something still in the infected immigrants mind. Maybe that was the most torturous part of the virus, it kept hold of a small part of your consciousness.

With the infected loosing interest in the three living souls, they began to venture out once again. Roderick and Dr Chekov would search out whatever food was not spoiled or covered by the red mist. Then the bombs came down. The bombs destroyed most of the buildings and storage centres. Roderick and Dr Chekov still went out in search of food, Nina slept, her body was frail. It did not accept the medicine as well as the other two; it attacked both the virus and her body.

The door of the bunker opened and Dr Chekov came in. As much as he could he ran to Roderick. He whispered with a deep excitement, sharing a soft gaze with Nina. Then he thrust a box towards Roderick. "Look what I have found." Dr Chekov sat across from Roderick on his bed.

"Doctor what is it?"

"It's a radio." Dr Chekov's excitement was clear.

"Doctor, what exactly are we to do with a radio?" Roderick did not have the energy to feign interest.

"Roderick this is a two way radio, we can signal for someone to come for us." He watched a seed of hope enter Roderick's eyes but failed to take root. "We see the planes everyday. One of them will hear our call. They will retrieve us."

"Doctor are you sure?"

"Yes, of course. When I was in the military, we would use a similar radio." The youth of that time came roaring with hope. "The radio was to the South, amongst the military vehicles over run by the infected. I have tested it and it works. We need to send a signal out, to get their attention."

The two man sat in silence for a moment. Nina stirred and opened her eyes, she could see the two men with hope on their faces. "Roderick what is happening?"

"Dr Chekov found a radio. We are going to contact the planes over head."

Nina leant over the bed and the little that was in her stomach hit the bucket. "I don't know how much longer I can hold on for."

Roderick knelt beside her, he brushed the hair from her face.

The medicine caused a fever in her whenever she had it administered, the nausea was ever present. He wiped her brow and looked at her as she fell back to sleep. Roderick turned to Dr Chekov, "We must try Doctor".

For three days the two of them sat out in the open, connecting the radio to an antennae that was once used for the military to communicate back to base. They sent messages of hope, for the people who attacked August to send help. Each day they would watch for the infected to leave, then they would send their message. Signalling for help, help from anyone.

For three days they tried. Taking it in turn, each repeating the message. When they slept they heard their voices going into the sky. They hoped their fate would not be defined by the evil they experienced, their messages were a manifestation of hope.

Dr Chekov sat at the machine, sending out their message of hope. They saw planes over head, those who they called too. Dr Chekov called to Roderick, "Look behind you." Roderick turned around. He had just left the bunker, checking on Nina, she was deteriorating quickly. Behind him were three infected at the bunker door, they banged on it. Their returned aggression was unlike anything they had been displaying in the last few weeks.

Then from the building to the right of Dr Chekov three more infected came out. "Doctor they've ambushed us." They walked towards them, that unnatural gate sparked a deep fear. "Leave the machine."

Dr Chekov stood, holding the cricket bat out in front of him. They had found it in the storage lockers. Sporting goods that were meant for the immigrants withheld.

The three infected advanced and Dr Chekov swung at them. "Doctor you must run."

"They will not leave until they have destroyed us. They have us caught."

Dr Chekov swung at them again, "You two must sur-

265

vive." He stepped forward and struck the one walking out in front. The wet thud was loud, taking away much of its face. The noise attracted all six of them.

"Doctor we can do this together." The three from the door ran towards the doctor. They ignored Roderick and focussed on the Doctor. They were protecting each other.

"Roderick my son, run, we cannot hold them all off. Run to your wife, keep her safe and wait for them to come. You will be my legacy, I will have done one good thing."

The infected engulfed Dr Chekov, for an old man he was adept with a bat. It reminded him of his childhood. The roar from his school mates as he struck the ball. He was a talented batsman, if his love of helping people had not be so strong he may have been a professional.

All his might was behind his next swing, he crushed the head of the next infected that came close. All together they advanced and Roderick saw Dr Chekov go down, there was so much red. When the doctor stopped moving three of them turned their attention to a stunned Roderick. They walked towards him and he ran for the bunker. With all his strength and with Dr Chekov in mind he ran.

The bunker door felt light under his panicked grasp. He closed it tight and leant against the door. He watched it, hoping that the Doctor would follow. It was a wish, one that would never be. Then there was a banging, the infected were at the door once again.

Roderick walked into the bunker and Nina saw his eyes, "Roderick, where is Dr Chekov?"

"They have him, he died fighting to keep us safe." Nina looked at him confused, "He is dead?" Roderick cried, the tears fell fast. He believed in that moment they were doomed. He believed that before long they would be dead. His hope was gone with the doctor, he would be glad for death.

For four days the infected banged on the door, relentlessly and without pause. For four days they listened to their future. Who would tear apart the other first? For four days a constant sound. Then it stopped and the door opened.

CHAPTER TWO

Kate woke to a man in tactical gear standing over her. This was not the wake up call one expected in a luxury hotel. The rude awakening assaulted her feelings of safety. The death threats against them appeared to diminish with the destruction of August. The man standing over her made assurances meaningless.

The pounding in her heart was instant and it took a minute to collect herself. "Ma'am we are moving you, your husband and William." He motioned to the men at the door. "These men will take you, we will give you a minute to get ready."

"Why are you moving us, what happened?" Kate's voice wavered trying to regain some control of her surroundings.

"There has been an attempt on your life." The man went to the window and looked to the street, "A man claiming to be apart of the Augustan resistance was found on site with a bomb." Kate was putting on clothes, the man seemed to not notice her half naked body.

"How did you stop him?" Grant was getting dressed also, his habit of sleeping naked was slightly embarrassing in that moment.

There was a noise from the radio, "We need to go now." There was an urgency in his voice and posture. He grabbed the two of them and all rushed out the door. From behind them a gunshot and the window of the bedroom shattered. There was a gun fight in front of the building. The radios were alive, Kate felt a deep fear. The gunshots reminded her of Trevor West laying in his own blood. She felt sick with the image, terrified that it would be her fate too.

They met Bill in the hallway, his face showing the shock they felt. The three of them had flak jackets thrust to them. They wrapped themselves in what would bring them protection but no peace of mind.

They were quickly ushered into the utility elevator and rushed to the basement. Their guardian focussed on the door, listening to the voices on his ear. "We have all three," his voice was short and sharp. The elevator stopped and he exited first. He swept the area, "Follow me". They were flanked by four more men. All had guns drawn and were on high alert. They arrived to an awaiting black van, the door opened and they were pushed in. It took off quickly, the two men that sat with them held their guns tightly.

"What is happening?" Kate's attempt at calm escaped her and there was a deep terror in her voice.

"There is a group of Augustan citizens who have formed a resistance to what they see as UN injustice." There was a voice from the radio, "We are going to bunker 3 - 2." His focus was back on the three people whose fears had gripped them. "The resistance is attempting to kill people they see as responsible for the fall of August. We have been following them, we had no indication previously they were this capable."

"We are the enemies of these people?" Bill asked a question they all knew the answer too.

"We stopped the bomber before he was able to detonate." The van turned sharply, the wheels squealing.

There was absence in the van, no one had words to fill the void. The van made sharp turns pushing them from side to side. Everyone was frozen by what they lived through. Sadness from what their fellow countrymen were capable of. It was easier to believe that the fall of August was the result of one mans hatred. It was harder to realise many more were like him.

They were in the truck for less than 15 minutes when it came to a sharp stop. The doors jerked open quickly. Their guards jumped out and scanned with their guns, "We are here."

He motioned for the three of them and they followed his signs. They were in the depths of a building and took an elevator deeper.

"Where are we?" Kate broke the silence as they trekked into what felt like the depths of the earth.

"We are at a secure location controlled by the UN. No one knows this place exists." He dropped the gun to his side. "You will be safe here." He pointed them to a door and they walked into an apartment deep beneath the surface of the earth. "This space has two bedrooms and a kitchen. We have stocked it, you could live in here for two months quite easily."

"You aren't going to leave us here for two months are you?" Bill looked terrified, his claustrophobia getting the better of him.

"No, Sir" the soldier let his first smile show. "The lights have a UV filter, it will adjust to match the time of day and help you sleep."

"I don't think sleep is something we will be doing any time soon." Bill sat down on a couch, his eyes firmly on the floor.

The soldier paused for a moment, "You will be under 24 hour surveillance. We have our best men protecting you." He walked to the door, "The screen on the wall has a direct feed from the UN, any communication will come through there." He stepped out of the door, "There is a small booklet that will show you the finer points of the apartment." It felt like he was a hotel clerk welcoming them to a suite. If fear was not controlling, Kate may have offered a tip.

"Thank you for helping us." Bill stepped forward and shook the mans hand. "We appreciate your efforts."

"Of course, Sir," he closed the door and there was a loud locking sound. No one could break in or out. The three sat in silence, the threat of death scared each of them differently.

They spent a day in the apartment without speaking to another person. The three of them felt like the last people on earth. The screen illuminated, there was a ringing. Kate pressed the glowing button on the television remote and a face appeared on the screen. The three of them collected in the living area. "My name is Laurence Welsh, I am a UN officer and your official contact. I am tasked with keeping you informed of events."

"Have you found the people who tried to kill us?" Bill was animated as he stepped forward.

"We do not believe we have captured all involved, we are doing our best." Laurence Welsh moved papers around on his desk. "We have captured four members, they were all listed as Loyalists. They have not been overly forthcoming under interrogation."

Kate sat down in a chair, "They wont speak."

Laurence nodded in acknowledgement, "We may have a way to stop them. To have them loose faith in their cause."

"How do you expect to do that?" Kate kept her eyes on the screen.

"We have intercepted a communication from Charles Terri, we know where he is."

The three of their jaws dropped, "We thought he would be dead." Bill's statement started as a question but ended in disbelief.

"Charles Terri's body was never found. This has kept those Loyalists who made it to other countries hopeful. As it turns out they had reason to be."

"You will kill him wont you?" Kate had a note of fear in her voice.

"We will attempt to take him alive, so we can get him to surrender and stop the resistance."

Laurence watched the three of them look at each other. The conversation was absent of words but strong nonetheless. There was a tension that he interrupted. "There is one more event that you are to be made aware of." The three of them turned back to the screen. "The Chinese Air Force have received a signal from August, a call for help from the immigrant zone. They believe there are survivors, they are going in to retrieve them."

"How has anyone survived?"

"We don't know, we hope to find out soon."

The call lasted a few more minutes, mostly discussing when it would be safe for them to go to the surface again. Their thoughts went to the possible survivors and the capture of Charles Terri. From below the earth they felt helpless, like they were not apart of the world. They wanted to see the moment Charles was caught and meet the survivors. For the first time Kate truly wanted for Charles Terri's death not capture.

CHAPTER THREE

Charles Terri stood on the deck of the war ship Independence. The United Nations attack had crippled his fleet, the persistent surrenders crippled moral. The Augustan navy, a fraction of its once great might. The anti-missile artillery on board functioned adequately, the most technologically advanced to protect the President. This ship had been upgraded as the UN began to threatenAugust. It was built to be a sea fortress for the most important citizens. It was always considered an unlikely necessity, the belief in a victorious fate was strong.

The second wave of UN jets left the remaining ships relatively untouched. He watched them fly over head and to his beloved country. As they moved through the seas, he prayed for retaliation against those who acted against his great country. He prayed for vast numbers of dead military men.

The wind bit at Charles as he stood on deck. He thought it was his duty to watch over his flock. It was his duty to protect all his people. The UN organised strike had been severe, twenty ships of varying sizes remained. Seven remained in the convoy protecting their president. Three scouted for friendly space, the remainder surrounded the nation in combat.

Not all the countries agreed with the UN. Not all countries had so little morals that they would support the organisation that Charles Terri so detested. President Charles Terri did not enjoy the thought of running from his country, that was his reality. The only way to keep the remaining Augustan citizens safe was to run. They were running to a friendly country where they would request asylum.

General Morton stepped to his side and watched out at

the waves. The crew were indifferent towards their leader at this point. So many of their loved ones had died, so many lost. Their minds crafted to take orders, to be in service. This ingrained behaviour began to crack, but for the moment they were good seamen.

"Sir, it is not safe to be out here. If an enemy were to attack." He placed a hand on the Presidents shoulder, was he still a President if he didn't have a country to preside over? Were the people aboard enough?

"General thank you for your concern. It means a great deal to know that I have people who are thinking of my welfare." Charles Terri smiled and returned to staring back out to sea. The comment reflected the danger he felt his life was in.

"Sir, we are all loyal here, every man, woman and child on this vessel stands by your side. You could not have seen what the UN were to do. You could not have guessed their desperation, to use biological weapons. Sir, they have acted like the evil creatures we believed them to be. We do not blame you for their evil nature, we are solemn for what we have lost."

Charles Terri gave a small smile, if only these men knew the truth. If they believed the propaganda the UN forces dropped. It was just so preposterous, a President spreading such a disease amongst his people. All the propaganda in the world could not convince his people of that truth. The awful truth that he was the monster.

"General give me a moment please." Charles Terri brushed the hair out of his face. Looking to the horizon he let out a breath of despair. "If you would be so kind, I would like to address my people when I come in."

"Sir, we need to maintain radio silence. We are in significant danger as it is." He joined the presidents gaze to the horizon. "It will place a target on our back sir. They have stopped attacking us because they believe we are moving civilians."

"General they will place a target on my back." Charles Terri turned from the horizon. "I am aware of this. If they know I am on this ship, surrounded by civilians, they will take me alive."

"This is suicide sir."

"This is sacrifice, I cannot let them kill another Augustan citizen. When I am captured I want you to send out our surrender." Charles Terri contemplated life as a captured creature. "We will not make it to our destination General, I can see that now. There has been enough death, please allow me to save what is left of our nation"

General Morton nodded. "I will make the arrangements Sir." He walked off deck. These were the orders he believed should have been given some time ago. If the President was taken, the people would be spared. His people would be able to live and make lives. General Morton was the second most senior person on the ship, once the president was taken he would ensure the safety of his citizens. He looked back at the President, the propaganda gave him questions. He was a good soldier, he followed orders.

Charles Terri's thoughts were of his beautiful daughter Lauren. Her memory was being tarnished by the events that had preceded. He questioned the man he had become, allowing hate to poison him. The man that he had become would have disgusted her, the words his dead wife spoke were true. The truth that made him kill her.

Charles Terri sat down, it would be his last address as President. It would be the last time he would lead the country he loved. All the pain, death and suffering that he had caused. It was for her, for her people. If only he knew then, if only he knew what his hatred would create.

The man to his right with headphones on nodded to him. The floating citizens believed this would be a rallying cry. A speech to fortify the weary, to energise the masses. They were not expecting to hear the resignation of President Charles Terri.

"Ladies and gentlemen, loyal Augustan citizens." There was a break in the Presidents voice, "It is with a heavy heart that I speak to you tonight. Our country, our home has been taken from us." Charles wanted to slam his fists onto the table but the strength had left him. "The UN has destroyed all we had and all we hold dear. I ask you to pray for those lost souls.

"Tonight I have made a very hard decision, one that no leader makes with levity. Ladies and Gentlemen you must understand that I have made this choice so that you all can live safely and continue on with the traditions of our home. Tonight I am notifying the UN of my position, I will without resistance surrender my presidency.

"They will not stop until they have me, I will not allow them to hurt another Augustan citizen. To the members of the UN who have been waiting to learn my position. My latitude is 13.909327 and longitude -162.922093. I will be waiting for your arrival. I am unarmed and will not fight. I am onboard a ship of citizens, I am trusting in your civility not to hurt these people.

"To all the citizens listening to this, be strong, rebuild. We are August and we will not be defeated."

Charles Terri turned to the man operating the recording equipment. His mouth hung open. "Young man thank you for your service." Charles smiled and took off his headphones and walked out of the room.

"What have you done?" General Morton walked with the president, down the grey hallway. "You have endangered everyone on this ship."

"They will come for me, they will not hurt the innocent citizens who reside on this ship." Charles walked on.

"With all due respect sir, we don't know how they plan to attack." General Morton grabbed Charles Terri's shoulder, stopping him. "You have just endangered every person on this ship."

"General I have just saved everyone's life on this ship." Charles Terri looked at the Generals hand. It came off his shoulder, "They would have pummelled us until they killed me or destroyed every last one of our fleet. They would not believe of my death until they had my body. They would not have stopped destroying every last Augustan vessel."

Charles Terri continued to walk off, resolved in the fact that what he did was for the good of his people. He turned back, "General could I please ask you a favour before I go to my reckoning?"

"Yes, Sir." General Morton said with reservation.

"Could I please have your side arm?"

"Sir, can I ask what for?"

"They will be sending people here to kill me, you wouldn't forbid me some protection."

General Morton handed the gun to Charles Terri and watched him walk out onto the deck. Charles Terri enjoyed the wind on his face, his last moments of freedom. He watched over his fleet, his people who had suffered so much. He would give his life to protect them and this act was proof of that.

CHAPTER FOUR

Maria Singh was alone in the female bathroom, she looked at herself in the mirror. It had been so long since she took time for herself. She tied her hair into a bun and looked into her own eyes. She felt as if she had aged a decade. The stress of declaring war, of destroying a nation. This was not something she thought would be required of her. It was not something the UN was charged with, yet she made the call.

The UN office in New York had become her home, she was thankful for the showers. Her hotel room was largely vacant, she could not risk being away from her command. Maria had thoughts of Kate, the tremendous pain she must be feeling. Maria could not imagine how she would feel if her beloved India was destroyed. Of the friends and family who would be gone forever. Immense was all she could think.

Maria was devastated by the destruction, of August and that which continued across the world. No nation was spared the pain of the virus. Charles Terri's hate was so expansive it touched all corners of the globe. His self belief so detrimental that he destroyed a country. It saddened her that the world stood by until it was too late. That the human race had not learned from the mistakes of the past. How many tyrant had to rise and fall, before they would be stopped. Prior to the point of destruction. It pained her that she was handcuffed while Charles Terri treated those in his care so poorly. Handcuffed because the people of the world did not see their own being hurt.

The door of the bathroom swung open, her head of security knocked. He walked in upon her smile. "Gary, this is the ladies room. I'm not sure you're allowed in here."

"Ma'am General Xing is waiting for you in the boardroom." He didn't respond to her joke. In the four years he had been on her security team, not once did she see him laugh. It was not a thing that she would give up on easily.

"Thank you" she turned back to the mirror, "if you'll give me a moment to finish up in here."

"Yes, ma'am". He closed the door behind him. Maria looked back into the mirror. She promised herself when she found the time she would go away on holiday. Somewhere remote, where no one could reach her. She would go away and give her soul some time to heal, to wash itself of all the death and suffering her name would now forever be tied. She applied her lipstick, allowed herself to dream of that time for just a moment. Then she left the bathroom.

General Xing was one of the people she most enjoyed working with. He had the manners of a gentleman, like the ones her father instilled. He was honoured that she would learn Mandarin and he learnt some Hindi in return. He was grey from the many years he had been alive. His wisdom was quite profound.

General Xing smiled as Maria walked in the door, "Namaste Maria" he extended his hand.

"Ni Hāo General," they sat at the table, "I have been informed that you have some information regarding operations inAugust?"

"Yes, we have been picking up a message. This has been received for our last three passes over the immigrant zone."

"What does the message say?" Maria did not know whether to he hopeful or terrified.

"It calls for help." General Xing took a piece of paper from a uniformed man. "These are the co-ordinates. We would like to send a rescue mission, we have planes ready to go."

Maria looked at the paper, "General this is where we extracted the late Dr Fleming. Do we know who is sending the communication?"

"No Secretary-General, we would like to find out." General Xing stood, "Do we have the support of the UN to investigate this?"

"Yes General, we appreciate this information. You continue to be a strong ally and we thank you for that." General Xing turned to the man on his right and gave him the order to take action.

"Maria we will keep you informed." He began to walk out of the door, "I have matters to attend to."

"Yes, of course". Maria guided him through the door. She walked to her office and stood at the doorway. She turned to her security detail, "Gentleman if it's ok I will attempt to get some rest."

They nodded and she lay on her makeshift bed. She pictured the holiday that she would take and fell asleep.

Maria had been sleeping for two hours when the door to her office opened, a crack of light falling across her face. Her secretary apologised and she sat up. "Christine it's ok, what's happened?"

"General Hamilton is on the line, he has news about Charles Terri".

The name struck her, she sat up quickly. It took her only a minute to get ready. Charles Terri had disappeared in the malaise, gone underground and protected amongst the many who escaped to the water. The many ships they believed he was on had been destroyed. They had lost all leads. The one man in the whole world they wanted to put to justice. The one man the whole world looked for disappeared. The many ships that were out at sea carrying Augustan citizens were under suspicion but forces were stretched, they could not search all.

Maria sat in front of her screen and General Hamilton of the United Kingdom greeted her. "Ms Singh, we have received information about where Charles Terri is located."

"Who has this intel come from?"

"Charles Terri himself." The man on the screen stared through the monitor. He was proud that it was his men who found this.

"What do you mean, how has he told us about his where-abouts?"

"Charles Terri sent a message out, in it he gave us his co-ordinates." The man waved to someone off camera, "There was no attempt to hide the transmission. In fact he is calling us to him."

"How do we know that it isn't a trap? That we wont be sending more men in to face death at his hands?"

The message started to play, "Ma'am we are sending in our special forces teams. We will take all the necessary precautions. We will bring him in."

"When will you be starting this operation?"

"We have started already."

General Hamilton ended the call. Maria sat and listened to the end of the message. Then she started it again. For half an hour she listened to the message. She listened to the voice, to the man who had enacted so much on the world. She listened to the message hoping to understand his thoughts. Maria left her office to eat, the message still playing in her mind.

CHAPTER FIVE

The silence at the door took them both by surprise. It took a moment to comprehend the end of the sound. The virus had become stronger in their own body, the medicine had run out and they were over due for a shot. Both saw the red in each others eyes deepen, their movements became more difficult. The silence was a welcome relief from thinking about their eventual end, the moment that the virus was stronger than their resolve. Nina made Roderick promise to end her life before she became something so wretched. He reluctantly agreed.

They expected the banging to resume. After the ambush, occasionally the banging stopped but it was not for long. There was a deliberate clicking at the door, as if someone was trying to unlock it from the outside. Their fears spiked, the fear that these things could learn. What if they had watched them, worked out how to open the door. Nothing was out of the realms of possibility. History was constantly being rewritten, they were in a shifting world. The scratching at the door lasted a little longer, they huddled together. In times of fear or happiness they chose to be close.

The door creaked open; collectively they let out a breath. They were awaiting their doom, for death to appear. Four men came into the main area of the bunker, from their uniforms Roderick could see that they were not Augustan soldiers. They spoke in a language that was foreign to both of them. The fear on their faces must have struck the soldiers, one of them knelt beside the huddled couple. He spoke in an accent that Roderick's dilapidated brain finally realised was Chinese. "We are here to bring you to safety. We received your call for help." The absence of a response from the two frightened people gave the soldier pause. "You can come with us now. We do not have much time, we have woken a nest of those things. There will be too many of them soon." He extended his hand.

"We need some medicine; it has been too long since our last shot." Roderick looked at the man hopefully. "We are very weak, we can't hold off too much longer."

The man that spoke to them softly now yelled to the men and a soldier came running with a box in hand. "This man is Chén, he will administer the medication." He stood back and let the doctor do his work. He set the box down and motioned for them to lay down on their sides. He pressed on Roderick's neck warning him before the injection, then the cold of the needle came through sharply.

The liquid went into his body and started a war with the virus. Suppressing it and keeping it from destroying the person he was. At this late stage, not having the anti-viral for so long, taxed his body greatly. He began to see vivid and sharp lights, darting across his mind. His body shook and he began to convulse, throwing his body onto its back. The doctor with the help of the soldier turned him on his side and placed a leather strap in his mouth. Nina screamed, they jabbed him in the leg and his vision disappeared. He was sure this was death, empty and black.

Roderick woke on a plane, the soldier who showed kindness to them in the bunker sat watch. Nina was asleep, for a moment she was so still he feared deeply. Then he saw her take a breath. His heart beat again; he touched her and felt her warmth. It took some time for him to contextualise the plane, exactly what was occurring. He took a moment to catch himself, to feel his body completely his own.

"Would you like something to eat?" The soldier asked quietly, not wanting to wake Nina. "We have some food, it is not the most delicious but it is filling."

"Yes, thank you." Roderick smiled. "Where are we going?"

The soldier stood from his seat and took a pouch from a drawer. "We are heading to New York. You will start a new life there." He handed the pouch and a spoon to Roderick, "There has been much happening while you have been in the bunker. We were surprised to find anyone alive."

Roderick ate quickly, his stomach so hungry. "We heard the bombs, how many survivors are there?"

"Not many I'm afraid, most escaped to ships. The wealthy and powerful took it upon themselves to ensure their own safety." He bowed his head, "The virus ran through the immigrant zone quickly as you would be aware. Then they broke through the containment fences and took the city. The infection was spread quickly, there were very few survivors." The soldier bowed his head for the lives lost.

"The UN took the decision to eradicate as many infected people as possible and dropped bombs on the nation. That is what you would have felt in your bunker. We were able to eradicate much of the disease."

"What has become of August as a nation?" Roderick asked with a firm gaze on his hands.

"The nation has been destroyed." He said so with a quiet resolve.

"Good" Roderick said with an uncharacteristic hate. "I hope the people who escaped now live as immigrants. I hope they feel the pain that we have. Their hatred caused this; their treatment of us was appalling."

"We have watched in horror, it is with sadness that we could not help. Those who survived and were responsible will be brought to justice." Roderick did not feel any satisfaction from this. So much hurt had been inflicted on him, so many of his loved ones lost forever. Justice would never be served.

The plane hit turbulence and began to shake. They all strapped in for the bumpy ride back to the world, away from the horror of August. "Has the virus spread through the world?"

"Yes, it is the greatest pandemic we as a species have seen. The anti-viral is bringing some control but it will be some time before we can consider any sort of control." Roderick was saddened by the news. "The late Dr Fleming did a great thing, for the horrors he made he redeemed himself with that anti-viral."

"Dr Fleming is dead? How?" Shock at this news.

"I am afraid he took his own life, the weight of what he created was just too much for him."

Roderick said a quiet prayer for the doctor, hoped that he finally found some peace. "Thank you so much for what you have done for Nina and I. Can I ask you one more question?"

"Of course."

"What is your name?" Roderick said with a smile.

"Clint Hú." He extended his hand.

"Thank you Clint" He shook his hand with a deep gratitude. "Clint is not a name I would have guessed."

"My parents were big country and western fans." They both laughed, and rode out the turbulence. They chatted about more pleasant subjects from there on. Roderick was happy to have this sense of normality. Even on a rescue mission from a disease ridden nation, pleasant chatter was welcomed.

CHAPTER SIX

Carol Phillips held her new born tightly, she loved him more than any other. It was a cold winters day in New York and she rugged him up tightly. As they waited for the bus she sang to him. She was a performer before she was a mother. Touring as a back up singer, working with some of the greatest musicians. Her break never came, she thought it never would, then she had Griffin. He was her break; the lacking in her life was complete with him.

The people waiting along side them listened to her. They enjoyed the pleasant distraction from the harshness of the weather. Griffin stirred and she stroked his forehead, checking his temperature. She held so much fear for him catching a chill, or over heating. Griffin responded to her voice, the softness made him go back softly to sleep. Griffin's dreams were always the most active when she sung him a lullaby.

The bus let out a slight squeal as it arrived. The same one took them on their weekly trip to the city. There was so much madness in the world, fear and anger seemed to consume. It was most imposing in the city. This was the reason she only made the trip on a day like today.

When the bombs first came she was eight months pregnant. The virus spread quickly through the city and its outer limits. She avoided it for so long, her protective nature attached to the life in her belly.

The day she heard the screaming of her elderly neighbour her instincts overcame her logic. The old ladies belly, out sizing her own. Then she popped and covered Carol in a red mist. Just like that Carol and her new born were infected and joined the red eye population.

The anti-viral was widely distributed; unfortunately the elderly and weak were susceptible to the disease. It attacked them so savagely; they were not strong enough to hold it at bay. Throughout the city people fell to it. The anti-viral was effective but by no means perfect and there was a great deal of death. She stayed indoors to protect her little child. Protect him from the horrors that inhabited the world.

The bus ride had now become much more pleasant then when she first required it. She made friends with the driver, he was a volunteer shuttling the infected into the city for their weekly shots. They exchanged pleasantries, never about the darkness. Today with Griffin sleeping the bus driver politely smiled. He warned all to be quiet, to be sure they didn't wake the little boy. The driver listened to her sing and it made him happy, it also made him miss his family.

The drivers name was Patrick Cox, a retiree. His wife was ill before the war; she had such a sensitive disposition that he believed her heart problems worsened due to the pain around her. She had been ill for so long, her precious heart beating so weakly. She was one of the few who died of something other than the virus. Patrick didn't have any biological children; his beautiful Reggie couldn't conceive.

This too stole some of her heart, he knew it. Instead of dwell on their hardship they volunteered and made the lives of many orphans all the better. He may not have had blood relatives but he had much love. Brian drove the bus to help all those people who had no one. He drove the bus to keep them safe and their dignity in tact.

The bus came to a stop outside the big grey building, now housing hundreds of medical professionals. They were there to ensure the disease spread no further and that those who contracted the disease could continue to live.

Carol walked inside; the white was medical and reassured the many who walked through its doors. There were big hallways with small rooms off of them. The rooms were big enough for a bed, a chair and a technician. After the anti-viral was produced they trained thousands of people to administer it. Point and shoot, that was the basis of their training.

Carol took her number and sat on the plastic chair. Griffin stirred with hunger; her little man was growing so quickly and drank his bottle. He loved his food just like his father did. Carol burped him and he went back to sleep. She kissed his forehead and felt it for a temperature.

A man stepped out of a tiny room and called her number. He wore a lab coat but was not a doctor. He was a technician, one of the many. "183" he called out. He watched her stand and walk in his direction.

When Carol entered he was cold to her, his eyes weren't red. One of the very few who worked in here that wasn't infected. "Could I please see your injection card?" She handed it over to him. He put it into the computer and her file came up. "Your results from last week's test show that the virus is still in remission."

This was good news, if the virus wasn't in remission you were quarantined. She wasn't concerned about the results; if the virus had begun to take over they wouldn't have waited for her weekly visit. The man looked at Griffin; he saw the red of the little babies eyes. "Can I have his card?" Carol handed the card, he flashed up on the screen and it blinked green.

"Lay him down on the cot please, I'll administer to you first." He was very matter of fact. Carol put Griffin down and kissed him. She climbed on the bed, turning on her side. "Please hold still" He wiped the area and then inserted the syringe, the liquid was very cold. It took only a moment and then she was done, safe to walk the streets without fear of inflation.

"The technician last week gave Griffin a sedative before the injection." Carol rubbed the back of her neck. "Could you do the same?"
"Yes, it's standard procedure for those under ten." He seemed annoyed by the question. Griffin cried when the needle went into his thigh. Carol sung to him, her voice and the sedative

calming him. "Could you please roll him over?"

She took him out of his blankets and laid his limp little body on its side. The technician inserted the needle and she fought back tears as the liquid entered her tiny man. She wrapped him back up, "Thank you." She left the room before the tears came. She was so terrified for what this little boy's life would become.

Carol ran to the bathroom and cried with the unconscious body in her arms. This was her normal now. Tears dropped on his blanket and she wiped at them. Carol only allowed herself to cry when Griffin could not witness it. She let the tears flow, turning her head so the blanket remained dry.

Carol splashed water on her face, her eyes puffy. She looked at the helplessness of herself, the red that controlled. The red that would control her little babies life. She gave herself a moment and then walked to the bus, she wanted to be at home more than anything in the world.

Patrick was always so kind to her on the ride home. He could see that being in the building crushed her. Holding that limp little body was a dagger to her heart. He spoke about life with his wife and all the people they helped together. He allowed her to peer into his past to take the focus from her present. He enjoyed sharing the stories, it allowed them to live on through other people.

CHAPTER SEVEN

Charles Terri was on deck, sitting on a fold out chair. The leader once powerful now reduced to plastic furniture atop his floating manmade country. He sat quietly waiting for the UN thugs to arrive; gun in hand. He knew this would be the last time he could consider himself an Augustan citizen. This action would set in motion a chain of events that would eradicate August as a nation, but would keep his citizens safe. He sat quietly and waited.

Charles Terri's true motivations were not completely clear even to him. Everything he fought for would be over. His actions would be viewed as a surrender; proving the image of him the UN perpetrated. Historians would put him amongst the most wretched of people, this he was sure. His failures may have been great, but their reasons sound. He was leader of all Augustan citizens; their futures were what he fought for.

Charles Terri recalled the moment they fled. That was the precise moment his failings gripped him. As he sat on deck, he wanted to ensure the world knew it was not the people of August who were to blame. These were his decisions and his actions. He wanted to take on all responsibility, to ensure the hatred was directed at him. He would die a martyr, if it meant his people could live happy lives.

The ship swayed on the waves and Charles Terri thought back to all that came before. All the struggles and his goal of a unified and strong August. He thought of the UN and their insistence of control. If it were not for them, he would not have needed to act in such an extreme manner. His resignation of President was an act of condemnation on their irresponsibility.

It took little more than an hour before he saw the first helicopter. The black monster seemed to be a myth until the loud sound came. There were four in all, an overreaction to one man's surrender. They came in quickly, two landing on deck and two staying in the sky. Their massive guns focused on him.

Twelve men jumped from the two helicopters. Guns drawn, they advanced on him. Their tactical gear was as black as the helicopter and no less terrifying. Four meters in front of him, he showed the gun. "Put the gun down or we will be forced to engage."

"Before you take me I have a message for the people of the world." Charles Terri demanded at them.

"You will be given a chance to speak. You are under arrest for human rights abuse; we have been tasked with taking you into custody."

"I will not resist and neither will my people. This is a surrender from all levels of August. You have won, the UN and its illegal activity has triumphed." Charles Terri held the gun tight. "I have instructed my men to surrender; you will face no resistance in taking our ships. We will show you a dignity that you have stolen from us." Charles Terri turned the gun to himself, fitting it snugly under his chin.

The men scanned the area, they assumed that this would be a sign to ambush but could see no other living soul on deck. "Charles Terri, I will repeat you are under arrest for human rights abuse."

"Sir, you will hear my message and then I will give you the joy of my capture."

There was a voice in the soldiers ears, "We will allow you to speak but you have two minutes and then we will take any actions necessary."

"It will only take a moment." Charles dropped the gun to his side. "The action taken by the UN has caused irreparable damage to my people and country. The demonising of our nation

291

has caused hate to be heaped on our good citizens. I am standing before you, President Charles Terri and I say that I take full responsibility for the actions of my nation. If it necessary heap your scorn on me."

Charles Terri drew the gun on himself. "I say to my people I have failed you. My failures should not cause punishment against you. The atrocities the UN has perpetrated will haunt those in charge till the day they die. Shame on you Maria Singh, and shame on you Katherine Laurie, your treachery will not be forgotten. I hereby resign as President of August. God bless August and her people, for they are the greatest on earth.

"To my people stay strong; my love, devotion and life was always yours." Charles went quiet. "To my Lauren please forgive your father, pain corrupted him."

The men stepped forward, "its time to go" they shouted loudly. They took two steps and Charles Terri lifted the gun to sit under his chin.

"This was a resignation not a surrender, long live August." Charles Terri pulled the trigger. There was a loud shot; the men took a step back. Charles Terri's body dropped to the ground, no hint of the life that once possessed it.

The men ran to him, they checked his vitals. "Charles Terri is dead". There was confusion on the other side, "We did not engage, Charles Terri shot himself." The men took the body and brought it on the helicopter. The news of his death went across the world quickly, there were many dry eyes.

The ships that constituted the Augustan nation did as their late ruler demanded. They surrendered without a fight. They showed the dignity he spoke of. The ships were brought to many ports, split up to stop resistance. They were now prisoners of war. The rich and powerful of August were no longer in positions of affluence. The very people who made those who sought asylum suffer were now preparing to start their lives as immigrants.

Long live August, August has fallen.

EPILOGUE

CHAPTER ONE

Carol came out of the shower, enjoying the alone time for the moments they lasted. There was a crash from the lounge room, with a towel wrapped around her she went to investigate. "Griffin, what are you doing."

He turned around, caught, "I was throwing the ball to Bella."

"What is the rule about throwing the ball in the house?" Carol used her most stern voice, it felt uncomfortable.

"Not to throw the ball in the house."

"And what were you doing?"

"Throwing the ball," he looked at his feet feeling shame. "But Bella wanted to play with the ball." He pointed the blame at their little white and champagne Chihuahua; she looked up at Carol and panted. She tried really hard to be angry at them, she failed.

Carol walked over and hugged Griffin, then leant down to pat Bella. "We will take Bella for a walk when we get back." She took the streamer that hit her in the face down. "I thought we agreed that you were going to clean this?" She was referring to the decorations from his birthday party.

"Yes, but I like it like this."

"Why do we need a giant five on the wall?" Carol pointed taking care to hold onto her towel.

"How else will people know I'm five?"

"I'll tell them." Carol turned to walk back into the bathroom.

"You wont have to if we leave the five on the wall." He yelled after her, his cheeky personality becoming more defined.

Carol looked into the mirror and began to dry her hair. She was amazed at being the mother of a five year old. She could remember carrying him in her arms, he was so small. Now he was so independent, she missed him being completely reliant on her.

Today was their appointment to get the anti-viral. She was glad it was no longer a weekly requirement. The less time spent in the city the better. The implant went under the skin at the base of the skull. Three months of freedom and no needles into the spinal column. The government said it was safer, more effective and cost much less. All things she was happy for.

Griffin hated days like today. It hurt to have the implant put in, no matter how much numbing cream they used. Even though he got a day off of school, he hated today. There was another bang from the lounge room. "Griffin, if I come in there and that five isn't down we're not going for a walk." She could hear him scrambling.

Walking Bella was one of his favourite things to do. The two of them were inseparable. She was worried about getting a dog; she never had one growing up. The bond they had, made her so pleased with the decision.

Carol dressed and walked into the lounge room. Griffin did what he was asked and took down the five and also a few layers of paint. Griffin looked guiltily at her and shot a smile, it melted her heart. "Griffin, do you know how to paint a wall?" He shook his no, "Well you are going to learn today." "Awesome." He took his mother's hand, "Do we have to go today?"

"Yes, baby, it will make sure that we stay healthy and strong. It will be over quickly and then we can have fun for the rest of the day."

"Ok, then can I have an ice cream?" He looked up at her, Bella could tell they were talking about food and looked up as well.

"It's so cold, do you really want ice cream?"

"Yep, Bella does too."

She looked at the two of them, "As soon as we get back we can go and get some. Now put your jacket on, we need to leave."

Griffin ran to his room to get ready, Bella jumped on the

couch. "Come here". She picked her up and put a jumper on her. She got cold easily, Griffin ran back out, "Ready".

Patrick smiled and said hello to the both of them as they hopped on the bus. "Patrick," Griffin spoke to him as he pulled onto the road, "do you know how old I am?"
"You're five."
"How did you know that?"
"Well, there was a big five on the wall." Patrick laughed.
"See mum, that's how people know." He flashed her his cheekiest grin.
"Very good," she leant into the chair and watched the passing scenery. Griffin and Patrick talked about his party the weekend before, and how much fun they had. Patrick had become like a grandfather to Griffin. Carol was happy for it, her parents had passed away and she was an only child. She liked that Griffin could have some family. Patrick had become like a father to her, he guided her and she called him when she feared for Griffin.

The bus pulled up in front of the building. The grey had gone; they resurfaced it to give it a friendlier appearance. It was now white with green and yellow accents. "Mum do we have to?"
"Baby, I'm sorry but it is very important. We would get very sick if we didn't do it." She knelt down to him. Looked into his red eyes, the horror of the colour had disappeared and all she saw was him.

Hand in hand they walked into the building and took a number, it was like being at a deli. There were much less people working in the building now, the weekly need subsiding meant less man power. "Phillips, Carol and Griffin." They walked up to the lady calling their name, "Come this way".

The two of them followed her, Griffin squeezed tight on his mother's hand. They walked into a room and the lady closed the door behind her. Carol looked at the cot in the corner and remembered Griffin as a baby. "Now you look a little scared". She pointed to Griffin and he nodded. "My name is Mac, and I am the best at doing this I promise. What I will do is rub some of this on your neck so it doesn't hurt."

"But it does hurt" he spoke from behind his mother.

"I know honey the old one wasn't very good. This one is my special recipe and I promise it will work." She rubbed the back of his neck and he held tight to his mother. "I will make a bet, if this hurts then you can have this cape." She pulled out a piece of cloth with an S on it. His eyes lit up and he took hold of it. "If it doesn't hurt then I get to have the cape."

"But it won't fit you." He said committing to the pain for a reward.

"Well, we will have to see." She smiled and that put Carol at ease. "Can I please have your cards?"

Carol handed them over and she watched them get inserted into the machine and their names glow green. She turned back around, "Now let's see if I can keep my cape." Griffin jumped up onto the table, and for the first time in this place he smiled. The technician leaned over and felt for the old implant. Mac made an incision and took the old one out, inserting the new one. She put two tiny stitches in. "We are all done." Griffin sat up and felt his neck, his face showing amazement. "So do I get to keep my cape?"

"That didn't hurt." He almost looked upset by this. "Yep you can keep it," he held it out upset.

"You know what, it looks like it will fit you better. How about you keep it but bring it back every time you have to come in." She smiled at him, "Deal?"

"Deal."

Carol had her implant changed and was also amazed by the lack of pain. Even in this world of infected people and death all around, there were people wanting to do better. They walked out, and Carol passed the bathroom she used to break down in. She was so scared about bringing a life into such a terrifying world. The world was still a terrifying place and it was still just as horrible, but now she had her superman. She didn't need to break down with a superhero in her world.

CHAPTER TWO

Kate sat in the back of a lecture theatre, Grant was lecturing on global politics. He was so passionate, intensely knowledgeably and looked at home in front of the crowd. The preceding years had been difficult for the three of them. Grant missed being a teacher, giving something to the next generation. The death threats kept them confined to bunkers and safe houses, always moving to ensure their lives were not taken. The threat was a heavy one to bare. They were happy as their lives slowly gained some normality.

The threats did not subside until they moved from New York, away from the influx of Augustan immigrants. New York and the United States did an exemplary job of welcoming the poor and huddled masses of Augustan citizens. With the poor and unfortunate came the bitter and resentful.

It was heart breaking to be removed from their country-men, but with such blame heaped on Kate it was the only way. Their move to the United Kingdom allowed them a freedom they had not experienced in so long. Being able to walk the streets without fear.

Kate and Grant split their residences between London and Cambridge. Universities competed to have Grant take a professorship with them, his choice of Cambridge felt right to him. Living in between London City and Cambridge was diffi-cult as they missed being together. When classes were in ses-sion Grant lived close to the university. They made every effort to see each other.

The lecture wrapped up and she sat and waited for the last students to disappear. She was so happy that he was back doing what he loved. "My dear that was a very engaging lecture" she kissed him and felt the warmth lacking when they were apart.

"I am so glad you could come, how's work?" He packed his briefcase and they walked out together.

"Busy, and frankly at times depressing," they left the building and strolled across the gardens. The grass was so green, the flowers so bright. "Every other day we learn of another person that worked in my administration being a loyalist."

"Darling the lengths these people went too." He paused, they sat at Grant's favourite café. The waiter came over and smiled, "Michael the usual please, darling what would you like?"

"Just a water please," she looked over at Grant, his beautiful green eyes holding her. "No, a hot chocolate, diet be damned."

"Very good ma'am" Michael smiled to her.

Grant looked into the courtyard and then back to Kate, "They were well funded and smart people. They knew the political sphere because many of them built it. The August you were elected to was a myth. I am afraid that the real country was the one working in the background."

"That is all too clear now." She was still hurt by the depth of betrayal, or maybe that she was fooled by the myth. "Every day we investigate the people that stowed away on the ships. All those people had enough money to arrange their transport to safety. The poor and sick left to die on that forsaken island. Every day we need to investigate if they were just selfish or criminal."

"What is the distinction?"

"In reality there isn't one, in reality we are trying to work out if they were loyalists or not. Then we have to determine how much they knew and acted on. Five years and we are no closer. Many burnt their identification to hide from responsibility"

The drinks came and Michael put them down on the table. "Ma'am please accept this from me." He placed down a cup cake, frosted so decadently. "Diets are no match for my red velvet cupcakes."

"Thank you, this is defiantly a welcomed surprise." She placed her hand on his, "You have made my day." Michael walked off smiling.

"Those are the best cupcakes you will eat, they're not on the menu. That right there is a sought after item."

"Well, then," she stuck her fork into it and tasted. She smiled to Grant and kept eating, happy to be absent of words.

"Kate have you considered accepting the teaching post they keep offering you?" He continued even though it was clear she was lost in the cupcake. "It would be much less torturous on you, and your knowledge would be an asset to any institution."

Kate savoured the flavour for a moment before responding. "Grant, when all of them have been processed I will consider it. Bill and I hold information that is of critical importance." She sipped her hot chocolate and the warmth filled her stomach. "My duty is to ensure those responsible are not allowed to flee without being held accountable for the horror they caused. It is something I need to do, torturous or not."

They each allowed a moment of silence, letting the subject disappear into the gardens. "How has Bill been? He has been noticeably absent."

"He has fallen in love, he spends every spare moment with Baldric." Kate smiled happy for her dear friends joy. Grant chuckled into his coffee, "Really Grant?"

"It's a ridiculous name," he laughed again and Kate joined him. "Stop it, he is very nice. He is very good at settling Bill's nervous nature." She had to avoid eye contact or else they would both have a laughing fit. "They are very much in love; they look like we did when we first started dating. It's very nice to see."

"I am happy for him; it has been a difficult few years." He smiled to her in his most mischievous way. "I am glad he found his very own Baldric." The two of them laughed, it was infectious.

They finished their drinks, careful not to mention August or Baldric. "Michael that was the most delicious cupcake, I would like to have one each time I am here."

"Only because you are married to my favourite customer and lecturer" He smiled to them. She liked Michael, the destroyer of diets.

The two of them walked hand in hand through the grounds. "Grant I was thinking that I would spend the night." She liked being close to him.

"I would love that. We can go to my favourite restaurant and make an evening of it."

"That would be nice." She squeezed his hand and he squeezed back.

"I will be damned if I am showed up by Bill" he paused and waited till she was looking into his eyes. "And Baldric". They erupted in laughter.

CHAPTER THREE

Roderick sat at a café sipping on his cappuccino. Coffee had always been a luxury in his life, even now when it was a staple, he drank it with scarcity. The waitress kept her eyes on him the whole time; they were suspicious of the infected. Suspicion unlike he experienced in August, this time it was concern not hatred. His red eyes made it visible, marked him as one of the infected. She turned and served another infected lady, the un-infected were always so careful around them. Never sharing cutlery and God forbid they shook hands.

In all that he now had, these little annoyances quickly disappeared. For the first time in his life he was happy. Nina walked over with the three little ones. A consequence of the virus was it caused the host permanent infertility. Any chance they had of becoming parents had well and truly disappeared. With so many children orphaned they used their parental wanting to take care of three little girls.

They ran as soon as they spotted him, "Daddy". He hugged them tight, his little family brought him such bliss. Nina kissed him, "Roderick, you were meant to put this suit into the dry cleaners. What must the people at the University think?"

"I am a renewable energy scientist; most people think I am much too overdressed."

"Most people are wrong." Since the oppression lifted she became herself, slowly and more everyday he fell more in love with her. She was a strong leader, she led her family and community. She helped Roderick up when he wanted to fall. "Please leave it on the table tonight and I will bring it in tomorrow."

The waitress came over and spotted the family of infected, and her chilly disposition continued. "What can I get for you?" The girls so excited about their trip into the city exploded in requests.

"Chocolate milkshake" Lidia blurted out, she was the eldest. Seven years old but acted more senior. The other children waited till she spoke before joining in.

"Babycino" Clarissa sat on her father's lap; she loved the drink because it was a copy of his. She most loved to be with him. She had been left for so long when her parents died that she didn't speak for a year. She developed a bond with Roderick, she loved him dearly.

"Strawberry milkshake please," Lorraine said. She was the youngest and ordered the drink less for its taste and more because it matched her dress.

Nina smiled and looked at the menu, after water being a luxury for so long she often froze in moments like these. Roderick touched her hand; she smiled at him thankful for his intrusion. "I will have an iced tea, please". The waitress walked off and Nina took a breath, settling the butterflies in her stomach. "Dear, how did you manage to get the rest of the day off?"

"Well, I thought to myself, would I rather be in the lab or take my lovely girls shopping for dresses." The girls heads whipped around and let out a collective gasp. Roderick smiled at Nina.

"In that case you will be on your own." She kissed him on the cheek for his kind gesture. "I need to go back to the centre; they need me to help take care of the children. We are short staffed as usual."

"Could you not have someone take over for you?" His eyes pleaded with her.

"We are under resourced as it is." She looked at the three girls. "You four will have a fun day without me."

"Ok my love." They were now both watching the children, so happy with their new little lives. The drinks hit the table and the girls were quiet. "We will buy you something special then."

"That would be lovely."

Nina kissed them all goodbye at the train station. She was off to tend to the needy. Her tribulations caused in her a wanting to help. "Now girls, what shall we buy your mother?" The girls erupted in discussion. Roderick felt his heart repair a little, becoming lighter. Those little girls were his saviours, he was blessed.

CHAPTER FOUR

Maria Singh walked to the podium; the crowd was quiet and waited for her to speak. For five years she was the very public face of the organisation tasked with cleaning up the virus. The expectations were that as a world they would ensure its eradication. This did not eventuate. The first world countries ensured their peoples safety first and the third world was left. This created areas over run by the virus, with no other option but to burn people. In these areas fear ran rampant. An accusation was all that was needed to spark a fire.

The fear of these people caused atrocities to happen across the globe. It was a fitting legacy for Charles Terri. For five years she fought the destruction he caused, for five years she pushed for help.

"Ladies and Gentleman, today we are here marking the fifth anniversary of the fall of August. With it we saw the greatest virus the world has ever been subjected to. This disaster has shown us the darkest elements of the human being. It has shown us the depth we are willing to plummet for our own selfish endeavours.

"It is not only those who caused the plight who have shown their awful nature. We have, the many who sit within this hall showed our ugliness. It has been five years, five years for us to help those less fortunate. Third world countries are wallowing in the disease and we send nothing more than tokens of help." The floor erupted; Maria had lost all ability to manage her tact. She looked up from her script leaving it never to be heard.

"How long will it be before we are able to stand up and

forever say we are one? Have we not had enough pain from segregation? You all sit still, while we have man, woman and child dying all over the world. They could be saved if only you saw them as one of your own. Shame on you!

"Has this tragedy not taught us the value of a human life or have we learnt to hide our greed better? We have camps of people dying, waiting for asylum and we say we have enough. We have met our quota while people die. Starving to death while we sit on the mounds of food we throw out daily. We have too much and still we say we will not share. Shame on you!

"We have thousands, if not millions on the island, waiting to be treated. The world health organisation waits for the funds to find a cure. Still we wait. Hoards of people on the island, shipped there because we will not care for them. The funds do not come; they should be better spent on frivolous means. Shame on you!

"People are dying and we sit here and do nothing. It is more than I can bear; it is an example of our human condition.

"We are bound to repeat these atrocities and for that I say, shame on you!

"No longer will I be the face of idle, no longer the face of narcissus. I resign from my post and all affiliation with this organisation." Maria was furious; the years of watching people suffer infected her soul.

"August has fallen but it has risen again in your hearts."

Maria left the stage; the moment of silence was met with incensed shouts. She retired to her office for the last time. Seeing the true human spirit appear from behind the veil damaged her completely.

August has fallen but it has risen again in your hearts.

ABOUT THE AUTHOR

Byron Gatt

Byron resides in Melbourne, Australia with his wife Jayde and little ones: Lily and Freddie (Chihuahua's), Button (bunny) and Truffle (Green Cheek Conure). Unlike the sterotypical author Byron finds creativity in being around his loved ones, but does love a good whiskey.

A word from the authour:

"Making up stories has been my passion for as long as I can remember. As an intensely shy child, it was a way that I could understand the world, and communicate with others. I remember discovering novels in primary school and loosing myself in these worlds. No pictures but full of vivid imagery."

Thank you for reading, and expanding this story.

If you'd like to get in touch email: Byron@byronwrites.com